FAKING WITH THE ENEMY

MILESTONE MISCHIEF #2

PIPER JAMES

For all those couples who love to hate and hate to love…it can be fun, walking that thin line between the two.

1

Nate

*E*ver had one of those days when everything seemed to go to shit, and you just couldn't drag yourself out of the muck? Yeah? Me, too.

"Damn that woman."

I'd been staring at the blank form on my computer screen for at least ten minutes, the flashing cursor mocking me as I fought the urge to toss the laptop out the nearest window. Mr. Stevenson was waiting for his quote, and I could see him checking his watch for the hundredth time through the glass partition that separated my office from the waiting room.

I should've been done with it seven minutes ago, but I was having trouble focusing.

Damn her.

Shaking my head and taking a deep breath, I began to type.

Brake pads are at fifteen percent in front and twenty percent in

back. Recommend replacements, as well as a new air filter, tire rota-
tion and windshield wiper blades. Total cost: $200

I tapped the keys that would send the quote to the tech's tablet and leaned back in my chair. I could've recommended a dozen other repairs and upgrades, but Mr. Stevenson was retired and living month-to-month on meager social security checks. I knew he couldn't afford to pay anything but the bare minimum, which was why I only charged him half the labor costs and discounted his parts whenever he brought his truck in.

Of course, *he* didn't know that. He'd flat-out order me to charge him full price if he did. His pride wouldn't allow him to accept anything less.

With that task off my plate, my mind refocused on what had recently become the bane of my existence—Charity Glasscott.

Her high-heeled shoes had tapped their way across the concrete floors of my shop this morning, the noise echoing around me like a bad omen as her smile sent a shiver skittering down my spine. A shiver of revulsion.

I'd made a mistake—a big one.

Two weeks ago, after a couple of beers with my best friend Dane, she'd walked into the bar with that pretty face and those long, luscious legs and set out to turn me into another notch on her bedpost. Maybe I was horny. Maybe I was just bored. Whatever it was, I'd shrugged at Dane and agreed to let Charity take me home.

When it was over, she was a boneless mess, puddled in her sheets with a satisfied grin on her face. The whole thing for me was barely above a "meh" on the sex scale, but I was careful not to let her know that. I didn't want to hurt her feelings.

God, I wished I had.

Because one taste of my *magic dick* was never enough.

I barked a self-deprecating laugh at the thought. Back when I was younger, my older brother Rafe constantly tried to curb my gluttonous sexcapades. He told me they'd get me in trouble one day, and I'd always scoffed at his efforts.

I'd told him it wasn't my fault. That my *magic dick* had become the stuff of legends, and girls were coming out of the woodwork to experience it for themselves. How was I supposed to resist? I was only human.

I was such a fucking cocky idiot back then. And apparently, still was.

Charity had walked right into my office and told me in no uncertain terms that she wanted me again. When I tried to let her down gently, she'd gone on the offensive with calculated candor. She wanted me in her bed, and she always got what she wanted.

And if I refused her demands, she would go straight to daddy.

Normally, I would have laughed at the threat, but her words had sent a new chill prickling down my spine. Her father was Chester Glasscott, owner of Milestone Bank and Trust...the very bank that holds the loan for my shop, Walton's Auto Repair.

Charity didn't mince words, telling me outright that if I didn't fall into line and become her lover, exclusively, she'd go to her father, give him some sob story about how I'd used and abused her, and have him fudge the numbers to make my loan fall into default.

I could lose my business. And depending how depraved Charity's lying mouth became, I could lose my freedom.

I could lose everything.

I'd considered giving in. I could give her what she wanted...maybe. I was so pissed and frankly, *appalled* by her demands, I wasn't sure I could even get it up for her at this point.

But where would it end? Would I be stuck, performing for her every whim until my loan was fully paid off? I still owed ten years' worth of payments.

No fucking way.

I'd considered applying for a new loan at a different bank, but unfortunately, MB&T held a monopoly in Milestone—there were no other choices. And the national bank chains had only offered me exorbitant interest rates. I was stuck.

Between a rock and a hard place.

"Hey, Nate," Dane said, poking his head through my door. "It's almost closing time, and I've got Jason pulling in the cars. Do you need anything else?"

"No," I said. "You go ahead. I'm just going to finish up here, then I'll lock up."

"You okay?" he asked, stepping fully into my office and closing the door behind him. "You seem...off."

I knew what he was asking. He'd seen Charity come in, and had caught my eye through the glass window while she'd been laying out her demands. It had been obvious I was pissed, and he'd raised his eyebrows before pointing at himself then at me, silently asking if I'd needed his help.

I'd shaken my head slightly at him, and he'd shrugged, leaving me to handle it on my own. Now, though, was another matter.

"You've been in a funk since that chick from the bar showed up here earlier. What did she want, anyway? More sex?"

He wiggled his eyebrows suggestively, and my frown deepened. The mischievous glint disappeared from his eyes, and his lips turned down as he waited for me to answer.

"Charity Glasscott. Daughter of Chester Glasscott," I said.

"Why does that name ring a bell?" he asked, scratching his head.

"Because he owns the bank."

"Oh, that's right," he said, cocking his head. "What did she want?"

"You weren't wrong," I sighed. "She wants more sex."

"And that's a bad thing, because…" he said, waiting for me to finish the sentence.

"Because I don't want to," I said, "and she threatened to have her father put my loan into default if I don't give it up—wherever and whenever she wants it."

"What the fuck?" he shouted. "That's bullshit. Not to mention illegal. You should go to the cops."

"I don't have any proof, Dane. And besides, who's going to believe me over her? She's one of Milestone's elite, while I'm just a grease monkey who barely graduated high school."

"Nate," he said, his voice deep with reprimand.

"I know," I said, waving a hand in the air. "I've made something of myself, and I should be proud. I *am* proud of what I've accomplished here, Dane. And Charity Glasscott could take it all away, just like that."

I snapped my fingers and slumped back into my chair. What a fucking nightmare.

"All of your hard work has turned this place into a success," he said. "Just apply some of that cunning and work ethic into getting out of this situation, and you'll figure it out."

"You think so?" I asked, arching one brow at him.

"I know so," he said, turning to leave. "Good night, boss man."

"Night, Dane."

I sat in silence, my brain working overtime to come up with a solution. I couldn't see a way past this, and I was becoming more and more agitated as the minutes ticked by. I had to figure something out, because becoming Charity Glasscott's whore was not an acceptable choice. Not by any stretch of the imagination.

My phone chimed with an alert, and I groaned as I read the message. It was a reminder from my sister Lola that we had dinner plans tonight with Rafe. We were meeting up with his girlfriend—though I wasn't sure *girlfriend* was the right word for her—and his best friend from work.

Ivy Anderson. If anything could take my mind off the shit storm that hit me today, it was her.

2

Ivy

$\mathcal{I}$ did *not* want to go to this dinner tonight. I loved Rafe like a brother, and Jessa was such a nice girl. If I'd been invited to join just the two of them, I'd be all in. But that wasn't the case.

Rafe's brother and sister would be there two, and he expected me to act as a kind of buffer between them and Jessa. I told him he was being an idiot, but he was fighting his feelings for her and wanted everything to stay casual and light.

And that meant not having her as the only non-family member at a family dinner. Which was where I came in.

Rafe's sister Lola was a total sweetheart—kind, considerate, funny, and uber-smart. She was six years younger than him and still in college. She'd graduate next year, a full year early, with a degree in business, and Rafe was so proud of her.

He'd finished raising her after their parents died when

he was eighteen, and she'd turned into a wonderful woman. *She* wasn't the problem with tonight's dinner.

It was Nate Walton that had my nerves tangling up like puppet strings. And I hated myself for that.

My mind drifted back to when I'd first met Nate. I hadn't been in Milestone long, moving here after earning my nursing degree and scoring a job in the emergency room in the town's only hospital. Rafe and I had been working together for a few weeks, and he was fast becoming my best friend.

When he'd introduced me to Nate and Lola, I'd been smitten with both of them. Lola, with her quiet sweetness and Nate, with his effervescent charm—they'd both won me over within minutes.

Nate, especially. He had this magnetic force about him, and I was powerless to resist. Not only was he hot as hell with those dark, Hispanic looks and bright blue eyes, he emanated this flirtatious charm that warmed my heart.

And other parts that had lain dormant for a long, long time.

For a while, it seemed like something sparked between us. Flirty banter, steamy gazes, and seemingly innocent brushes of a hand kept me keyed up and ready to explode for weeks. I wanted to jump his bones, despite his being Rafe's brother and theoretically off-limits.

Best friend code be damned. I'd rather ask for forgiveness than permission. Nate Walton would be worth whatever grief Rafe heaped on me afterwards. I just knew it.

I never acted on my attraction, thank God, because I couldn't have been more wrong about him. I'd seen it with my own eyes, and no amount of bleach could scrub the image from them.

I slumped onto my couch as the memories of that night assailed me.

"Excuse me. I'll be right back."

As Nate said those words, his gaze burned into me, bright and hot like a sunburst. He stood from his chair, giving me one last look before navigating his way through the tables toward the hallway where the restrooms were located.

We were at Hero's Pizza and More, having dinner with Rafe and Lola, and his electric blue eyes had been burning holes through me the entire time. He'd always been playful with me, throwing out phrases with double-meanings and seductive winks as if he were daring me to give into him. But tonight was different.

His whole demeanor was darker. More intent. His gaze was filled with need, and every time his shoe brushed against mine under the table, one corner of his mouth turned up, showcasing a deep dimple I wanted to explore with my tongue.

Slowly, he'd licked the hot wing sauce from his lips while he stared, making me press my thighs together. My panties were soaked, and an aching emptiness inside me begged to be filled…by his cock.

It was a dangerous game we were playing, shooting off fireworks while hoping Rafe and Lola didn't notice.

And now, what? That look he gave me as he left the table ordered me to follow him. Could I really do this? Could I satisfy my need for Nate Walton in a public restroom? Should I?

I knew I shouldn't, but that didn't stop me from making my own excuses and leaving the table. I was no longer in control. My libido had taken over my brain, and I was going to taste Nate right now, consequences be damned.

When I reached the small hallway, my eyes flicked between the two doors. I wasn't sure, exactly, where Nate went. Nor did I think I had the guts to push my way into the men's room looking for him. What if some dude was in there taking a piss at the urinals? Gross.

Shaking my head, I pushed open the door to the ladies' room. I froze, my brain not quite deciphering what my eyes were seeing.

Nate had his back against the far wall, his eyes squeezed shut as if he were in pain…or in the throes of pleasure. A woman was leaning into him, her mouth on his neck as her hands fumbled with the buckle of his belt. He raised his hands to grasp her shoulders, and I bolted.

I ran back to our table, mumbled off some bullshit excuse about being nauseous to Rafe and Lola, and rushed out of the restaurant, eager to get away from Nate Walton. From his lying eyes and treacherous smiles. From my most utter and extreme humiliation.

I opened my eyes and pulled myself from the memory. It had been years since that night, and I still remembered it as if it had happened yesterday. And it still hurt, no matter how many times I told myself it shouldn't.

We weren't together at the time. I'd misread his signals. It was *my* fault for letting his sly flirtations get under my skin when it was just fun and games to him.

It didn't matter. I'd decided that night, while my tears soaked my pillow, that Nate Walton would never hurt me again. A seed of hatred sprouted in my heart, and I nurtured it. It grew, unchecked, until I couldn't stand to breathe the same air as him.

I never hesitated to let him know how much he disgusted me. And he never asked why. Not once.

His lack of curiosity over my sudden personality transplant made one thing clear to me—he already knew the cause of it. Which meant he either knew I'd seen him with that tramp and didn't care…or the whole thing had been some cruel, twisted set up meant to cut me deep.

While I didn't want to believe the latter to be true, the idea that Nate had trifled with my emotions like that wouldn't fade.

And now, I'd let Rafe rook me into yet another family dinner. He'd begged me to come. He was fighting his feelings for Jessa, trying to keep things casual because of some unrealistic pact they'd made when things started between them.

I could see that he was fast on his way to love, but he refused to open his own eyes and thought my presence would make everything more relaxed.

As if. When Nate and I are in the same room, there's nothing relaxing about it.

A horn honked outside, and I knew my time was up. Rafe insisted on driving me, like he feared I would flake out if left to my own devices. And I might've, too.

This dinner was going to be hell.

~

"*A*ren't you going to say hello to me, Ivy?"

"Go fuck yourself, Nate."

The words flew from my mouth before I could stop them, and I felt the heat of a blush riding my cheeks. We were sitting around a large table in the middle of the restaurant, and I was tucked between Lola and Jessa—as far away from Nate as I could get. And yet, he may as well have been sitting on top of me with the way I was reacting to his proximity.

This was going to be bad.

"I'm sorry for these two, Jessa," Lola said right before Nate grunted in pain. She'd obviously kicked him under the table. "I don't know why Rafe thought it would be a good idea to bring them together like this, *again*."

"Is it so wrong that I want my family and my best friend to get along?" Rafe asked.

I snorted, but held my tongue. Nate mumbled something under his breath, and Lola frowned at Rafe.

Our waitress materialized beside the table, taking our drink orders while batting her eyelashes at Nate. He slouched in his seat, giving her the sexiest bedroom eyes he could muster as he bit his lower lip and ordered a drink.

All of the tactics he'd used on me, once upon a time. Jealousy warred with hatred inside me, turning me into a mass of fried nerve endings.

Jessa let out a loud snort as Nate asked the waitress for a sex on the beach, easing some of the tension inside me.

"Really?" she asked, the word dripping with sarcasm.

"What?" he shot back. "Maybe I like fruity drinks that don't taste like alcohol."

"You know she's a bartender, right?" I cut in, backing Jessa up. "She can spot a skanky guy ordering a skanky drink to try to get laid a mile away."

Nate's eyes narrowed as Jessa lifted her fist toward me. I raised my own fist and bumped it against hers. Victory zipped through me, making me smile maliciously as Nate frowned.

"I'm disappointed in you, Jessa," Nate said, a sorrowful look on his face. "You're supposed to be on my side."

"And why is that?" she asked, her smile growing wide.

"Yeah, why is that?" I repeated. Then, for good measure, I added, "Chicks before dicks, asshole."

"You wouldn't say that if you'd taken a whirl on this di—"

"That's enough, Nathaniel," Rafe growled, cutting off his crude comment. "What the hell is wrong with you?"

"Sorry," Nate mumbled, more toward his brother than me.

So much for me making things more comfortable at this shit show of a dinner.

Thankfully, our waitress approached, easing the tensions as she handed out our drinks. Unfortunately, she continued to flirt with Nate. He reacted to her advances more humbly than before, doing nothing to encourage her. But the damage had already been done.

"So, Lola, how is school going?" Jessa asked, thankfully changing the subject to something more palatable.

Lola gushed over her classes for a few minutes, but as soon as she finished, Rafe stood up.

"Jessa, can I speak to you privately, please?" he asked, holding out a hand to help her to her feet.

She took his hand and they walked out, leaving me alone with Nate and Lola. The poor girl tried to get the conversation going several times, then sighed with relief when the waitress came to take our orders.

Nate ordered for the table, and I didn't argue. I was already embarrassed by how I'd reacted to his earlier digs, so I kept my lips sealed and my eyes downcast.

After several tense, silent minutes, Jessa returned, alone.

"Everything okay?" Lola asked.

"Yeah, I'm good," Jessa said, sitting back down beside me.

My gaze scrutinized her face, one eyebrow arching as I gave her a knowing nod. Whatever they'd talked about out there, the conversation had ended with Jessa having a toe-curling orgasm. It was written all over her face with her bright, shining eyes and rosy red cheeks. Her face flared brighter with a blush, and I laughed. Lola and Nate looked at me like I was crazy, making Jessa chuckle.

"You chicas are loco," Nate mumbled, which made Jessa and I laugh even harder.

It felt good, forgetting my beef with Nate for a moment and just having fun. I made a mental note to make plans to hang out with Jessa more before she headed back to her home in Atlanta...*if* she headed back.

"What's so funny?" Rafe asked, slipping into the chair beside Jessa, and she whispered something in his ear that seemed to satisfy his curiosity.

The conversation picked up after that, and Nate and I took every opportunity to make little verbal stabs at each other. Lola quietly reprimanded her brother, and Rafe and Jessa remained completely unscathed in their little bubble of romance.

We'd barely finished eating when Nate threw his napkin onto his plate and stood up. He tossed three twenties onto the table, saying, "Thanks for this *lovely* dinner, Rafe. Come on, Lola. Let's go."

He stalked away, leaving Lola to squirm uncomfortably. Rafe gave her a warm smile and stood to hug her goodbye. She waved at Jessa and me before turning to chase after her brother.

"What is up with you two?" Jessa asked, cocking her head at me.

"Nothing," I said, flinching at how rushed and fake the word sounded. I let out a sigh, hoping it came off more realistic. "He just rubs me the wrong way, and I guess the feeling is mutual."

"Don't ask me. They've been like that since they met," Rafe said when she turned to him.

Not since we met. There were a few weeks of excitement and... hope. Before the night Nate showed his true colors.

"You guys ready?" I asked, eager to change the subject. "Rafe and I rode together, so—"

"You can take my car," Rafe cut in quickly. "I'll ride with Jessa, and you can pick me up for work tomorrow afternoon."

"Sounds good," I said, taking the keys from him and grabbing my purse from the back of my chair. "Jessa, I had a lot of fun tonight. We should hang out some time."

"Sure," she said, smiling back at me.

"You two kids have fun," I sing-songed, shooting Rafe a wink before turning to leave.

I hurried across the lot and climbed into Rafe's SUV before the two of them even made it outside. I watched them hop into Jessa's Jeep, all smiles and anticipation while my own mood dropped even lower. I was happy for Rafe. Jessa, too.

I was strong enough to admit I was a bit jealous of what they had. They were both in denial about how strong their feelings were growing, but I could see the hearts in their eyes, even from a distance.

I wanted that for myself, and I was beginning to think it might never happen.

3

Nate

$\mathcal{T}$he Bullpen was pretty crowded, even for a Saturday night. Dane and I were sitting at the bar, nursing beers and watching game four of the World Series on the big screen in front of us. I'd taken off my jacket and hung it over the back of my barstool, the heat of the crowd warming me from the outside as the alcohol did the same to my inside.

"Rafe's girlfriend isn't working tonight," Dane mused, his eyes roaming over the two bartenders running themselves ragged.

"It's moving day," I said, taking a swig of my beer.

It had been a crazy few weeks since our disastrous "family" dinner, and Rafe and Jessa had pulled their heads out of their asses—with a little help from me—and decided to admit their feelings to each other. Jessa decided to stay in Milestone, running this bar for her father and giving her relationship with my brother a real shot.

And today, she moved into my childhood home with

my brother. I was happy for him. For both of them. But I still had a very big problem, and being in this place reminded me of how it all got started.

As if reading my mind, Dane asked, "Anything new with the Charity situation?"

I shook my head. "She keeps texting me, telling me she knows I want her and that I should just stop fighting myself."

"Any new threats?"

"Nothing concrete. She's too smart. She knows if she gives me *anything* to use against her, I will. In a heartbeat. But the implied threat is always there. Her last text said her patience was growing thin, and that I only have two weeks to decide."

"So, what are you going to do?"

Before I can answer, a woman sidles up to me, pressing her breasts against my arm. "Hey there, sexy. Can I buy you a drink?"

"That's sweet of you, but I'm good," I said, tipping my half-full beer in her direction.

I tried not to make too much eye contact, hoping she'd take the hint and leave. She was hot and seemed to be willing, but I wasn't in the mood. Besides, letting a horny woman pick me up in a bar was what got me into this mess in the first place.

Her fingertips drifted over my thigh as she angled herself forward, giving me a better view of her tits. And while those plump orbs and forward behavior might've tempted me in some past life, right now, her aggression annoyed me.

"Hey, darlin'," Dane said, leaning back to see around me. "What's your name?"

Her eyes flashed from me to Dane and back again, like she was giving me one last chance to take the bait before moving on. When I glued my eyes to the television screen on the wall, she shrugged and sauntered around to snuggle up against him.

Dane tilted the neck of his beer in my direction, and I clinked mine against it. Like some kind of reverse wingman, he offered himself as a pinch hitter to keep me from having to be rude. I took another drink of my beer, ignoring the cooing noises the woman was making as Dane wrapped his arm around her.

How had I ever found that attractive? The insincere pandering used to boost my ego and make my dick twitch with desire. Now it just annoyed the shit out of me.

Maybe Charity Glasscott had ruined me for quick, easy hookups. Maybe I was just in a bad mood, rightfully so. Or maybe I was just growing up.

Whatever the reason, I wasn't feeling it. I rapped my knuckles on the bar, getting the bartender's attention. I signaled for my check, then drained the rest of my beer.

"Where are you going?" Dane asked, only half his attention on me as his new friend explored his chest with roaming hands.

"Home," I said, then nodded toward the woman. "Have fun."

I handed the bartender my credit card and climbed from the barstool before slipping my jacket on. Signing the check, I left a decent tip and slid my wallet into my back pocket. Patting Dane on the back, I slipped away, pretending not to notice the brunette walking toward me, her hips swaying like there was an R&B record playing in her head.

I made a beeline for the door, not looking back to see her disappointed expression. I couldn't help but think something was wrong with me as I made my escape. Where I should've been hot and ready to indulge the sexy brunette's advances, I'd felt nothing but revulsion at the thought of entertaining them. Outside, in the brisk October air, relief washed through me.

"Maybe I should ask Rafe for a physical," I mumbled, shaking my head as I made my way to my car.

Something was definitely wrong with me.

I ran a fingertip over the glossy black hood as I rounded the car. I'd restored the sixty-six Mustang with my own hands. It had been nothing more than a rusted out skeleton, and I'd spent more than a year tracking down parts to return it to all its glory. It was my pride and joy.

I slid into the leather seat and cranked the ignition, my whole body relaxing as I tapped the accelerator and revved the motor. The sound was my favorite song, the vibration my favorite melody. This car was perfection, and she was mine.

I took the long way home, driving up and down deserted country roads where I could really let loose. Shifting quickly through the gears, I gunned it, letting the speed fill my body with adrenaline. But the usual excitement wasn't there, and my dilemma with Charity kept sneaking in and dampening my high.

"Damn it," I grunted, turning the car around.

I headed home to my quiet apartment. I tossed my keys on the table and grabbed a water bottle from the fridge, then slumped onto my couch. Clicking on the television, I tuned in to see the end of the baseball game. I tried like hell to lose myself in it, but my mind kept circling back to Charity and her demands.

I had to come up with something. The thought of giving her what she wanted was intolerable.

My phone chimed, and I picked it up to see a text message.

Dane: *Dude, that bitch was crazy. She tried to pull my cock out right there at the bar. I barely escaped.*

A laugh burst through my lips. Some guys might enjoy being manhandled in public, but not Dane. He was a bit of a romantic, and tried to make even casual hookups feel special. I teased him about it mercilessly, but deep down, I had nothing but respect for him. He was one of the good ones.

Me: *You mean you didn't let her choke your chicken before you left? I'm revoking your man card.*

Dane: *Ha. Ha. You don't know how accurate your phrasing is. She locked my wrist in a death grip when I tried to stop her. My chicken would've been choked, for sure.*

I laughed again, imagining his face as some horny chick tried to pull out his dick while he fought her off. I knew what he was doing, sending me these ridiculous texts. And it was working.

Me: *Thanks, man. I needed that.*

Dane: *Any time, bro. Come up with a plan yet?*

Me: *I got nothing.*

Dane: *Hmm. Too bad you don't have a girlfriend. That would be one surefire way to put a stop to Charity's game.*

I leaned my head back and dropped my phone on the couch beside me. Could Dane be right? Would my being in a relationship make Charity back off?

Probably not. Girlfriends come and go. She could simply wait it out, or demand that I break things off with this supposed girlfriend to be with her.

No. It would have to be something serious. Like…an engagement.

I sat forward and propped my elbows on my knees. I'd have to find someone who would be willing to go the whole nine yards—date me, wear my ring, and maybe even move in with me—to make it look like the real deal.

But it would also have to be someone I could trust not to develop feelings for me. I refused to escape one trap, only to be locked in another. It had to be strictly business, with each of us getting something we wanted out of the situation.

But what did I have to offer in return? It had to be tempting enough to make a woman put her life on hold for God knew how long to help me out.

I shook my head. I'd worry about my payment later. First, I needed to find a woman. *The* woman.

Someone who would never develop romantic feelings for me, but could pretend well enough to fool everyone. One face popped into my head, but I brushed it aside with a mutter.

"No fucking way."

4

_____

Ivy

"So, how are things?"

I couldn't help but tease Rafe when he walked into the E.R. with that cheesy grin on his face. His life had changed so much since Jessa stumbled her way into it, and I couldn't have been happier for him.

"Things are good, my friend," he said his smile growing even bigger. "Things are *real* good."

"Ugh, you're positively sickening," I said, hip-checking him as he passed by me to get to his locker.

"Hey, you encouraged this," he accused with a laugh.

And I had. I'd seen right away how good that girl was for him. He just needed a little nudging in the right direction to see it for himself.

"Oh," he said, spinning to face me. "Jessa and I are hosting a Halloween party at our place this weekend. Tell me you'll come."

"Of course, I will. Why do you think I wouldn't?"

He shrugged. "Nate."

I shook my head. "It's fine. It's a big house. I'm sure I can avoid him."

"Are you ever going to tell me why you hate him so much? I just don't get it."

"I don't know, Rafe," I lied. I knew exactly why. "Haven't you ever known someone who just rubs you the wrong way, no matter what they say or do?"

"Not really," he said. "I mean, he's my brother, and I love him, but I know he's not perfect. He's cocky and stubborn, but most women find those traits attractive when it comes to Nate."

"I'm not most women," I said, refusing to meet his eyes.

Rafe could usually read me like a book, but this subject was one I wanted kept close to the vest. My reasons for hating Nate were too personal...and too embarrassing. Luckily for me, I'd hated him long enough that Rafe didn't even remember the short time that I didn't.

"Oh, that's me," he said as a nurse paged him over the intercom. "I gotta go. So, can I tell Jessa you'll be there?"

"I'll be there," I said, waving him off.

My shift was over, so I grabbed my things from my locker. Checking my phone, I realized I had a string of text messages. Jessa had added me to a group chat between her and her two besties, Karly Brooks and Felicia Stone. They were going out for a girls' night tonight, and they wanted me to come.

I started to reply that I was dead on my feet after my shift, so I couldn't make it. I stopped typing mid-sentence and took a deep breath. I *was* tired, but I also dreaded going home to my empty apartment.

Me: *I'm in.*

I hit send before I could talk myself out of it, and was rewarded with a slew of celebratory texts from all three of them. A smile curved my lips, as anticipation shimmered through me.

A girls' night out was just what I needed.

My long, hot shower revived me, and I slipped into my favorite blue jeans and a pink top before perusing my boot collection. Western boots of every color, height, and toe-shape were lined up in my closet, and I tapped a finger against my lips as I tried to decide which ones to wear.

My eyes landed on my newest pair, the ones I hadn't even worn yet. Brown leather with a snip toe and a western heel, the stitching was in bright blue and pink, making them perfectly matched with tonight's outfit. I smiled as I grabbed them from the rack and went to sit on my bed.

Rafe had bought me these boots when I balked at going to dinner with his family. Yeah, it was a bribe, but when he offered, I couldn't resist. They were gorgeous, and they fit like a glove.

My phone chimed, and the newest text told me the girls were here to pick me up. According to Karly's messages, I was morally and legally obligated to get schnockered tonight as the newbie in their group. Like some sort of initiation.

I wasn't opposed to it. Lord knew, it had been a long time since I really let loose. I was actually looking forward to it.

"Let's do this," I muttered as I grabbed my purse and tucked my phone inside before heading out and locking up.

The girls had the windows down and were screaming at me to hurry up over the music blaring from the speakers. I shook my head and laughed, even as I picked up the pace.

This was going to be one wild night.

~

"*T*ell me what you're looking for in a man," Felicia said, her words slurring the slightest bit.

Or maybe it was my hearing that was slurring. Wait, that didn't make sense. Could hearing slur?

"Ivy, focus," Karly said, slapping a hand against the table. "We're doing something very important here."

My eyes darted to Jessa, who was leaning back in her chair, laughing at us. She was the designated driver for the night, sipping on lemon water and quietly enjoying our drunken antics.

We'd somehow ended up at her bar The Bullpen after Karly and Felicia had declared the first two places "boring as bananas." Whatever that meant.

"I don't know, really," I said, answering Felicia's request for a list of desirable attributes for my dream guy. "He'd have to be nice, I guess."

"Bor-r-r-ring," Karly yelled, stretching the word out. "I think you need a hot bad boy to release your inner vixen."

"I don't know, Karly," Felicia said, her eyes narrowing on me. "He could be nice in the boardroom and naughty in the bedroom."

"That doesn't even make any sense, you drunk bitch," Karly shot back. "Why would Ivy want some stuffed suit who works in a boardroom? She needs someone who drives fast, talks slow, and isn't afraid to get down and dirty."

"It was a euphemism, dumbass," Felicia shot back.

Shit, this was getting out of hand. I didn't want them fighting over me or what my supposed dream guy should look like. This was supposed to be a fun girls' night out.

"Don't worry," Jessa said, leaning in close to speak directly to me when she saw the concerned look on my face. "They're always like this. Watch."

She nodded toward Karly and Felicia, who were still bickering. I looked over just in time to see Felicia's fist strike out and pop Karly's right boob. Karly squealed as her hand came up to rub the spot.

"Hey," she complained, her bottom lip poking out.

"That's payback for last time," Felicia said, her smile victorious.

I looked back at Jessa, my eyes wide, but she just laughed and shook her head. I picked up my beer and took another sip. These girls were crazy.

And I think I liked it.

"Anyway, *Ivy*," Felicia said, stressing my name, "back to your dream guy. What's he look like?"

Nate Walton's face flashed through my mind, and I gasped, inhaling the sip of beer I'd been attempting to swallow. Jessa patted me firmly on the back as my lungs spasmed, harsh coughs wracking my body as they tried to dispel the liquid.

"Are you okay?" Jessa asked.

"Yeah," I croaked, coughing again. "Wrong pipe."

"So, dream guy?" Karly asked, getting the conversation back on track.

"Blonde. Brown eyes. Tall and skinny."

The words flowed from my lips without any real thought, describing attributes that just happened to be the complete opposite of Nate. It wasn't intentional, and it also wasn't true. With his dark hair, sandy complexion, and bright blue eyes, Nate's face was…perfection. At just shy of six feet tall with lean, corded muscles, his body made me want to run my fingertips all over it.

No. Bad, Ivy. He's detestable, and you hate him.

"Huh," Karly said. "I wouldn't have guessed that. Let's see."

She raised up in her seat, making a show of looking

around the bar. After a second look, she slumped back into her chair with a shake of her head.

"Nope. No candidates here, tonight."

"That's fine with me," I said, my words definitely slurring. "I'm not really looking for a relationship right now, anyway."

"Who is?" Felicia asked. "Take Jessa, for instance. That girl had more relationship-anxiety than everyone in this bar, combined. Now, look at her."

I looked at Jessa, who wore a huge grin. I smiled back at her. She was in love, and she made Rafe happier than I'd ever seen him. I threw an arm over her shoulder and squeezed.

"I'm so happy you and Rafe found each other. You both deserve it."

My voice sounded weepy and emotional—thanks to all the bottles of beer I'd downed—but I didn't care. Finding true love might not be in the cards for me, but at least my best friend had found his.

And I whole-heartedly approved.

5

Nate

I should've left the moment I saw them sitting there. Instead, I found a table in a darker corner and nursed my beer, watching them like some stalker in a made for TV movie.

I knew if Jessa spotted me, she'd bring my presence to the rest of the table's attention. And if that happened, things were going to get weird. Not because of Jessa—that girl was practically a member of the family after moving in with Rafe.

No, it was because of Ivy, our feud, and my psychotic plan of asking her to be my fake girlfriend, or fiancée, or whatever. It had seemed like a logical solution before. Being in a committed relationship would get Charity off my back, and having Ivy play the part would be perfect because there'd be no chance of her developing real feelings for me in the meantime.

But seeing her now, so relaxed, smiling and laughing... it was so at odds with the perpetual angry face she wore around me. It had me all twisted up inside, and as I sipped my beer, my mind wandered back to when we'd first met.

I'd been instantly attracted to her. I wanted to run my fingers through that long, blonde hair. I wanted to taste her lips and every other inch of her skin, and I wanted to count every freckle scattered across her nose and cheeks. She was beautiful, funny, and way too smart for a grease monkey like me.

And for a while, it seemed like my interest was reciprocated. Her blue eyes sparkled with hunger when she looked at me. Her cheeks turned pink and her eyes darted away when she'd realize she'd been caught looking. Even now, desire flickered inside me when I thought about it.

Then suddenly, everything changed. No more stolen glances. No more pretty blushes. I'd been shocked at first, not knowing what had happened to change things. I tried to talk to her, but she avoided being alone with me for even a second. And as her animosity grew, mine spiked up to match it.

Maybe she'd only been toying with me. Maybe she realized I wasn't good enough for her.

Or maybe my big brother warned her off. She was his best friend, and I had a reputation of being a bit of a player. If he gave her details of my track record with women, that would explain her sudden standoffishness.

But would that make her *hate* me?

"Whatever," I mumbled, taking another drink of my beer.

It was a long time ago, and it didn't matter. There was enough animosity between us now to guarantee we'd never actually like each other. Which made Ivy Anderson the perfect candidate for my plan.

I just needed to figure out how to convince her of that.

~

$\mathcal{I}$ stood on the porch of my childhood home, my toe tapping against the wood as I waited. I nodded at the guests as they arrived for Rafe and Jessa's Halloween party, my eyes constantly searching for the one person I wanted to see.

I'd come straight from work, wearing a pair of dirty coveralls with wrenches poking out of the pockets and brake dust smeared across my forehead. Not very original, but it would work for a costume. Besides, I had other, more important things on my mind.

I'd made the decision—I was going to talk to Ivy.

A ball of dread formed in the pit of my stomach. Talking to Ivy was…difficult, at best. But what I was about to propose? I'd be lucky if she didn't laugh in my face before heading inside to tell everyone my idiotic request so they could all have a good chuckle.

I pushed the doubts away and strengthened my resolve. I could do this. I could convince her. She loved Rafe like a brother, so there was no way she'd leave me hanging and let my business go under because of a little animosity. Right?

My internal debate screeched to a halt as Ivy's car pulled along the curb. I was off the porch and striding toward her before she could even shift into park. She yelped when I opened the door and slid into the passenger's seat, flinching back against her own door.

"You know, you should really keep your doors locked when you're driving alone," I chided, pulling the door closed behind me.

"What are you doing?" she demanded. "Get out of my car, Nate."

She turned off the ignition and moved to open her

door, and my hand shot out to grasp her arm. She froze, her eyes darting to my fingers, and I quickly released her.

"I'm sorry. Please. I really need to talk to you," I pled, hoping she'd see the sincerity on my face in the dim glow of the streetlight through the windshield.

Her hand released the door handle, but the tension I could feel coming off her in waves didn't ease in the slightest. Silence reigned between us for several moments, and I realized she was waiting for me to speak. I shook my head and angled my body toward her.

"Thank you," I said softly, then took a deep breath. "I have a favor to ask. A huge one."

Her eyes narrowed as she asked, "What kind of favor?"

"I need you," I said, pausing to order my thoughts, "to help me out with a little problem I have. No. Scratch that. It's a huge problem, and you're pretty much my only hope."

"Just spit it out, Nate," she ordered.

"Okay. So, you know Milestone Bank & Trust?"

"Our town's only bank that *everyone* uses? Yeah, I know it," she shot back.

"Well, the owner, Chester Glasscott, has this daughter—"

"I am not helping you hook up with the next notch in your belt, Nate," she said, her voice angry.

I held up my palms. "Woah, there. Don't be ridiculous, Ivy. That's not what I was asking."

Shit. This is not going well. Backpedal. Backpedal. Backpedal.

"Sorry," I said, apologizing for my tone. "Please, hear me out."

"Fine," she said, crossing her arms over her chest.

"Charity Glasscott, who I made the mistake of sleeping with one time, has decided she wants me, permanently," I said, opting to be one hundred percent transparent. She made a disgusted face, but didn't respond, so I went on. "She threatened the shop, Ivy. She said if I don't fall into line and give her what she wants, she'll have Daddy alter my loan payment history to make it look like I'm in default. I could lose everything."

"That must've been one hell of a night," she deadpanned.

"Ivy," I said, my voice deep and chastising.

She rolled her eyes. "That sucks, but what does it have to do with me?"

"I have a plan, but, like I said, I need you."

"To do what?"

Her voice raised in pitch as if she were truly afraid of my answer. My hand itched to reach out and touch her. To wipe away her anxiety and make her feel more relaxed. But I knew my touch would have the opposite effect, so I kept my hands to myself and prepared to spit out the whole crazy idea.

"If I were in a real, committed relationship, she might give up and move on."

She blinked several times as if processing my words. Obviously not getting it, she said, "And?"

"And I want you to pretend to be my fiancée to get her to back off."

There. Like ripping off a Band-Aid.

And with the way her head flew back, that Band-Aid took some leg hairs with it.

Harsh laughter burst from her mouth, filling the space between us with mockery and disdain. I remained silent until her dark humor faded, and she blew out a breath while wiping the tears from her eyes.

"Good one, Nate," she said. "You really had me going there. You know it's Halloween, not April Fool's Day, right?"

She was openly mocking me now, and I felt my anger rising to the surface. "I'm being serious, Ivy."

"How can you say that? It would never work, Nate. We hate each other."

"I've never hated you," I whispered, cutting off whatever she planned to say next.

She paused for a moment, her expression softening the tiniest bit. "A mutual dislike, then. Why don't you just contact the police?"

"I don't have any proof. She spelled it out for me one time, and ever since then it's been nothing but hints and innuendos."

"But surely you have proof of payments to dispute whatever claims they make. Right?"

"Of course, I do," I said defensively before looking down at my lap. "It's just…a few of them were late."

"What? How did that happen?"

The shop is my pride and joy. She knows that, so her incredulous reaction was expected. I would *never* let my payments fall behind. And technically, I didn't. I leaned my head back to stare up at the roof of the car.

"Several months ago, I hired a new office manager to help out at the shop. She was in charge of answering the phones, processing payroll, and sending out the bill payments from the business account. My first hint that something wasn't right was when the electricity went out."

"She wasn't paying it?" she asked, her face softening with sympathy.

"No. I was an idiot. I watched her like a hawk for the first three months, and she was perfect. Every task was completed in a timely manner, no mistakes. I became too comfortable, trusting her to continue to do her job."

"But…you didn't see that the money for the payments wasn't being deducted from your business account?"

"I said I was an idiot, didn't I?" I snapped. She flinched, and I backed down quickly. "I'm sorry, Ivy. I shouldn't speak to you like that, no matter how upset I am."

Her suspicious expression returned, and it wasn't totally unfounded. I'd spoken to her way more harshly over the last few years. But in my defense, my nastiness was usually a reflexive reaction to her own unpleasantness. I forged on before I lost her completely.

"I was wrapped up in a rebuild, working long nights after-hours to get it finished. Between that and the nonstop line of cars coming through the shop during regular business hours, I grew too dependent on her to take care of all the administrative stuff. Like I said...idiot. I don't know what happened or when things shifted, but she stopped mailing out the checks I was writing."

"Wait. Wait," she cut in, her eyes wide. "You still write checks?"

"Yes," I said defensively. "I feel more comfortable with a physical paper trail for my records. Call me old school."

"How'd that work out for you?" she mumbled before her hand shot out to pat my knee. "Sorry. That was uncalled for."

With a gasp, she yanked her hand away from me as if it burned. Like she only just realized she was touching me and couldn't believe the gall of her fingertips. Meanwhile, I was deftly ignoring the sparks of electricity tingling from that simple touch.

"It's okay," I croaked out before clearing my throat. "The gist of it is, she was stashing the envelopes for all of my monthly expenses into her desk drawer to send out *later*." I lifted my hands to make air quotes with that last word. "Everything fell behind...with my business loan not being paid for three months. I fired her ass, called the bank, and the manager was very sympathetic. I paid the overdue amount and everything was fine."

"Until Charity's threats," she added.

"Exactly. I don't know if she somehow got a peek at my account, or if she's just bluffing, but it's too much of a risk. My now-sullied payment history is a real problem. Maybe they're empty threats. Maybe not. I don't know, but I can't take that chance."

"And that's where I come in," she said softly before meeting my gaze. "You want me to pretend to be in a relationship with you to…what? Make her forget about you and your magic dick?"

I flinched. *Damn it, Rafe.* Of course, he would tell her about that.

"Ivy, please. Name your terms. I'll give you anything."

She grew silent, still looking in my direction but not really focusing. After several tense moments, her gaze locked back onto mine.

"Why me?"

"Because you're the only person guaranteed not to catch feelings while we're pretending," I said simply. "You and I can treat this like a business deal, and when it's over, it's over." When she didn't respond, I added, "Please, Ivy. Say you'll do it. Say you'll help me out of this. I'll give you anything. Anything you want."

I knew I sounded pathetic, begging like that. But I was desperate. If Ivy refused me, I had no idea what I was going to do.

"I need some time to think about it," she murmured.

I nodded and, without saying another word, got out of the car. It wasn't a *no*. If Ivy needed time, I'd give it to her.

I just hoped she wouldn't take too long to decide.

6

_____

Ivy

$\mathcal{H}$oly hell. What just happened? Did Nathaniel Walton just asked me to pretend to be his…? It's so ridiculous, I can't even bring myself to think the words.

I knew Milestone was no hot mecca of young singles looking to mingle, but Nate could've asked literally *anyone* else—assuming they were unattached—to do this for him, and they would've jumped on the opportunity in a hot second.

Nate was a young, healthy, successful guy with an undeniable sexual appeal—

Nope. Stop it, Ivy. None of that.

Physical attributes aside, Nate was smooth. He could've sweet talked any number of women into pretending to be his girlfriend. No. *Fiancée.* And if Charity Glasscott refused to back off, how far was he planning to take this?

I shook my head. It didn't matter. No way was I going

to agree to his ridiculous plan. It was a dumpster fire waiting to happen, and I had no desire to get burned.

I took a deep breath of the crisp night air and blew it out. The noises from inside reminded me I should be in there, enjoying Rafe and Jessa's Halloween-slash-housewarming party. But still, I didn't budge from my perch on the back steps. I was still reeling, and it was too soon to come face to face with Nate. I needed to figure this out on my own, without his magnetic blue gaze influencing me.

Because, despite all the hate we thrusted in each other's directions—or maybe because of it—he still had the ability to affect me.

The back door swung open, and I tensed, only to relax when I saw it was Jessa.

"Mind if I join you?" she asked, parking next to me before I could answer.

"Of course," I said. "I was just getting some air."

"Not having fun?" she asked, and the weight of Nate's proposal suddenly felt too heavy to hold on my own.

I couldn't talk to Rafe about it for obvious reasons, and Jessa was my closest girlfriend. Of course, *she'd* tell Rafe…

"It's not that," I said with a sigh. I needed to get a different perspective, so I admitted, "It's Nate."

"What's the deal with you two?" she asked.

"When I first met Rafe at the hospital, we became instant friends," I said softly, realizing I needed to go back to the beginning. "I immediately felt this kinship with him, like he was a long-lost brother or something. But when I met Nate, my feelings were anything but sisterly."

I barked out a self-deprecating laugh, which Jessa seemed to ignore.

"You were attracted to him?" she asked.

I gave her an incredulous look. "Have you *seen* him?"

"Eh," she said, holding out a palm and tilting it back and forth. "He's alright."

"Whatever," I said, laughing for real this time. Then I sobered. "I thought I felt a connection. I was so into him, and I thought he liked me, too. But I was wrong."

"What happened?"

"I caught him fucking some waitress in the bathroom at Hero's."

"Shit," she groaned. "I'm sorry, Ivy."

"It was a long time ago," I said, waving a hand in the air. "I'm over it."

"Then why are you sitting out here all alone?" she asked, lifting one eyebrow.

"Because he approached me tonight with a proposition. One I'm having trouble refusing, even though I *know* I should run fast in the other direction."

And as the words flowed past my lips, I realized they were true. Despite my logical brain screaming at me, begging me to avoid Nate and this harebrained scheme, something deep inside me wanted to help him. Maybe it was because he was Rafe's brother. Rafe made me feel like part of the family, and family didn't turn their backs on each other.

Another voice in my head whispered, *"Bullshit,"* but I ignored that, too.

"What is it?" she asked, and it took me a second to decipher the question.

"I can't say," I said, realizing she wanted to know what the favor was. I didn't know if it was supposed to be a secret or not, so I decided to err on the side of caution. "Anyway, thanks for listening. I'll figure it out. Let's go back inside."

I stood up with those quickly spoken words, and

though Jessa's expression was skeptical, she nodded and led the way.

I spent the next hour avoiding Nate, never allowing myself to be caught alone. He didn't try to force his presence on me, but I got snagged by the pleading glances he sent my way too many times to count. He was wearing me down, and I hated the fact that he was doing it so effortlessly.

Was I really that weak? That a few earnest looks from across a crowded room would make me putty in his hands? No. If I was going to agree to his outlandish scheme, I needed to get something out of it, too.

Something concrete. Something invaluable. Something to make the pain of pretending with him worth it.

I let my gaze wander over him when his attention was diverted by Lola. His costume was equal parts uninventive and sexy as fuck—the mechanic's coveralls accentuated his broad chest while leaving enough to the imagination to make a girl want to strip them off to discover what hid underneath. I forced the mental image from my head and focused on the obvious.

Nate was an auto mechanic. And while his shop didn't provide the service to general customers, I knew he had a talent for body work, too. His precious Mustang was a testament to his skill.

And suddenly, I knew what I wanted.

As if he could hear my thoughts, Nate looked my way, catching my eye with a hopeful expression. Steeling my spine, I jerked my head toward the front door before walking out as I tried, in vain, to keep my pace slow and steady. My heart was pounding, and I forced myself to believe it was because of what I would get out of this deal. Nothing more.

Hell, I didn't even know if he'd agree to it. But he had said *anything*.

I walked to my car, and smashing the button on the fob to unlock the doors, I slid in behind the wheel. The passenger door was banging closed before I even got settled, Nate's blue eyes burning into my profile. It was even worse than I imagined when I turned to meet his gaze. I nearly melted on the spot from its intensity.

"I've decided on my terms," I said.

"Anything," he shot back quickly. "Whatever you want, it's yours."

Whatever I want? No. Down girl. Bad Ivy.

Clearing my throat, I nodded toward his car parked in the driveway behind Rafe's SUV. "You rebuilt that thing pretty much from scratch, right?"

His head turned slowly, his eyes wide as he focused on what was obviously his pride and joy. His head whipped back toward me, his eyes narrowed as that blue gaze burned into my skin.

"You want my car?" he asked, though it sounded more like an accusation.

Oh, this is too easy.

"You did say you'd give me anything I wanted, Nate," I replied, my voice firm as I tried like hell not to laugh.

I didn't want his car. I knew how much that thing meant to him, and I would never ask him to part with it. But a devil inside me wanted to know just how far he'd go to get me to agree to this fake engagement.

"I did say that," he murmured, his eyes losing focus as he considered my price.

A myriad of emotions played across his features, ranging from outright obstinacy to careful deliberation to grim acceptance.

"Fine. It's yours."

My head flew back with surprise as I stared at him with wide eyes. Did he really just agree to give me his most prized possession? No, not *most* prized. The most important thing to him was his shop, and it was quickly becoming obvious that he really would do anything to protect it.

"Relax, Nate. I don't want your car," I said, injecting enough flippancy into my tone to cover the sudden wave of respect that filled me at his sacrifice.

"You don't?" he asked, sounding so relieved, I couldn't contain my chuckle.

"No," I said. "I only mentioned it because what I want is a custom rebuild."

His dark eyebrows pulled down as he considered my words. His gaze roamed the interior of my car, and I could practically see the wheels turning in his head. My low-budget economy car was no collector's prize.

"Not this car," I clarified, and he blew out a relieved breath.

At my glare, he held up his palms. "No offense, but there isn't much I could do to make this thing look better. And I know it runs good, because I personally take care of the service and repairs."

He flinched slightly, like he hadn't meant to let that little nugget of information slip. I took my car into his shop for regular service…it would be stupid of me not to. Walton's was the best shop in town, and Nate grudgingly gave me the family discount—which meant free labor and parts for cost.

But I just assumed Dane or one of the other mechanics took care of it. I had no idea Nate, himself did the work. I shook my head to clear it. I needed to refocus on the issue at hand.

"You know my father passed away five years ago, right?" I asked, and he nodded. "Well, he had this project car that he'd been tinkering with for years. A gift for my mom that he never got a chance to finish."

"What kind of car?" he asked, his eyes gleaming in the dim interior vanity light.

"A fifty-five Bel Air convertible," I said.

He whistled long and low. "A classic. Could be hard to find parts for it. How much work is left to be done?"

"I have no idea," I admitted. "It's parked in a barn behind the house, and I haven't been back there since my dad died. It was…too hard."

"And now?" he asked, his voice filled with a soft concern that warmed my insides uncomfortably.

"Now, I think it would be the perfect Christmas gift for Mom from me *and* Dad."

"Christmas?" he croaked, his eyes flying wide again.

"Do you think you could do it?" I asked. "I know it's only a couple of months away…"

"I won't know until I can get a peek at it," he admitted. "But if it can be done, I'll do it."

He let that sink in for a minute, his eyes never leaving mine. A prickly sensation I couldn't define tattooed up my spine. Maybe it was anticipation. Maybe it was foreboding. Whatever it was, it wasn't entirely unpleasant.

"So, do we have a deal?" he asked, holding out a hand between us.

I sucked in a breath and slipped my hand into his, giving it a firm shake. "You fix my mom's car, and I'll be your devoted fiancée until Miss Glasscott backs off and you figure out the whole loan thing."

"Agreed," he said, pumping my hand once more, then squeezing it slightly before letting it go. "I'll call you tomorrow, and we can iron out the details."

Then he threw open the door and slipped out. Turning, he propped one arm on the top of the door frame and the other on the roof so he could lean back inside. Giving me a smile that had my traitorous toes curling, he patted the roof with his hand.

"Thanks, Ivy. You're really saving my ass."

He pulled out and slammed the door, striding away before I could even respond. *And* giving me a delectable view of said ass.

I tore my eyes away from it and banged my forehead lightly against the steering wheel.

What had I just gotten myself into?

7

Nate

"So, Nate, how are things going with you?"

I jerked at the sound of my name, my eyes flying up to meet Jessa's. Most of their guests had trickled out over the last hour, with Lola and I being the final two remaining. We were sitting in the living room, and I'd been zoning out while the conversation flowed around me.

I couldn't get Ivy and the deal we'd struck out of my head.

"Things are good," I said, leaning further back into my chair. "Why do you ask?"

"No reason," she said, tilting her head to peer at me. "You just seem distracted, and Ivy said something about a proposition…"

Her words trailed off suggestively, and Rafe straightened to glare at me. "What kind of proposition?"

My gaze shot back to Jessa and narrowed, but she just shrugged and grinned, the little imp. I was sure that whatever Ivy had told her, it had been vague. If Jessa knew the whole of it, she'd have run straight to Rafe and they'd both be up my ass.

No, this was a fishing expedition, and I wasn't biting.

Or maybe it was the perfect opportunity to put my plans into motion. I just hoped Ivy wouldn't hate me even more for this when she found out about it.

"Oh, yeah," I said, shrugging like the whole thing was no big deal. "I asked her out."

"You what?" Lola and Rafe shouted the words in perfect synch while Jessa's mouth fell open in shock.

"What's the big deal? She's attractive, brilliant, and single. Just like me," I said, adding a cocky grin at the end for good measure.

"Are you forgetting that she hates you?" Lola asked.

"Yeah, why does she hate you? I've always wondered, but she always get squirelly and brushes off my questions," Rafe added.

"I have no idea," I replied honestly. "But she must not hate me as much as we all thought, because she said yes."

"She did?" Jessa asked, her eyes wide with disbelief.

"You're hell on a man's ego, Jessa Maddox," I groused. "Why is that so unbelievable?"

I puffed out my chest and gave her my sexiest grin. Her mouth snapped shut, and she burrowed closer to my brother.

"Because you're an asshole to Ivy every time you see her," Rafe supplied, his arm closing around his girl.

"Maybe she likes it," I shot back coolly, but everything inside me rejected the idea.

Ivy most certainly did not like it when I was an ass, and I made sure to *always* be one around her. Why was that? Because I'd been insulted by her sudden rejection of me so many years ago? Or did I crave something more than the disinterested antipathy she showed me before I started trying to get a reaction out of her?

"Anyway, that's in the past," I said, shaking off the thoughts. "Ivy and I are putting away the past and moving forward."

"I still don't understand," Lola said, scrubbing a hand down her face.

"You'll get it when you're older, kid," I said ruffling her hair.

"I'm not a kid anymore, jerk-face," she grumbled, making me laugh.

"I don't know what you're doing, Nate, but you better not hurt her," Rafe said, his warning tone like a stab to the gut.

Whose side was he on, anyway? Obviously not mine.

"And what if she hurts me?" I shot back, trying to sound flippant.

But the joke fell flat. Everyone in the room was certain that if anyone was doing the hurting, it was going to be me. And to their credit, it was usually an accurate assessment.

But this time, with *this* girl, I wasn't so sure.

~

*M*e: *Hey, do you have time to talk?*

I watched my phone screen for the tell-tale dots that would show Ivy was responding, but nothing happened. Pushing my disappointment away, I dropped my phone to the bed beside me and flipped through the TV channels.

It was ten in the morning, so I was reasonably sure she wasn't sleeping. The shop was closed on Sundays, so I was free, and I'd hoped she would be available to work out the details of our agreement. Now that she was on board, I was eager to get started.

The sooner I got Charity Glasscott off my back, the better.

My phone chimed, and I bobbled it in my haste to pick it up. Cursing, I forced my movements to slow, and opened my messages.

Ivy: *Sure. Should I come over so we can talk in person?*

My shoulders slumped with relief. I hadn't realized it, but I'd half-expected her to change her mind after a good night's sleep. I'd been preparing myself for her to explain that she'd come to her senses and realized what a terrible idea this whole thing was.

But that wasn't happening. We were really going to do this.

Me: *Absolutely.*

Ivy: *See you in thirty.*

Her response came through with no delay, and I smiled as I leapt to my feet. I only had thirty minutes to make myself and this apartment presentable. Not because I wanted to impress her. No. I just…wanted to make sure she didn't take one look at my place and decide I wasn't worth the trouble.

"Yeah, that's it," I muttered, shaking my head as I carried dirty glasses to the sink before picking up three days' worth of dirty socks from the floor.

After making sure the rest of the living room and kitchen were tidy, I rushed into my bathroom to freshen up. I quickly rejected the idea of another shower. I'd already taken one before I plopped my ass on the bed to watch television. I did, however, add another layer of deodorant and a spritz of cologne after re-brushing my teeth.

A small voice in my head questioned why I was going through the trouble, but I ignored it. I gazed at my reflection, briefly considering changing out of my t-shirt and sweatpants before rejecting the idea. Women liked men in sweats, right?

"Ugh," I groaned, flicking off the light as I walked out.

I was acting like a schoolgirl with her first crush. Ivy knew me. She knew what an asshole I was and still had agreed to help me by being my *fake* fiancée. Fake, as in not real. Pretend.

I didn't need to impress her or try to look good for her. Hell, I didn't even *like* her. She was a means to an end, and that was it.

I needed to get my head on straight and not confuse gratitude for something else. Something deeper. I could be congenial for the sake of our working relationship, but I needed to make sure it ended with that.

A few minutes later, a knock sounded at my door. When I swung the panel open, Ivy gave me a tight smile.

"Hi," she said, looking more like a prisoner headed for execution than an excited fake-bride-to-be.

"Hi. Come on in," I replied, moving aside to let her enter.

"Thanks. Nice place," she said, her eyes scanning the living room. "It's homey."

"Thanks," I said, trying to see my apartment through her eyes as she wandered around the living room.

The oversized leather couch in dark brown contrasted nicely with the cream carpet. The wooden coffee table matched the end tables, and a large screen television hung on the opposite wall. Pictures of my family dotted the walls in identical frames, including one of Rafe and Ivy. They were dressed in matching scrubs, each with an arm wrapped around the other and big, cheesy grins on their faces.

Ivy stopped in front of it, her eyes widening before she turned that blue gaze on me. "Where did you get this?"

I shrugged. "Rafe."

My nonchalant reaction and the answer were grossly understated. I'd forgotten I'd hung that picture, or I would've taken it down before she got here. I'd also technically gotten it from Rafe—as in, I'd downloaded it from his social media and had it printed and framed without telling him.

That was in the early days, when Ivy and I still had a few sparks firing off between us. I didn't really know why I'd left it up all these years. I'd told myself it was a good picture of my brother and his best friend, and it wasn't weird. If Ivy were a guy, I wouldn't have given it a second thought.

Thankfully, Ivy moved on, her eyes scanning the other photos on the wall. Me, in front of Walton's during our grand opening. Lola at her high school graduation. Rafe at that same event. The three of us one Christmas. My car, the day I'd picked it up from the paint shop.

Finally, she turned and looked at me expectantly. I held out an arm toward the couch, inviting her to sit.

"Can I get you anything? Water? Coffee?"

"No, thank you," she said, perching on one edge of the sofa.

I nodded and sat down at the other end, leaving as much space between us as possible. Ivy seemed to relax a bit, angling her body toward me.

"So, where should we start?" she asked.

"I'm not sure—"

"I think we need to establish a set of rules," she interrupted, the words spilling from her in a rush.

"Okay," I said slowly. "What do you have in mind?"

She gave me a tight smile as she pulled her phone from

her purse. Tapping the screen a few times, she swallowed visibly before taking a deep breath and reading aloud.

"Rule number one: No sex."

My head flew back as if she'd slapped me. Sex actually hadn't even crossed my mind. Ivy and I barely tolerated each other in the best of times, so the idea that something intimate might spark between us seemed ludicrous.

Or maybe not…

The fact that Ivy felt the need to add that as rule number one on her list was interesting. Very interesting, indeed.

8

Ivy

Oh, my God.

The look on Nate's face was my first clue that I'd fucked up. Royally. Making "no sex" a rule had seemed perfectly logical last night, when I was lying in bed, constructing my list. We were playacting for Charity's benefit. None of this was real, so there was no reason to complicate things by fooling around in private.

Yet, as I watched his lips curve up into an entirely-too-sexy-for-my-own-good smirk, I realized that making it a stated rule—the very *first* stated rule—had been a mistake. It only served to make Nate think I had been contemplating having sex with him. Which I hadn't. Much.

"Okay," he said slowly, dragging the word out for far too long. "No sex. Got it."

"Ugh, I hate you," I mumbled, rolling my eyes.

"So, no hate sex, then?"

"Shut. Up," I growled, turning my eyes back to my list.

"Rule number two: We need to tell Rafe the truth. I don't want to lie to him about this."

"Agreed," he said. "I don't want to lie to him, either. Or Lola, for that matter. Jessa brought you up last night, and I told her and the others I'd asked you out. But they know us too well. They'd never buy that we're suddenly engaged after one date."

I gave him a firm nod. I wanted to ask him what she'd said. Had she told him what I said about why I hated him? No, she wouldn't break my confidence like that, and Nate would surely be asking me about it now if she had. So I let it go and moved on.

"Rule number three: No seeing other people, even if you think you're being discreet. I don't want to go through all of this just to fail because you can't keep your *magic dick* in your pants."

He scrubbed a hand down his face and groaned. "Can you please stop saying that?"

"What?" I asked, fighting a grin. "Magic dick?"

"Yes, that," he growled. "I admit it. I was a cocky bastard in high school. I'm not that guy anymore."

"Aren't you?" I shot back, arching one eyebrow.

"Okay, maybe a little," he replied, a smile tugging at his lips. "But I haven't called it that in years, and I'm going to beat Rafe's ass for telling you that."

I returned his smile, then realized I was doing it and cleared my throat. "Anyway, that's all I've got for now. Anything you'd like to add?"

"I'd like to amend rule three to include you keeping it in *your* pants, as well."

"Of course," I said, feeling my face heat. "That was implied."

His saying that was a moot point. I had no prospects and hadn't in a long time. It was almost embarrassing, how long it had been since I'd gotten any dick. Magic, or otherwise.

"Rule number four," he said, pulling me out of my depressing thoughts, "when we're in public, we need to show affection. Milestone is a small town with lots of gossipmongers, so word will get around if the community's newest it-couple are acting frosty toward each other."

I nodded and started typing, adding the rule to the list. The couch dipped, and my gaze shot to Nate, who was sliding closer.

"What are you doing?" I asked, my nerve endings firing sparks as I attempted to burrow further into my corner.

"We need to practice," he said, closing the gap between us even more. "How are we going to make this believable if you can't even sit close to me?"

He had a point. I forced my body to relax, and didn't flinch away when he closed the distance between us completely. His thigh pressed against mine from hip to knee, and before I could react, his arm stretched across the back of the couch.

When his fingertips brushed gently against my shoulder, I leapt to my feet and dodged around the coffee table. My gaze darted around the room before finally settling on a spot just above his head.

"Can I, uh, use your bathroom?" I stuttered, inwardly flinching at the nervous vibrato in my voice.

"Sure," he said, then pointed. "It's through there."

I nodded awkwardly and forced my feet not to run as I headed in the direction he pointed. I ended up in a masculine bedroom and backtracked several steps when my eyes landed on a very large, very *inviting* bed. *Why did he send me in here?*

"Sorry," Nate called out as if reading my mind. "This

is a one bedroom, one bathroom apartment."

I nodded and moved forward, averting my eyes from that bed as I passed by. Inside the bathroom, I closed the door and locked it before leaning back against it. After taking a few deep breaths, I moved to the sink and braced my hands against the countertop. Staring into the mirror, I frowned.

"He doesn't affect you. You don't want him. You don't even like him," I whispered as I turned on the cold water.

Cupping my hands under the flow, I splashed my face. Grabbing a hand towel from the nearby rack, I patted it against my skin to dry it. I froze, inhaling deeply as the scent of Nate's cologne filled my nostrils.

Jerking the towel away, I chastised myself as I firmly hung it back where I'd found it.

No, Ivy. Bad. You don't like it, and you don't like him. He's an ass. A womanizing, philandering ass.

Steeling my spine, I unlocked the door and threw it open. I shrieked and stumbled back a few steps, pressing a palm to my chest to hold my heart in. Nate stood just outside the door, his long arms braced against the doorjamb.

"Jesus, Nate," I breathed. "You scared me."

"Sorry," he said, his smirk telling me he wasn't sorry at all. "I just came to check on you. I couldn't remember if I replaced the toilet paper roll, or not."

I shook my head and tried to push past him, but he didn't budge. My chest brushed against his, making my breath catch in my throat before I took a quick step back. I ignored the tingling in my nipples as I leveled him with an angry look.

"Excuse me," I gritted out.

He pushed away from the doorjamb with a soft smile, moving to the side to let me pass. I hurried through his bedroom, not breathing until I was safely back in the living room. Being alone with Nate near his bed was unacceptable.

Because it was inappropriate. *Not* because I didn't trust myself not to spread my body across that mattress like some pagan offering to the gods of magic dick.

"I need to go," I whispered, grabbing my phone and my purse.

"Where are you going?" Nate asked when he came in and saw me grabbing my things.

"I've...I just have to go. Sorry," I said in a rush as I practically jogged to the door.

"But we're not finished," he argued. "We haven't even ironed out any of the details yet."

"Sorry," I repeated, throwing his front door wide. "I'll call you later."

I slammed the door behind me and ran all the way to my car, not pausing until I was safely inside. Taking a few deep breaths, I pulled up the list on my phone and furiously typed in another rule.

Rule number five: No falling for Nate Walton.

~

"Hi, Mom," I called out as I pushed through the front door of my childhood home.

I'd made the decision to go home before leaving the parking lot of Nate's apartment complex. It took an hour to drive there, which gave me plenty of time to think about my deal with Nate. About his fingers brushing my shoulder. About my chest leaning into his. About his bed.

I shook off the thoughts as Mom rounded the corner from the kitchen, a big smile on her face. "Ivy, honey, what a surprise!"

"A welcome one, I hope," I teased, rushing forward to wrap myself up in her warm embrace.

"Of course, it is," she said, squeezing me tightly.

My mother was the best. Always warm and welcoming, and always smelling like fresh baked bread. Or, like today, cookies.

"Are you baking?" I asked, inhaling the sugary scent.

"Is it Sunday?" she shot back, giving me a wink. "Come on. I just pulled some snickerdoodles out of the oven."

Once we settled at the table with coffee and cookies, she gave me a stern look. "Now, tell me."

"Tell you what?" I hedged, taking a sip of warm liquid gold.

"Tell me why you came here out of the blue, needing your mama's arms and reeking of quiet desperation."

"Tell me why you feel the need to wax poetic," I shot back.

"Ivy."

"Jeez, Mom. I'm fine. I missed you. That's all."

"Mm hmm," she muttered. "Eat your cookies. You're too skinny."

I rolled my eyes but did as I was told. The sugary-cinnamon goodness melted on my tongue, and I moaned with pleasure. She could end wars with these things.

"How's everything at work?" she asked, apparently letting her accusations of ulterior motives drop. For the moment.

"Good," I said. "Busy, but good."

"And Rafe?"

I rolled my eyes at her hopeful tone. She loved him more than I did, and had always not-so-secretly hoped we'd end up together like those silly friends-to-lovers romantic comedies she watched on cable television.

"Rafe is really good, actually. He's got a girlfriend, and she just moved in with him."

"No," she said, her voice dramatically low. "I'd hoped…"

"I know what you hoped," I cut in, "and I've told you a thousand times it was never going to happen. Besides, you're going to love Jessa. She's funny and smart and perfect for Rafe."

"And she's okay with him having a woman as his best friend?" she asked arching one silvery-blonde eyebrow.

"Of course. We've actually become close, and she introduced me to a couple of her friends. We all go out together for girls' nights and stuff."

"Well, I like her already," she said, giving me a warm smile.

She'd been on my case to make some girlfriends forever. She tried to convince me that working all the time and only socializing with Rafe wasn't healthy, and I could finally admit she'd been partially right. Hanging out with Jessa, Felicia, and Karly had been like a breath of fresh air, giving me something I didn't know I'd been missing.

"And what about your love life?" she asked, pulling me from my thoughts.

I tensed, not knowing how to answer the question I should've known she'd ask. The question she *always* asked. Nate and I had agreed to tell Rafe and Lola the truth, but we hadn't discussed my family. I could trust her. That wasn't the problem.

The problem was, I knew she'd disapprove. And try to talk me out of it.

"Ivy?" she asked when I didn't respond with my normal denials and assurances that I didn't need a man to be happy.

"I'm seeing someone," I blurted, my face heating with

the lie.

"You are? Who is he?"

Her expression lit up with excitement, and I nearly caved and admitted the truth. Instead, I said, "Nate. Rafe's younger brother."

"But…I thought you couldn't stand him. Did something change?"

"I guess he grew on me," I muttered stupidly.

Of course, I'd complained to Mom many times over the years about what an asshat Nate was. Of course, she was confused by my sudden change of heart. And then… she was smiling.

"Like Emma and Hook in *Once Upon A Time*?"

I pictured Nate in a black leather jacket, with black eyeliner making those blue eyes pop, and I had to shake my head to clear the image. I started to make some deadpan comment about real life not being like fantasy television, but the hopeful look on her face stalled me.

"Sure. Why not?" I drawled, giving Mom an indulgent smile.

She twittered a dozen questions that I tried to answer as vaguely as possible. She wanted details, but I didn't have any to share. Maybe I should've stayed at Nate's until we'd worked them all out. We were surely going to have to agree on an ironclad story before we told anyone else we were together.

"Hey, Mom, is the Bel Air still out in the barn?" I asked once she'd ran out of questions about my new romance.

"Yes, of course," she said, her expression filled with confusion. "Why do you ask?"

"I just wanted to go see it," I murmured.

"The key is on the hook by the back door," she said softly.

I nodded and stood up, giving her a hug before walking

away. Snatching the key from the hook, I slipped through the door and jogged down the back porch steps. The property was over an acre with a large wooden barn near the back fence. Dad had used it as a workshop, spending every weekend out there trying to bring the old car back to life.

I slipped the key into the padlock on the barn door, and it made a rusty screeching sound as I twisted it open. Swinging the large doors wide, I wandered inside and flicked on the lights. As the fluorescent bulbs blinked to life, my eyes settled on the red and white beauty before me.

The hood was still up, the engine in pieces like Dad had left it that awful Saturday afternoon. He'd taken a break for lunch, and halfway back to the house, he'd dropped to the ground. Mom had found him like that a few minutes later, laying on his side, clutching his left shoulder.

He'd suffered a major heart attack, dying in my mother's arms before the ambulance had even arrived. I was still in school, finishing up my nursing degree. I'd never forget the tremor in Mom's voice when she called me that day. She'd broken down into sobs before she even got all the words out.

I ran my fingers over the faded paint of the trunk and tried to imagine what the car would look like once Nate finished with it. He was talented, and I had no doubt if anyone could bring her back to life, it would be him.

Mom had a lifetime of memories with Dad that she cherished, but this car was an unfinished chapter. Driving it would bring a sense of peace and closure to her that I knew she was missing. I wanted to give that to her.

And if pretending to be in love with Nate Walton was the cost, I'd happily pay it.

I just had to keep my temper—and my heart—locked up behind a wall of indifference. I could do that. Right?

9

***

Nate

"Hey, Nate, that catalytic converter for the Chevy came in. Mike is putting it in, now. Should be ready to go by two."

I nodded absently, my eyes glued to the selection of diamond rings on my computer screen. Which one would Ivy like best? I had no idea. And I didn't want to spend a small fortune on something she'd hate, fake engagement, or not.

"Hey, you okay?" Dane asked, stepping all the way through my office door and closing it behind him. "You seem...distracted."

I minimized the screen on my computer as he neared and looked up at him with a fake-as-shit smile. "I'm good, bro. How are things going out there? Did the cat come in for that Chevy?"

"Dude. What the hell is going on with you? Did you get another threat from Charity?"

"No," I said, sighing. "It's not that."

He stared at me with an expectant expression, waiting for me to cave. And I *would* cave, no doubt about it. Dane had this way of waiting someone out, and his patience practically forced the truth into the open. It was a sorcery I wished I'd possessed.

"What I'm about to tell you stays in this room," I said, and his face twisted up like I'd just insulted him.

"That goes without saying. You know that," he said.

"Sorry. I'm not thinking straight." I paused for a moment to gather my thoughts before leaning back and scrubbing a hand down my face. "You remember when you told me it was too bad I didn't have a girlfriend? That if I did, she would solve all my problems with Charity?"

"Yeah," he said, drawing the word out like a question.

"Well, I decided you were right. At least, mostly right. I don't think a mere girlfriend would stop her, but a fiancée would."

Dane's expression turned shell-shocked for a moment before he burst into laughter. Loud guffaws echoed off the walls, irritating me beyond reason. When he saw my pissed-off frown, he sobered.

"Wait. You're serious?"

"As a heart attack," I said. "And I already talked Ivy into doing it. She'll pretend to be engaged to me, and I get to restore her mother's fifty-five Bel Air convertible. It's a win-win."

Dane's eyes widened into saucers as his mouth fell open. "You mean *Ivy Anderson*?"

"The one and only," I said.

"No wonder you're out of it today. It's going to be a shit show, dealing with her and pretending to be in love. Why in the hell would you pick her, of all people?"

My back teeth clenched as I fought the urge to leap over my desk and punch Dane in the jaw. He must have seen the murder in my expression, because he flinched and held up his palms in surrender.

"Sorry, man. I didn't mean any insult." His eyes narrowed and he cocked his head. "Why are you being so touchy? I thought you hated her?"

My muscles relaxed, and I leaned back with a sigh. "I don't hate her. I never did, really. But she hates me. And that's what makes her so perfect for this. She's guaranteed not to get attached. It's one hundred percent business."

"And does *she* know that restoring a classic Bel Air is on your bucket list?"

I laughed. "No. I sold it like it was going to be a chore. She wants it done by Christmas, and I played up how hard it might be to find parts for it that quickly."

Dane whistled. "Six weeks? That's going to be tough. Do you know how much work it needs?"

"No," I said, the smile finally leaving my face. "I guess her dad was restoring it for her mom. He died suddenly, without warning, a few years ago, and Ivy wants to surprise her mom with it as a Christmas gift."

"That's really nice," Dane said, his eyes unfocused for a moment before he zeroed back in on me. "So, she pretends to be your fiancée to get Charity Glasscott off your back, and you get to do something you've always wanted to do for her in return. Am I getting this right?"

"That about sums it up," I said.

"So what has you in a funk? It seems like you've got it all figured out."

"Not everything," I said, pulling the browser back up and turning the monitor so he could see it.

He let out a low whistle as his eyes drifted from ring to ring. "Pricey."

"Yeah, and I don't want to choose the wrong one. Which one do you think she'd like best?"

Dane shrugged. "Hell if I know. I don't really know her that well, man. Why don't you ask Rafe?"

"I haven't told him yet," I admitted as movement through the glass behind him caught my eye. "Oh, shit."

I turned my screen back and closed out the browser as my office door creaked open, and my sister slipped through.

"Hey, Lola. What brings you by?" I asked.

"Hey, Nate," she said, then looked at Dane. "Hi."

"What's up, cutie?" he asked, his tone entirely too flirtatious for my liking.

"Goodbye, Dane." My voice was an octave deeper and brooked no argument.

He rolled his eyes and stood, giving my sister a comically wide berth as he moved around her toward the door. As he passed through the doorway, he paused and turned back to Lola, his eyes giving her a slow up and down.

"Looking good today, Lola," he said, giving her a charming wink before his eyes cut back to me. "Real good."

"Out!" I shouted, pointing a finger.

Dane smirked and turned to go, whistling a peppy tune as he sauntered away. I shook my head, only taking a moment to plot his death by dismemberment before turning my attention back to Lola. I motioned her into the chair Dane vacated.

"You know he does that just to mess with you, right?" she asked.

"And it works every time," I mumbled. "So, what's up?"

Lola lived in the dorms at her university, which was a half an hour away. It wasn't like she was just in the neighborhood and wanted to stop by. There had to be a reason.

"Actually, I was hoping you could take a look at my car," she said. "It's been making a weird knocking sound."

"Oh, I see," I teased. "You're not here to see me. You just want to use me for my boss mechanic skills."

She tilted her head. "If it's too much trouble, I could just ask Dane—"

"Shut your mouth, woman."

She chuckled, but something about it seemed off. I studied her for a moment, noting her bright eyes and pink cheeks.

"Are you sure you're okay? You're not getting sick or something, are you?"

"What? No. I'm fine." She stood up and adjusted her purse strap over her shoulder. "Can someone give me a ride to the house so I don't have to wait here?"

"Did you call Rafe? You know he doesn't live alone anymore."

"Yes, *Dad*. I did," she said, rolling her eyes. "Rafe is at the hospital, and Jessa is at her dad's."

"Okay," I said, raising my hands. "We just don't want a repeat of what happened before."

I trembled with a whole-body shiver, and Lola laughed. When Rafe first started dating Jessa, we'd shown up for one of our usual family dinners…which Rafe had forgotten about. Jessa let us in while Rafe was in the bedroom, and he'd come running out bare-assed naked with a handful of condoms.

I didn't know if I'd ever fully recover from the sight. At least, not without psychotherapy.

I grabbed my keys, tasked Dane with pulling Lola's car into one of the bays, and drove her to Rafe and Jessa's. It was still weird thinking of our childhood home as *their* place, but I was getting used to it. Rafe was happy, and that was all that mattered.

On my way back to the shop, I pulled into a strip mall that housed a women's boutique, a tailor, and a few other high-end stores. Down at the far end, I pulled into a parking spot and took a few deep breaths to chase away the nerves.

If I was going to do this, I was going to do it right. I climbed from the car, slamming the door behind me in my haste. Striding forward, I jerked open the glass door and walked inside the brightly lit space filled with glass cabinets.

"Hello, sir, and welcome to Winchester Jewelers. How may I help you today?"

I inhaled deeply, let it out slowly, and said, "I need an engagement ring."

10

Ivy

"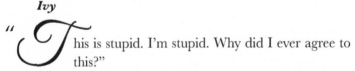his is stupid. I'm stupid. Why did I ever agree to this?"

I was staring at myself in the bathroom mirror—*Nate's* bathroom mirror—where I'd escaped to as soon as he'd let me in his front door. I must've seemed like some kind of maniac, asking to use his toilet instead of saying hello like a normal person.

I didn't know why I was so nervous. I'd known Nate for years, *hated* him for nearly as long, yet here I was with sweaty palms and pits, trying to decide if I could actually follow through with my end of the deal.

Actually, I was lying to myself. I knew why I was nervous.

Nate. He'd been almost...charming the last time I was here, and it had reminded me of Original Nate. The Nate I'd wanted to bump uglies with every time we breathed the same air. The Nate whose smile was sexy and secretive, not cocky and annoying. The Nate who'd stolen my breath away every time he turned those baby blues on me.

I steeled my spine and gritted my teeth. I could do this. I just had to remind myself that Nate was a class-A asshole, and that this whole relationship was a business deal. He would get Charity Glasscott off his back, and I would get my mother's beloved Bel Air restored. Then we'd go our separate ways—or, at least, back to loathing each other whenever we occupied the same space.

End of story.

I washed my hands for show and walked through his bedroom with my eyes plastered to the door. I didn't even glance at the bed once, making myself proud. I could totally do this.

My internal monologue and my feet screeched to a halt when I walked back into the living room to find Nate on bended knee. He was holding up a small, velvet box, the lid open to reveal a sparkly diamond.

My entire body flashed hot as my pulse pounded in my ears. Nate gave me his best shit-eating grin as he placed his free hand over his heart.

"Ivy Marie Anderson, will you do me the great honor of being my fake fiancée?"

When I didn't move or speak, he climbed to his feet and walked toward me. Reaching forward, he took my hand and placed the box into my palm. With eyes so wide they burned, I studied the ring nestled in white silk folds.

The center stone was a clear princess cut gem surrounded by a row of smaller diamonds. The band was a pretty rose gold that sparkled with diamonds studded down each side. I was dazzled by its brilliance, unable to even form a coherent thought.

"The jeweler said it's called a halo setting," Nate offered when I didn't speak.

"How did you know my middle name?" I asked, my eyes never leaving the ring.

"What?" he asked, obviously confused.

"My middle name. You said Ivy *Marie* Anderson. How did you know it?"

I knew I sounded ridiculous, latching onto something so mundane while I was holding a fucking engagement ring in my hand. But it was too much. My brain went a little haywire, so I'd just said the first coherent thought I had.

"I don't know," he replied. "I must have heard it from Rafe at some point."

I nodded, and my eyes still hadn't strayed from that glorious ring. It was perfect in every way, and something I would have dreamed of receiving from a real boyfriend under different circumstances. Its perfection made this whole situation feel almost...icky.

"Ivy. Do you like it? We can go trade it for something else if you don't," Nate said, filling the awkward silence.

"No!" I shouted, pulling the ring into my chest and finally meeting his gaze. "I mean...yes. I like it. It's fine."

For a fraction of a second, his face fell like he was disappointed with my mediocre response. He quickly smoothed out his features and gave me a smile.

"Good. Try it on. Let's see if it fits."

When I didn't move, he plucked the box from my fingers. Pulling out the ring, he tossed the box aside and held out his free hand. Ever so slowly, I placed my left hand into his, my whole body shaking with unexplained nerves. With gentle movements, he slipped the ring onto my finger.

"Look at that. Perfect fit," he said, his thumb brushing across my knuckles before he released me.

It did fit perfectly, and it looked amazing on my hand. I

balled up my fist and shoved it into the pocket of my hoodie as I swallowed thickly against the emotion clogging my throat. I looked at Nate and forced a smile to my lips.

"Thanks. It's great, really. Should we sit down and get started?"

The whole reason I'd come over was so Nate and I could write our story, so to speak. We'd known each other for years, but we didn't really *know* each other. The only thing we'd shown each other was sarcasm and anger, so he'd suggested a little "getting to know you" game to learn the finer details. We also needed a plausible story to explain how we were suddenly engaged when no one knew we were even dating.

Milestone was a small town. If we were dating, everyone would know. Which meant...

"When was the last time you had sex?" I blurted as we took our seats on the couch.

"Excuse me?" he asked, looking utterly shocked.

My face heated with a blush, but I pressed on. "How long has it been, Nate?"

"A gentleman never tells," he shot back with an arched brow.

"We both know you're no gentleman, and you need to tell me. You know how this town is. If you've been sleeping around like I'm pretty sure you have, how are we supposed to sell this relationship? I refuse to be seen as some chump who ignores your indiscretions and stays with you."

He sighed and leaned his head against the back of the couch. "I guess you're right. The last person I slept with was Charity, and that was four months ago."

"Really?" I asked, honestly shocked.

I'd had this unwanted image in my head of Nate sleeping with a different girl every week...if not more often than that. Working all the time and only hanging with Rafe meant I wasn't privy to a lot of town gossip, though I had overheard a few stories of clandestine affairs at the grocery store and in the coffee shop I frequented. So I knew people talked. They just didn't talk to me.

"Really," he said. "I'm not the whore you seem to think I am, Ivy. Do I have a problem getting some ass when I want it? No. But I have to be careful. When I'm not, shit like this happens."

And *there's* the Nate I love to hate.

"Fine," I grunted. "So I guess we've been dating for almost four months."

"Wait. Wait. Wait. You haven't told me how long it's been for you."

"Next subject."

"Come on, Ivy. It's only fair. And a fiancé should know these things."

"It's been longer than four months, and that's all you need to know. No one is going to ask you about that."

It had been much, much longer than four months for me. I was embarrassed to admit it, but it had been nearly a year since I'd dated anyone, and that guy had only lasted a couple of weeks. He couldn't handle my busy schedule or the fact that my best friend was a guy. I had a feeling the latter, rather than the former was the real reason he'd ended things. Jealous bastard. He wasn't even that good in bed.

"Fine. I'll take it, but I reserve the right to ask again." Before I could argue, he went on. "What's your favorite color?"

"Blue," I said without thinking as I stared into his *very* blue eyes.

"Mine, too," he said smiling. "Thongs or granny panties?"

"What?" I exclaimed. "You don't need to know that."

"Sure, I do. What if I want to be seen buying my lady some lingerie? I need to know what you prefer."

"Wouldn't that be about what *you* prefer?" I asked, arching a brow.

"Usually, yes. But I think I want my fiancée to be comfortable when she struts around our bedroom in silk and lace."

I rolled my eyes, conceding. "Neither. I like bikini-cut underwear and bras with no underwire."

His eyes fell to my chest, and I was suddenly glad I'd thrown on my bulkiest hoodie. At least, I told myself I was glad. My heart didn't seem to get the memo as it picked up speed.

"What size?" he asked, licking his lips.

"Nate." His eyes darted up to meet mine, one dark brow arched. "Ugh, you're such an ass. I wear a 36C."

He nodded, and one corner of his mouth turned up. "I wear a medium, and I prefer boxers to briefs. You know, in case you'd like to shop for me."

"Not happening. Next subject."

We spent the next hour discussing safe topics—brands of toothpaste, favorite foods, how we take our coffee. Things like that.

He told me all about opening the shop and how successful it had become, and I told him about college and the joy I found in my work. He described his relationship with Dane, who was his best friend as well as his employee, and I told him how I was becoming close with Jessa and her friends.

I told him how losing my father had affected me and my mom. And, though I knew the story from Rafe, Nate told me his experience with losing first his mother in an accident, then his father to suicide.

"He left us. On purpose. We were just kids, and he *decided* to leave us all alone."

My eyes burned with emotion as I let him get it all out, uninterrupted. I felt a little ashamed that I'd never really believed him capable of deep, emotional feelings. All I saw after that night at Hero's was a shallow, soulless whoremonger.

"Enough of that," he said suddenly, clearing his throat. "On to the good stuff. Top or bottom?"

"Wh-what?" I stuttered, shocked out of the haze of empathy I'd been swimming in.

"Which do you prefer? Top or bottom?"

"You don't need to know that," I said, sniffing primly.

"Sure, I do."

"No. You don't."

"Ivy, how am I supposed to order your drink if I don't know which you prefer?"

"Huh?" I asked, completely confused.

"Top shelf or bottom shelf? Belvedere or Smirnoff? Milagro or Jose Cuervo?"

"Oh, uh, I like light beer, actually."

"Good to know," he smirked. "But what did you think I meant?"

"Nothing. I don't know," I blurted, my face hot with a blush.

"Oh, you dirty little minx," he grinned. "You thought I meant in bed?" He tilted his head. "Which *do* you prefer?"

"You're an asshole," I said, "and I think that's enough for one night."

He was mocking me, reminding me of why I'd spent so long hating his cocky ass. *Ugh, stop it Ivy. No thinking about cocks or asses. Not when it comes to Nate Walton.*

"Ah, come on, Ivy. I was just messing with you. Sit back

down," he cajoled, laughter crinkling his eyes and making them appear even bluer than before.

I needed to get out of there.

"Goodnight, Nate."

11

_____

Nate

"*Hi*."

"What are you doing here?"

Ouch. That was not the reception I was hoping for. But, in all honesty, I *had* just shown up at Ivy's work out of the blue.

It had been a few days since our little study session at my house, and I thought it was time to present ourselves as an engaged couple to the public. The sooner Charity heard I was in a committed relationship, the sooner she'd back off and forget about me. This whole thing would be over, and Ivy and I could go back to our normal lives.

"Is that any way for you to greet your man?" I said, giving her my sexiest smirk.

"I'm working, Nate," she said, her finger swiping the screen of a tablet as her toe tapped rapidly against the tile floor.

"Sorry," I said, "but I wanted to do this face-to-face."

That got her attention. She looked up from her tablet, her expression equal parts inquisitive and anxious. She brushed a lock of hair back from her face, and I noticed her hand was bare.

"Where's your ring?" I asked, unwilling to examine the sudden rush of disappointment and possessiveness that coursed through me.

"Oh, it's in my purse," she said, tucking her hand into the front pocket of her scrubs. "I don't wear it at work."

"Why not?"

"Why are you here, Nate? I really am busy."

I pushed down the frustration I felt, silently deciding to examine it more carefully later, when I was alone. This was a fake engagement. I had no right to feel slighted because Ivy didn't wear the ring twenty-four-seven.

"Have dinner with me," I said, keeping my tone even. "We need to be seen together in public."

Her lips curved up the slightest bit with my first words, then fell with the last. She gave me a distracted nod.

"Okay. Pick me up at my place at eight."

She turned and strode away, disappearing around a corner. Her response had been tepid, at best, but I would take what I could get. Did I expect her to jump for joy at the prospect of going out with me? To swoon?

No. And I needed to keep my head on straight. Ivy not liking me was the reason why she was so perfect for this act we were putting on. No feelings would be hurt when it ended.

"Hey, what are you doing here?"

I spun around at the sound of that deep, familiar voice. *Shit.*

"Hey, bro. I was just in the neighborhood and thought I'd stop by to say hi."

Rafe looked at me like I'd grown a second head. I'd never "popped in to say hi" before, and there was no logical reason for me to do so now. His eyebrows raised in question, and my shoulders slumped.

"I came by to see Ivy."

"Why would you do that?" he asked, his narrowed eyes spearing me on the spot. "I know you said you asked her out, but I honestly thought you were joking."

"Do you have a few minutes?" I asked.

It was time to tell him. It might be the coward's way out, but at least here he wouldn't have time to chew me out. I could spit it all out and escape when his next patient needed him.

He led me into an empty exam room and shut the door behind us. He opened his mouth to question me, but before he could utter a word, his pager beeped. He checked it with a curse before narrowing his gaze back on me.

"Duty calls," I said, grinning. "I'll just see myself out."

"We're going to talk about this later, Nate," he said.

I gave him a little salute before swinging open the door and sauntering out. I'd worry about Rafe's possible reaction to my deal with Ivy later. Right now, I needed to get ready for my date.

The date that would hopefully be the beginning of the end of Charity Glasscott's presence in my life.

~

"*Y*ou look…nice."

It was all I could do to keep my tongue rolled up in my mouth as Ivy stood before me in the doorway to her apartment. She was wearing tight jeans paired with a baby blue sweater that looked so soft, I wanted to rub my hands all over it. The neckline hung off one shoulder, revealing an expanse of smooth skin that made my mouth water.

Clearing my throat, I offered her an elbow. "Shall we?"

She gave me a soft smile before stepping out and turning to lock up. Her ass looked amazing in those jeans. I quickly raised my eyes as she turned back to face me. She slipped her hand over my still-extended elbow, and I noticed she was wearing my ring.

My lips curved up without my permission, and I quickly wiped it away. The only reason I was happy was because Ivy was following through with her end of the deal by wearing my ring. I could practically see the end of Charity's plot against me. That's it. Nothing more.

I walked her to the Mustang's passenger door and held it open while she climbed inside. She looked almost startled for a moment, like she couldn't believe I was being a gentleman. I wanted to feel offended, but I couldn't.

I was self-aware enough to realize I'd never really shown Ivy this side of me. She'd only seen the douchebag I *wanted* her to see. An exaggerated version of myself that only came out for her. As I rounded the hood to the driver's side, I made a decision.

I wasn't going to pull any punches with her tonight. I'd give her Nate two-point-oh—the affectionate, romantic, chivalrous side of myself I rarely let the world see.

I ignored the little voice in my head that asked me *why* I wanted to impress Ivy. I didn't. It was just fun, giving her the unexpected and watching her reactions.

"Any new threats from Charity?" Ivy asked as I started the car.

"No. She's been quiet for a couple of weeks," I said, pulling away from the curb and heading toward town.

"I don't understand why you don't just call her and tell her you're engaged," she said.

I shook my head. "The direct approach doesn't work with her. She's stubborn and will just refuse to accept it... like she's refused my attempts to put her off. She'll think I'm making it up." I paused to grin at her, and my breath caught when she smiled back. I cleared my throat and went on. "But if she hears the news mixed in with idle town gossip, she'll come sniffing around to see if it's true."

"So, she'll believe the gossip, but not when it comes straight from the source? That doesn't even make any sense."

"I know," I said, "but that's been my experience with her. You know, the first time I saw her, I asked her out? She said she knew I was a mechanic and turned me down, flat."

"What?" she exclaimed, a sarcastic look of horror on her face as she mocked me. "What the hell is wrong with her?"

"I know," I said, smiling. "I'm a catch. Anyway, she heard some rumors about me, came sniffing around, and wouldn't take no for an answer."

"What? About your magic dick?" she asked, making me flinch. Then she laughed. "Sorry. It was just too easy. I'll stop. I promise."

"Anyway," I said, stressing the word. "I figured, *why not?* Worst. Mistake. Ever."

"Okay. I get it," she said. "So, where are you taking me?"

"I wanted to take you someplace casual, where we can just relax and enjoy a meal. I thought Hero's would be the perfect spot."

"Hero's?" she asked, her voice unnaturally high.

"Yeah," I said, glancing at her quickly before returning my eyes to the road. "Is that okay?"

"Yes," she squeaked before clearing her throat. "Hero's is fine."

12
———

Ivy

This was *so* not fine. How was I supposed to sit through a meal with Nate in the place where my hopes for us had been blown to hell? I hadn't been inside the place since that night. And now Nate was taking me there for our first fake date?

I didn't know if I had the skills to pretend like I was happy and in love in the one place I never wanted to step foot into again. And I certainly couldn't go anywhere near that ladies' room.

Oh, God. What if I had to pee?

Just the thought made my bladder spasm to life. Now I really did have to pee. Great.

"Stay right there," Nate said after parking the car.

He climbed from his seat and jogged around the front end, stopping beside my door. Pulling it open, he held out a hand to assist me.

"I can do it myself," I growled, ignoring his gesture.

Once I was standing beside him, he shrugged and

pushed the door closed. Before I could pull away, he twined his fingers through mine and brought my hand up to his mouth. His lips brushed softly over my knuckles, sending a shiver racing down my spine.

I smiled, putting on the show I'd agreed to. My insides were churning with dread as he led me to the entrance and pulled open the door. I extricated my hand from his and stepped inside Hero's for the first time in years.

Scents of pizza, hot wings, and garlic bread assaulted my nose, the usually pleasant aromas making my nausea intensify. My eyes flew first to the empty table where I'd sat with Rafe and his family, trading hungry stares with Nate. Then I looked toward the short hallway where the restrooms were located.

Where I'd seen Nate fucking some random stranger against the bathroom wall.

My steps faltered, and Nate's palm immediately pressed against my lower back to steady me. My first instinct was to shy away, but I forced myself to appear grateful for his touch. People could have been watching, and this was my part to play.

Nate guided me toward a more private booth in the corner, waiting until I'd slid into one side before he claimed the other. At least, I thought he was going to sit across the table from me. Instead, he slid in beside me, stretching his arm across the back of the booth behind my head.

I scooched away from him, tucking myself into the corner, but he only followed.

"We have to make this look real, Ivy," he murmured quietly.

I forced myself to relax, not even flinching when his fingers stroked my hair. This was all an act, and being here only solidified how much I hated Nate. My mixed emotions settled down as I grabbed onto that loathing.

"Is this okay?" he whispered, tugging lightly on my hair.

I nodded, even as my mind screamed "No!" He opened his mouth to say something else, but a waitress approaching our table stopped him.

"Hey there, Nate," she said, her tone much too sultry to be considered professional. "Can I get you something to drink?"

Her eyes never left the man at my side. It was if I were invisible. Could she not see me tucked against Nate? The fact that he commanded her attention so fully made me unreasonably angry at both of them.

"I'll have a light beer. Whatever you have on tap," I said, leaning closer to Nate as I laid my hand on the table.

That did the trick. Her eyes followed the movement of my hand, widening when they spotted the sparkly rock on my third finger. Her gaze collided with mine, wide with shock, before darting back to Nate.

"I'll have what she's having," he said smoothly before turning his head to press his lips against my temple.

The waitress stuttered something about getting our drinks before spinning on a heel and practically running away. I watched her go with a strange sense of satisfaction before Nate chuckled.

"Now, that's how you stake your claim," he whispered, his breath on my ear making me shiver.

"I wasn't..." I said, my words trailing off. *Wasn't I?* I brushed the thought off, saying, "Is that another of your many conquests?"

"Conquests?" he asked, his tone matching his offended expression. "Do you think I've slept with every woman in Milestone?"

I shrugged, lowering my gaze back to the diamond ring. "Kind of."

"Well, I hate to disappoint you, sweetheart, but that's just not the case."

"But I see you didn't answer my question," I shot back, meeting his eyes once more.

Without blinking, he pressed his palm against the side of my neck and tilted my chin up with his thumb. "No, Ivy. I've never slept with her. I just eat here a lot. I know everyone on the staff."

As far as I could tell, he was speaking the truth. Some of the tension left my back and shoulders as unwanted relief filled me. I shouldn't have been relieved. Who Nate slept with was his business, and had no effect on me, whatsoever.

"Were you jealous, Ivy?" he teased, the deepened rasp in his voice making me tense up again—this time for a whole different reason.

"I have to go to the bathroom," I blurted in a panic before silently cursing myself.

I did not want to go into that room, but it was too late. I'd already said it, and Nate was slipping out of the booth to let me out. I held my breath as I squeezed past him and took slow and measured steps toward the restroom.

I could do this. It was just a fucking bathroom. And I really did have to pee.

As I pushed open the door, I saw it like it was happening all over again. As if I'd somehow travelled back in time, I felt every one of my hopes for Nate and me shatter as small pale fingers fiddled with his belt buckle. I heard the woman's moan as she sucked at his neck, and Nate's hands moving to her shoulders to pull her closer.

I shook my head to clear it and charged into the room like I was on some sort of mission. Locking myself in a stall, I concentrated on going through the motions, leaving no room in my mind to dwell on the memory of Nate and his mid-meal liaison.

After flushing and stomping out of the stall, I washed my hands and dried them, keeping my eyes down and my jaw clenched. I needed to pull myself together.

A fake engagement for a fully-restored car. That's all this was. Nothing more.

With that wall firmly rebuilt around my heart, I left the restroom and headed back to the table. Nate made a move to get up and let me back in, but I quickly quashed the notion by sliding onto the seat across from him. A look of disappointment flashed across his features before he wiped it away, giving me a blank stare.

"Are you okay?" he asked.

"I'm fine," I said quickly. "Did the waitress come back?"

"Yeah," he said. "I ordered a large pepperoni and bacon and some hot wings. I hope that's okay."

I nodded as Nate pushed a full glass of beer toward me. I picked it up and chugged half of it before setting it back down. I wiped the back of my hand across my mouth with a sigh.

Nate remembered my order from all those years ago. Or maybe he'd asked Rafe. Or maybe we just liked the same toppings on our pizza. Something warmed in my gut, and I told myself it was the alcohol.

I grabbed the glass and drained it, earning a quizzical look from Nate.

"I'm so thirsty," I said, flinching at the lame excuse.

With a slight nod, Nate raised his hand to get the waitress's attention. He held up two fingers and pointed to his beer, which was still half-full. Then he smiled at me, and I cursed the butterflies fluttering in my stomach at the sight of it.

Nate stretched an arm across the table and wiggled his fingers. When I just stared at it, he whispered, "Take my hand, Ivy. You may not want to sit beside me, but you still have a part to play. We need to sell this."

"Right," I murmured under my breath and placed my hand in his.

I ignored the shiver of pleasure that raced through me as his fingertips tickled the sensitive skin of my wrist. I stared into his eyes and gave him a tight smile, imagining my mother driving that Bel Air, her hair blowing in the wind as she cruised around town with the top down when the weather warmed.

I could handle a little discomfort for her happiness. I could handle Nate Walton.

"You look like you're in pain," he said with a slight smirk before squeezing my hand. "Is this so terrible?"

I was saved answering by our waitress, who shuffled up to the table bearing two beers. Another server followed behind her, holding a tray on each hand. I gently extracted my hand from Nate's under the pretense of grabbing my glass. As the server set down our pizza and wings, I took a long swig of my drink.

"Can I get anything else for you?" the waitress asked, keeping her eyes on me.

She thinks Nate's off-limits, I thought. *Well, isn't he? Technically speaking?*

"We're good. Thank you, Heather," Nate said.

She nodded—at me—before turning to scurry away. Nate chuckled, bringing my eyes to him. I shot him a questioning look, and he shrugged before serving me a slice of pizza.

"It's not so bad, having a fiancée. I can actually eat in peace without…"

His words trailed off, and I arched a brow at him. "Admirers buzzing around, begging for scraps?" I offered.

"Something like that," he said holding a tray toward me. "Wing?"

"Sure," I said, plucking one from the tray.

Then, out of pure habit, I stuck my sauce-covered thumb in my mouth and sucked it clean.

13

Nate

Oh, sweet baby Jesus.

My eyes burned with the need to blink, but I held them open, unable to look away from Ivy sucking her fingers. My dick twitched, and I shifted my weight in my seat. She had no idea how beautiful she was—how sexy— and that fact only made her more desirable.

The food seemed to improve her mood, for which I was thankful. I was having a hard time figuring her out. She'd been fine when I picked her up. Friendly, even.

But then her whole vibe had changed, and she'd become skittish and grumpy. And I had no idea why. I played our whole conversation over in my mind, and I didn't think I'd said anything to piss her off or make her uncomfortable.

Ivy Anderson was a bit of an enigma.

And I didn't hate it.

Most of the women I'd spent time with were completely transparent. They'd use their words or their bodies to tell me exactly what they wanted. If we didn't want the same things, I'd let them know. All very straight-forward and for the most part, emotionless.

Ivy, however, kept me on my toes, constantly wondering what she was thinking. She'd spout angry or irritated words, but her eyes told me a different story. She'd feign indifference, but her blush showed me just how I affected her.

There was no denying it—despite years of animosity, I wanted her. And I was pretty sure she wanted me.

It was crazy. I didn't even *like* her very much. Or did I? I was so confused.

The one thing I was sure of was that if she kept sucking her fingers, I was going to do something ridiculous, like launch myself over this table and stick my tongue in her mouth. I shifted positions again and cleared my throat.

"How's the food?" I asked, taking a sip of my beer.

She'd already downed her second glass and ordered another. I thought about offering to get her some water, but quickly disregarded it. The devil on my shoulder wanted to meet Tipsy Ivy. Maybe she'd be more inclined to share the secrets hidden behind those blue eyes.

"It's good," she said, smiling at Heather as she approached with a fresh glass of beer.

I breathed a small sigh of relief. Ivy had been so sure I'd slept with the waitress at first, and while it shouldn't matter, I was glad I'd managed to disabuse her of the notion. I would never take Ivy somewhere where we might run into one of my ex-lovers on our first date. The fact that she thought I would kind of irked me, but I pushed the feeling away.

Ivy was smiling again, and I focused my full attention on her mouth. I wondered if her lips would taste like buffalo sauce and beer. I wanted to bury my nose in her neck, inhaling the sweet vanilla scent I'd caught a whiff of in the car.

I shook my head and took another bite of pizza. Nope. I needed to keep my head straight. This was a business arrangement. Nothing more.

"Did you figure out a way to sneak your mom's car out without her noticing?" I asked.

"I think so," Ivy said, picking up her purse and digging through it. She pulled out a keyring, handing it to me. "These are the keys to the barn and the car. I swiped them last time I was there."

She smiled, obviously pleased with herself. I ignored the feel of her fingertips on my palm as she handed me the keys, and I tucked them into my pocket.

"Whenever you're ready, I'll plan a shopping trip to get her out of the house. Can you send your tow truck to pick it up?"

I nodded. "I can drive it out there, myself."

"Good," she said, grinning. "Mom never goes out there, so I don't think she'll notice the key—or the car—is gone."

The alcohol seemed to be loosening her up, so I cocked my head and asked, "Can I ask you a question?"

"Shoot," she said, taking a long drink of her beer.

I took a fortifying drink of my own before asking, "What did I do that made you hate me so much?"

Her face paled. "I don't want to talk about that, Nate."

"Come on, Ivy. I want to know. It seemed like we..." I bit back the words I wanted to say—that it seemed like we were equally attracted to each other in the beginning. "I just want to know what I did."

"You didn't do anything," she gritted out. "Are you done? I'm ready to go."

"Ivy."

"No, Nate. I just want to focus on the here and now. The past doesn't matter."

I wanted to argue that whatever had happened in the past was affecting the here and now, but I kept my mouth shut. Ivy looked like she was teetering on the edge of panic, her fight or flight instinct leaning definitively towards *flight*.

"Sorry. I'll drop it," I said quietly.

"Thank you," she said before repeating, "Are you done?"

"Yeah," I said, catching Heather's eye and motioning for the check and a box for the leftovers.

Ivy drained the rest of her beer while I paid and packed up what was left of the pizza. When we stood to leave the restaurant, she slipped her hand into mine, and our fingers laced together. I knew it was part of the act, but my heart sped up at her unsolicited touch.

It was a silent drive to her apartment. Ivy was distant, staring out her window the entire time, and I didn't try to force conversation on her. When we pulled up outside her apartment, though, I couldn't let her leave without saying something.

"Ivy, I'm sorry if I made you uncomfortable. That wasn't my intention."

"It's fine," she said, sighing. "I probably overreacted. Thanks for dinner."

"You're welcome." As she opened the door, I leaned over and added, "I'll text you to plan our next date."

"Sounds good. Good night, Nate."

"Good night."

She climbed from the car without glancing at me and closed the door behind her. I watched her stride away, wondering if I should have offered to walk her to her door. Wasn't that what gentlemen were supposed to do?

Before I could finish the thought, she'd disappeared inside her apartment. With a sigh, I shifted my car into gear and pulled away from the curb. I turned on the radio, bobbing my head to the beat as my mind replayed the whole night.

Ivy was as beautiful as ever, but without the full force of her revulsion eliciting my own hateful responses, I noticed a few other things about her. Things I didn't hate.

The way her smile lit up her eyes. The feel of her hand in mine. The sweet-smelling softness of her blonde locks running through my fingers. The way she relished the food, sucking the sauce from her fingers with gusto before chugging her beer.

The way she staked her claim with the waitress, Heather, showing off the ring I put on her finger.

That was the part that had me on edge as I pulled into my own apartment complex. When Ivy had told Heather without words that I was off the market…that I was *hers*… I'd felt a certain satisfaction. Because that ring that made me hers also made her mine.

And I liked that feeling way too much.

Things were going so well, despite her initial weirdness when she found out we were going to Hero's, I'd felt secure enough to bring up the crux of our whole relationship— the catalyst that made Ivy go from flirty interested to coldly disgusted practically overnight.

I'd often wondered what happened to change her attitude toward me. I'd even suspected that my brother had warned her off. But while that might have made her more reserved, it wouldn't have caused her to turn into the hate-spewing she-cat she always showed me.

It was like someone had flipped a switch inside her, and I wanted to know why.

I heaved a sigh as I climbed from the car. I had to stop

worrying about it. This whole thing was a sham. A very *temporary* sham. It shouldn't have mattered why Ivy didn't like me.

The fact that she didn't was the whole reason I'd picked her in the first place.

Inside my apartment, I changed into a pair of sweats and stretched out on my bed. I tuned into the sports news channel, but my mind kept drifting back to Ivy. I tried to focus, to push her out, but thoughts of her kept sneaking back in.

I couldn't get the images of her licking her fingers out of my head.

I sucked my bottom lip into my mouth and bit it as I imagined those lips on my skin. Her tongue darting out to taste me. Her hands skimming over my chest, dipping lower...

With a groan, I shoved my hand down the front of my pants to grip my hardened cock. I began to stroke it, imagining Ivy standing before me. She had a fire in her eyes as her chest heaved with excitement. Her fingers took over for my own, pumping with enthusiasm before she dropped to her knees and—

I came with a growl, half-satisfied and half-pissed I finished before the fantasy came to an end.

I got up and stripped, tossing the pants into the laundry basket before heading into the bathroom to turn on the shower. As I waited for the water to heat up, I braced my hands on the counter and stared at myself in the mirror.

I'd just jacked off to thoughts of Ivy Anderson. Whom I was supposed to despise. My fake fiancée, who, in reality, hated my guts.

I was so fucked.

14

Ivy

𝓘 was a total basket case. Last night's dinner with Nate had been a series of highs and lows, but the crowning moment had been when he asked me what made me hate him in the first place. I'd frozen, then flat out refused to answer him.

Why? Was it because I didn't want to dwell on the past? Because I was still angry? Because we were in a quid pro quo arrangement that didn't require us to actually bond?

No.

It was because I was embarrassed. I'd obviously spent the first few weeks after I met Nate misreading his cues. I'd been attracted to him, and I'd thought he felt the same about me. To find him the way I did, getting it on in a public bathroom with another woman…it had devastated me.

And every ounce of anger I gave him over the next few weeks had been a result of that devastation. Then it sort of became par for the course. The rational part of my brain knew it was overkill, treating him the way I did after so many years had passed, but it had become a habit.

A habit that served to protect me from falling prey to his charm, his humor, and overall sexiness ever again. If I told him the truth, admitted that I'd been hurt by the realization that my feelings had been unrequited, I'd have been humiliated all over again.

He would have let me down gently, telling me he was sorry I'd been misled by his general flirtatious personality. He'd have told me we could be friends even after this whole pretend engagement was over. That one day we would laugh about the whole thing.

"No, thank you," I murmured quietly as I tapped the screen of my work tablet.

"Oh, hey, Ivy."

I whirled around, clasping the tablet against my chest as my heart stuttered back to life. "Jesus, Rafe. You scared me."

"Sorry," he laughed, holding up his palms. "I just came in to—what the hell is *that*?"

His gazed zeroed in on my left hand, and I looked down quickly, expecting to see a spider crawling across my knuckles. Instead, I saw a very large, very sparkly diamond.

"Oh, shit," I stammered, jerking my hand behind my back.

"Oh, shit is right," Rafe said, his expression bewildered. "Is that what I think it is?"

"Rafe, I can explain," I said, cursing myself for forgetting to take the damn thing off before work.

"I'm all ears," he said, closing the exam room door behind him to give us some privacy.

"This," I said, holding my hand up in front of me, "isn't what it looks like."

"It looks like a very big, very expensive engagement ring."

"Well, it is," I admitted. "But it's not real."

"So, it's a knock-off? Why would you be wearing a fake diamond?"

"No. That's not what I meant," I stuttered, shaking my head. Then I looked him right in the eye and said, "I'm pretending to be engaged. To Nate."

"What?" he shouted, making me flinch. "Why would you do that? Why would he…"

His words trailed off as several emotions flashed across his expression. Then he inhaled sharply and stabbed me with his brown eyes.

"The girl that's threatening him." I nodded, and he cursed quietly. "*This* is how he plans to fix it? Pulling you into his drama?"

"If Charity thinks he's in a committed relationship, she'll back off," I said, feeling oddly defensive on Nate's behalf.

"That's not your problem, Ivy," he shouted. He took a deep breath, shot me an apologetic look, and lowered his voice. "Why would you agree to this? You can't stand him."

"Well, I love you, and he's your brother," I said. He opened his mouth to protest, and I held up a hand to halt his words. "And he's going to finish restoring my mom's car."

Rafe knew all about the Bel Air and how much it meant to my mom. He knew I'd wanted to finish it for her, but classic car restoration could be pricey. I loved being a nurse, but I wasn't rolling in extra money.

"But—"

"No buts, Rafe. I'm doing something for Nate, and he's doing something for me. He asked me because he knew I could approach the whole thing as a business arrangement and not develop feelings for him. I said yes because he's my best friend's brother, he needed help, and he offered to give me the one thing I want more than anything else."

I ignored the little voice in my head that goaded me into admitting there might be one thing I wanted more than seeing the look of joy on my mom's face when she saw the car in all its glory—Nate. It wasn't true. I didn't want him. Not anymore.

"Are you sure you're okay with this?" Rafe asked, pulling me from my internal debate.

"I am. Dealing with your brother is a pain," I said, giving him a small smile, "but in the end, it will be worthwhile. It's only a few weeks of my time. It'll be worth it when I give Mom that car."

"Okay."

"Okay?" I asked, arching a brow. "Is that all you have to say?"

"Oh, I have plenty more to say, but I won't. You're a grown woman and fully capable of making your own choices. I'll support those choices, just like you've always supported me."

"Thanks, Rafe."

"You're welcome. I'll play along if anyone asks, but I won't lie to Jessa."

"Of course, not," I said. "I'd never ask you to lie to her."

He gave me a firm nod, then reached behind him to open the door. Then he held out a hand.

"Oh, my God, Ivy," he said loudly. "Congratulations! Let me see the ring!" I narrowed my eyes as I placed my left hand in his. He smirked at me as he bent over to examine it. "It's beautiful, just like you."

I looked past him to see a couple of coworkers crowded

in the doorway, expectant looks on their faces as they waited their turns to congratulate me and see the ring.

"Thanks, Rafe," I gritted out between clenched teeth.

"Anytime, bestie," he said, giving me a cocky wink before backing away and turning toward the women behind him. "She's all yours, ladies."

I spent the next twenty minutes gushing over my "relationship" with Nate, telling everyone who crowded into the empty exam room about how we'd dated quietly for a few months, fell in love fast and furiously, and ended up engaged. I smiled and giggled with them, all the while cursing Rafe for putting me in this situation.

Sure, Nate and I needed people to spread the word, but I'd kind of hoped it would be people in Nate's circle, not mine. I finally sent them all back to work and gave myself a moment alone to catch my breath.

This was harder than I thought it was going to be. Pretending to be in love with Nate when I had actual unresolved feelings for him was hell.

It would have been so much easier if I truly hated him.

After my shift, I grabbed my phone from my locker to find I had several texts—all from Nate.

Nate: *Hey there, my wife-to-be.*

Nate: *Nope.*

Nate: *Hey there, fiancée.*

Nate: *No, that's not right either.*

Nate: *Hey there, love monkey.*

Nate: *Yes! That's the one. What's up, love monkey?*

Nate: *Sorry, coming up with the perfect pet name is hard.*

Nate: *You can call me corn muffin if you want to.*

I found myself laughing despite trying really hard not to. Obviously, Nate hadn't let my frosty attitude deter him from his goal. He was still pushing forward with our fake engagement.

Me: *Hey, corn muffin, if you call me love monkey in public, I'm going to punch you in* your *love monkey.*

I tapped send without thinking, then panic formed a cold ball in my chest as I reread my words. They sounded flirtatious, and the thought that Nate might interpret them that way had my face flashing hot.

Nate: *Ha-ha. Got it. Love monkeys are for private time only.*

My face flamed even hotter, my embarrassment mixing with something else I wasn't ready to define. Something that had me clenching my thighs together as I pulled my jacket, purse, and keys from the locker and slammed it shut.

I hurried out to my car, sliding in behind the wheel and slamming the door shut before looking at my phone again.

Nate: *Seriously, though. I'm available tonight, if you are.*

My eyes widened as I tried to decipher the meaning behind his words. Available for what? To give me his love monkey?

Stop it, Ivy. That's obviously not what he means.

Nate: *To go pick up the Bel Air, if you can get your mom out of the house.*

Son of a bitch. The little, laughing-face emoji he added to the end of the last text told me he knew exactly what he was doing. Exactly what he'd made me think.

Me: *That's great! Thank you. I'll call her to see if she wants to go out to dinner, then get back to you.*

"Pretend like you weren't affected, Ivy. He only wants a reaction," I murmured before dialing my mom's number.

"Hey, baby," she said when she answered.

"Hey, Mom. How are you?"

"I'm good. How is everything with you?"

"Great, actually. I have the night off, and I want to take you to dinner."

"What's the occasion?" she asked, her voice skeptical.

"No occasion. I just want to hang out with my mom," I said, cringing at the defensiveness in my tone.

I needed to play this cool, or she was going to know something was up. I'd never been able to lie to her growing up. At least, not convincingly. She always knew when I was hiding something.

"Well, there is a new hamburger joint I wanted to check out," she said.

"Perfect," I replied. "I'll be there at six."

"Okay. See you then, honey."

"Bye, Mom."

After ending the call, I texted Nate.

Me: *It's all set. I'm picking her up at six for dinner. We should be gone by six-fifteen.*

Nate: *Perfect. Just shoot me the address, and I'll take care of the rest.*

Me: *Thanks, Nate. I really appreciate this.*

Nate: *Anything for you, love monkey.*

My lips curled up, and I was glad he couldn't see me. Cracks were forming in the walls I'd erected to keep him out of my heart. No matter how hard I tried to rebuild them, they crumbled a little more with every act of kindness. Every affectionate glance or flirtatious remark.

I actually kind of *liked* Nate.

And that was a big problem. A huge one.

15

Nate

$\mathcal{I}$ had my work cut out for me.

The Bel Air's engine was mostly intact. It needed some rewiring, a fuel injector, and a transmission, but I could tell Ivy's dad had put a lot of work into it before he passed. That would be the easy part.

The frame seemed to be solid, but the rear axle was bent and would need to be replaced. I'd also need to find new fenders, a front bumper, a radiator, and a new windshield.

Add in a paint job and new leather to reupholster the worn and cracked seats, this project wasn't going to be easy —or cheap.

And if I was going to finish it by Christmas, I needed to get started immediately. I just hoped I could find all the parts here, in the United States. If I needed to have something shipped in from overseas, it was going to cost me time and money I didn't have to spare.

But I couldn't deny the excitement in my veins as I

pictured what this car could be. What it *would* be. Because I *would* pull it off.

I owed it to Ivy for doing me this huge favor, sure, but I also couldn't deny that something else was pushing me to bring the old girl back to life. It would make Ivy's mom happy, which would make Ivy, herself, happy.

I tried to rationalize it all away. To convince myself I was just excited to finally have the chance to work on one of my bucket list cars. To tell myself that making Ivy happy was just a small victory in our ongoing battle of wills, that it would prove I was not the devil she seemed to think I was.

But the thought of making Ivy happy made my heart pound in my chest. Anticipating her smile of joy and gratitude made my breath hitch. The idea that finishing this car on time would soften her toward me—even the tiniest bit—brought a smile to my face I couldn't suppress.

I thought about my texts to her earlier. I'd been teasing her with ridiculous pet names, hoping to clear the air between us after that disastrous date. When she'd responded back—calling me *corn muffin* and threatening to punch me in the junk—I'd been...elated.

Her silliness had told me all I needed to know, that things weren't totally broken between us. That we'd be able to finish this ruse of an engagement, at the very least. I'd get Charity off my back, and things would go back to normal.

Normal. Did I really want that? Ivy going back to tossing barbed insults at me every chance she got, and me going back to exaggerating my player ways just to piss her off? Was that really where I wanted this whole thing to end up?

The stubborn half of my brain said yes. That Ivy and I

were just too different, and we were destined to live as enemies once the act was over.

The other half? Well, it held out hope that we could somehow come out of this as friends. Or maybe more…

I shook my head to clear the crazy thought. There was no way that was ever happening. There was too much water under that bridge. We could never go back.

I went into my office to sit down at the computer and start my search for parts, but my brain refused to cooperate. My mind kept drifting back to the early days, when Ivy and I first met.

The first time Rafe had introduced me to his new coworker, I'd been a little dumbstruck at how gorgeous she was. Blonde hair, bleached by the sun, soft blue eyes, and those cute freckles scattered across her nose and cheeks made her look like she should've been wearing a wetsuit and carrying a surfboard.

I'd seen the interest in her gaze, the way her eyes roamed over me when she thought I wasn't looking. I'd flirted with her, and she'd blushed, but her shy embarrassment hadn't stopped her from flirting back. As she and Rafe grew closer, I found myself getting jealous—which I'd thought completely ridiculous. I'd grilled Rafe on their relationship, making it sound like sibling teasing, until I was satisfied that his only feelings for her were ones of friendship.

Then I upped the ante. I made my intentions clear. I could feel the sexual tension between us growing thicker and thicker, and just when I decided to go for it, something changed. Drastically.

One night, we were playing footsies under the dinner table. The next, Ivy had basically disappeared from my life. It seemed as if she'd started deliberately avoiding me, and when I finally saw her again, she was a completely different person.

She was cold and distant, and when I tried to break through and figure out what had happened, she turned hostile. I reacted poorly, lashing out to soothe my hurt feelings, and things had been that way between us ever since.

If she would've just told me what happened to change things between us, I might've been able to smooth it over. I would've apologized and used my charm to win her back, but I had no idea what I'd done.

I heaved a sigh and pushed the past away. I started tapping the keys on my computer, looking up part numbers for the items I'd need to fix the Bel Air. That was what I needed to focus on. Fixing that car, and upholding my end of the bargain.

"Hey, corn muffin."

The voice startled me, and my rolling chair slid back a couple of inches as I jerked upright to see Ivy standing in the doorway of my office.

Like I'd conjured her.

"Hey, love monkey," I said, giving her a wide smile. "What are you doing here?"

"I just got back into town after dinner with Mom. I saw the lights on, and thought I'd stop by to get your first impression of the car and see how much work it's going to need. I hope that's okay."

"Of course," I said quickly, standing and moving toward her. "It's definitely a beauty. Your dad did a good job."

She gave me a misty smile, telling me I'd said the right thing. "He loved my mom, and he loved that car."

"I can tell," I said. "I've made a list of parts, and assuming I can find them all in a timely manner, I should be able to have her fully restored by the deadline."

"Really?' she asked, hope shining in her eyes.

I nodded. "Really."

And I would, if it meant seeing that happy expression on her face again.

"Nate, are you in here?"

My entire body froze as I recognized the voice calling out from the front door. I met Ivy's eyes, which were wide with question, and mouthed, "Charity Glasscott."

"I came by to see what you've deci—oh. Hi."

Her whole tone changed as she laid eyes on Ivy. Her eyes narrowed, scanning the full length of Ivy's body before settling on her face. My palm settled on Ivy's lower back, offering her support as well as showing Charity there was something between us.

Ivy's hand dug into the pocket of her coat. After a couple of seconds, she withdrew it and wrapped the arm around my waist. I assumed she'd taken off the ring while at dinner with her mother, and was surreptitiously putting it back on for Charity's benefit.

The weight of her arm across my lower back felt divine, and I had to clear my throat to speak.

"Ivy, this is Charity Glasscott. Charity, this is Ivy Anderson…my fiancée."

As Charity seemed to choke on her own spit, Ivy unwound her arm from my waist and offered her hand to the conniving witch. Charity took it, giving it a small shake. Her eyes grew wide when they landed on the ring, and her face turned an unflattering shade of red.

"Nice to meet you, Charity," Ivy said graciously before gently pulling her hand from Charity's grip.

"Since when are you engaged?" Charity spat, all pretense of civility gone.

I opened my mouth to give her a snide answer, but Ivy beat me to it.

"Oh, it was so romantic," she said, her eyes glistening with love as she looked up at me. "I know we've only been dating for a few months, but when he got down on one knee and told me I was the only one who would ever hold his heart, I had to say yes. And the *ring*." She held up her hand and wiggled her fingers. "Isn't it exquisite?"

"You never mentioned you were dating someone," Charity accused, refusing to look at Ivy and the sparkly diamond she was waving around.

"I didn't think I needed to explain myself to you. We barely know each other."

"You know what I said I'd do…"

"And what is that?" Ivy cut in. "What is going on here, corn muffin?"

Her face was so utterly bewildered as she looked up at me, her tone so sweet, I was having a really hard time keeping a straight face. Ivy was an A-list actor, and I couldn't have been more proud.

"It's nothing for you to worry about, love monkey," I cajoled, stroking a finger down her cheek. "Charity here just thought I was available because we were keeping our relationship under wraps like you wanted. Now she knows better. Isn't that right, Charity?"

I looked back at the bane of my existence, and she glared at me with hot, savage anger. I started to say something else, but the words flew right out of my head as Ivy's hand ran up the center of my chest. Her touch was like fire, sparking the embers of my lust to all-new heights.

When her fingers reached my neck, they curled around behind it and tangled in the hair at my nape. I'd never been so glad I'd put off getting a haircut before. Her grip tightened, and she pulled my head down, bringing our faces close together.

She locked gazes with me as her other hand fisted in

the front of my shirt. She paused to take a deep breath, tilted her head, and sucked my bottom lip into her mouth. Her teeth grazed it lightly, followed by a soft sweep of her tongue, and I completely lost my shit.

My hands flew to either side of her neck, my thumbs stroking her jaw as I took control. My tongue delved into her mouth for the first time, and all rational thought deserted me. All I knew was Ivy tasted like peppermint and heaven, and I didn't want to stop tasting her. Ever.

A small moan vibrated in her chest, making my dick stand up to attention. Before I knew what I was doing, I'd pushed her back against the nearest wall and hooked a hand behind her knee, pulling her thigh up by my hip so I could grind into her.

The fog of lust thinned when Ivy turned her head, breaking off our kiss. But it didn't completely dissipate. Still enthralled, I planted a trail of hot, wet kisses across her neck before sucking her earlobe into my mouth and biting down gently.

"Nate," she breathed, and it was the sexiest sound I'd ever heard.

I wanted to strip every scrap of clothing from her body and worship it for days. I wanted to run my tongue over every single inch of her to see if she tasted this good all over. My fingertips slipped under the hem of her shirt, teasing the soft skin of her waist before gliding upward.

"Nate, stop," she said, her voice only slightly stronger than before.

But it was enough to jerk me back to my senses, and I froze. Ivy and I were both breathing hard, and I slowly disentangled my body from hers and took a small step back. Ivy stayed where she was, leaning against the wall for support as her face flamed with a bright red blush—

whether it was from embarrassment or desire, I didn't know.

"She left," she said between harsh breaths.

"Who?" I asked, and Ivy's expression turned incredulous.

"Charity. You know, the person we were putting on that little show for?"

"Oh, right," I said, looking over to see she was right.

Charity was gone. And I'd honestly forgotten she was ever there. And that was something to analyze later, because I looked back to see Ivy edging toward the door. The rational side of my brain knew her leaving would be for the best—the smart thing to do—but the irrational side ruled by my cock wanted to shove her back against that wall and finish what she started.

"Well, hopefully that worked," she said, her voice a little too bright for my liking. "Maybe she'll leave you alone now. I have to go. Talk to you later."

Then she was gone, and I was left alone to figure out what in the hell just happened.

16

Ivy

*H*oly shit. What the fuck?

My brain was still in panic mode when I barged into my apartment and slammed the door closed behind me. I paced around the living room, my heart pounding a staccato beat as I wrung my hands together and silently questioned my sanity.

That was not supposed to happen.

Charity showed up, and I decided to play my part as Nate's loving fiancée—which required touching him, almost intimately, for *her* benefit. And I was fine with that. I'd expected it to come to that.

What I didn't expect was the heat that filled me as I ran my hand up Nate's chest, my fingers caressing every ridge and hollow. I didn't expect to feel his heart speed up as my palm glided over it, or to catch that little hitch in his breath when my fingers tangled in his hair.

And I didn't expect the entire world to melt away when our lips met.

One second, I was putting on a show for the bitch blackmailing Nate. The next, I was sandwiched between his chest and a wall, practically dry-humping him as he kissed me with what seemed like several years' worth of pent up passion.

It was overwhelming. It was exhilarating. It was the sexiest fucking kiss I'd ever experienced. Yet, here I was, alone in my apartment, filled with nervous energy as I paced with uncomfortably soaked panties.

I'd almost turned around three times during my drive home. My body urged me to go back and beg Nate to finish what he started. To give me that release that I *knew* would be epic. If the expertise of his mouth was any indication, that man would be a master in bed.

My train of thought led me down a dark road, bringing me to only one conclusion—Nate was that good because he'd had a lot of practice…like sex against the bathroom wall at Hero's kind of practice.

And just like that, the heat inside me evaporated. What had I been thinking? Of course, I shouldn't have stayed, allowing myself to sleep with Nate. It would've been a disaster.

Because while sex with him would have been something special to me, it would've been nothing but another Thursday night for Nate Walton.

I checked the time on my phone. It was only nine p.m., and I knew Jessa sometimes went out for girls' night on Thursdays with Karly and Felicia. I pulled up our group chat and sent a message.

Me: *Hey are you guys out tonight? I could use a drink and some girl talk.*

I walked into my bedroom and stripped out of my clothes before striding to the bathroom and turning on

PIPER JAMES

the shower. I needed to get the feeling of Nate's mouth and hands off of me before I drove myself crazy.

My phone chimed a few times, and I smiled as I read the messages.

Felicia: *We're at The Bullpen. Jessa's working, but she can take a break when you get here.*

Karly: *Hurry up. I've got a margarita with your name on it, but I WILL drink it if you don't get here soon.*

Felicia: *Please hurry. If Karly drinks any more tequila, she'll be dancing on the table, and Jessa will have to kick us out.*

Karly: *It could happen.*

Felicia*: It* has *happened.*

Me*: I'm just hopping in the shower, but I should be there in thirty.*

I set the phone down on the counter, twisted up my hair so it wouldn't get wet, and climbed into the shower to begin scrubbing the remnants of Nate's touch from my body.

~

"*H*ey Ivy," Karly shouted as I neared the table.

She stood up and wrapped her arms around me, and it wasn't until that moment I realized how badly I needed that hug. Felicia stood, too, hugging me as soon as Karly let go. Once we were all seated, I looked over at the bar and caught Jessa's eye. She gave me a little wave, then held up one finger to indicate she'd be over in a minute.

I turned back to Karly and asked, "Where's my margarita?"

"She drank it," Felicia said, rolling her eyes.

"In my defense, it was getting all melty and watered

down," Karly said. "Don't worry, I told Jessa to bring you a fresh one."

"Hey, Ivy. Here you go." I looked up to see Jessa setting a frosty drink down in front of me before sliding into a chair. "So, what's going on?"

I pulled my left hand from where I'd been carefully hiding it in my pocket and slammed my palm down in the center of the table. The girls seemed startled at first… before they noticed the ring.

Karly and Felicia's eyes rounded comically, but I noticed Jessa didn't seem surprised at all.

"You knew?" I asked.

She nodded. "Rafe told me about you and Nate."

"Nate," Karly squealed. "As in, *Nate Walton?*"

Felicia zeroed in on what Jessa had said. "You knew, and you didn't tell us?"

Jessa held up her palms. "Not my story. Not my place to tell."

"How did this happen?" Felicia asked. "I thought you couldn't stand him."

"I'll tell you everything, but you have to swear not to tell anyone. And I do mean *anyone*. If this gets out, it would be a disaster."

"You can trust us," Karly said, already leaning forward over the table with an anticipatory gleam in her eye.

"We won't tell a soul," Felicia promised, looking just slightly less intrigued.

I leaned forward and motioned for Jessa and Felicia to do the same, so we practically had our heads together. I told them about Charity and her threats against Nate and his business. I told them about our deal, our date at Hero's, and everything that happened tonight.

By the end, Karly was fanning herself. Felicia eyed me critically, and Jessa stared at me with compassion. Only she knew the truth behind why I hated Nate and the significance of him taking me to that restaurant, of all places.

"So, let me get this straight…you've hated him for years, but one kiss had you ready to get him naked and jump his bones?" Karly asked.

"Pretty much," I admitted.

"So, why didn't you?" Felicia asked, tilting her head. "If there's no feelings involved, it would've just been sex. And from the sound of it, *hot sex*."

"But he's not her type," Karly cut in. "Remember? She said she likes blonds."

"He's obviously her type if a kiss had her climbing him like a tree, Karly," Felicia said, arching a dark brow at me as she spoke.

I looked at Jessa, and she gave me an encouraging nod. She knew what I was asking, if I should tell them the real deal about my feelings for Nate. Honestly, I wanted to tell them everything.

"So, I kind of lied before," I started.

"Lied about what?" Karly asked.

"I don't really go for tall, skinny blonds. I only said that because it was the opposite of Nate Walton. He is one hundred percent *my* type."

"Why did you think you needed to lie to us?" Felicia asked, her expression inquisitive, but not hurt or angry.

"Because I was denying my feelings," I said.

I went on to tell them the same story I'd told Jessa at her Halloween Party. How the sexual tension I'd felt between Nate and I in the beginning led me to believe we could have something. How I'd followed him to the bathroom at Hero's that night and found him sexing up some waitress. How I'd turned bitter and hateful toward him, lashing out any chance I got until it became habit.

Felicia stared at me with her dark eyes for a moment,

then said, "It sounds like you hated his actions. But did you really hate him? Like, as a person?"

"Isn't it the same thing?" I asked. "Don't a man's actions prove who he is as a person?"

"People make mistakes," she said, shrugging.

"Yeah, just like I did tonight. Getting caught up in that kiss was a huge mistake."

17

Nate

I couldn't stop thinking about that kiss. As soon as I got home, I stripped and climbed into a hot shower, trying my best to think about my schedule for tomorrow, which car repairs needed to be completed, and where I might eat lunch.

But the thought of food led my brain to my mouth, which led me right back to how delicious Ivy tasted as I licked her skin. My cock pulsed, growing uncomfortably hard, and I curled my fingers around it to help ease the ache.

Bracing my free hand against the shower wall for support, I stroked my erection as images of Ivy played on repeat in my head. I could still feel her hand gliding up my chest, the feel of her teeth sinking into my bottom lip.

My hand moved faster as I remembered pushing her against that wall, devouring her mouth as her hips bucked against me. Her little moans rang in my ears, and my growl echoed off the shower walls as I came. Hard.

I huffed out a few shallow breaths as every muscle in my body seemed to relax. I thought I'd feel better, but jerking off in the shower left me feeling a little bereft. That was not what my body craved. I needed Ivy, to feel her naked skin rubbing against mine as I slowly inched my way inside her.

I turned off the water and grabbed the towel I'd hung over the door, concentrating on drying myself before I ended up uncomfortably hard again.

I threw myself across the bed, naked, and tried to clear my mind so I could go to sleep. It was still early, but after everything that had happened, I was bone-tired. Despite my best efforts, thoughts of Ivy kept creeping back in, so I rolled over onto my back and threw an arm across my eyes.

Why was I so affected by her? I couldn't lie, she was a beautiful woman. She was smart and had a big heart. And she was really funny when she wasn't actively spewing hate in my direction. That hatred had become a constant between us over the last few years, and I hadn't really thought of her in a sexual way in a very long time.

But this fake engagement had changed everything. Forcing ourselves to really talk to each other had opened my eyes, making me remember the early days. When I'd thought there might've been something between us.

And it made me remember how badly I'd wanted to take her to my bed.

I sat up, running a hand through my hair. My heart picked up speed as I wondered if sleeping with Ivy wasn't such a bad idea. We obviously had chemistry. That had been proven tonight as we basically lost our minds in front of Charity Glasscott.

The more I thought about it, the better the idea seemed. We needed to get it out of our systems. One night. That's all it would take, if I could get Ivy to agree to it.

I leapt to my feet and strode toward the closet. Pulling on a pair of loose jeans and a long-sleeved shirt, I felt better already. This was going to work. Ivy would agree, and we'd spend the whole night satisfying our needs together. The mystery would be gone, and we could ride out the rest of this fake engagement without all the tension.

It was the perfect solution.

$\sim$

I stood outside the door to The Bullpen, smoothing my shirt and running a hand through my still-damp hair. Luckily, I'd spotted Ivy's car in the lot as I drove by, saving myself a wasted trip to her apartment. Jessa's Jeep was also in the lot, which meant my brother's girlfriend was either working the bar, or she and Ivy were having a girls' night with their friends...or both.

"Just go in there, ask to speak to her alone, then spit it all out. What's the worst that could happen?" I mumbled before pulling the door open and striding inside.

She could laugh in my face. Or worse, call off our "engagement" and never speak to me again. But the minute possibility that she'd say yes, that I could have her in my bed within the hour kept my feet moving forward.

As soon as I stepped inside the bar, I spotted her. Ivy was sitting at a table near the bar with Jessa, Felicia, and Karly, her face turned upward as she laughed, exposing the smooth skin of her neck. I was suddenly convinced I was a vampire, because I wanted nothing more in that moment than to run my teeth over her throat, nipping and biting until she groaned with ecstasy.

Clearing my throat, I moved my feet, anxious to get

this conversation out of the way so Ivy and I could get to the good stuff.

"Nate. What are you doing here?" Jessa asked as I approached, her eyes narrowed into suspicious slits.

"Hey, Jessa. Ladies." I nodded at her friends before zeroing in on Ivy. "I came to offer my fiancée a ride home."

Felicia snorted, *loudly*, drawing my attention. My eyes darted between her and Karly. They were both shaking their heads like they didn't believe my excuse for a minute. My eyes moved to Ivy, who sported flushed cheeks and glassy eyes.

"You told them?"

She shrugged, and Jessa threw an arm across her shoulder, saying, "I told her it was okay. They're my friends. We can trust them."

I knew she was right. Those three were thick as thieves, and they would never tell a soul that Ivy and I were a charade. A charade that I was determined to turn into a reality...at least for tonight.

I looked back at the women and nodded. "I trust you." Then I refocused on Ivy. "Are you ready to go? I need to talk to you about something important."

"Boo," Karly yelled, tossing a knotted cherry stem at my face. "We're having fun, asshole."

I dodged the missile and turned to Felicia, who seemed to be swaying a bit in her chair as a sad country song played softly from the jukebox. Neither of them were in any condition to drive.

"Do you guys need a ride?" I asked, though the words felt like a machete to the gut.

I wanted to be alone with Ivy, but I couldn't, in good conscience, leave her friends here to make bad, drunken choices.

"I got them covered," Jessa piped up, lifting a glass of what looked like water in my direction.

I nodded and turned my full attention back to Ivy. She'd been quiet since my arrival. Too quiet.

"Will you come?" I asked, my overstimulated and undersexed body rejoicing when she nodded and said yes.

Yes. You will come. More than once, if I have anything to say about it.

I held out a hand and she took it, launching herself from her chair a little too enthusiastically, and her body slammed into mine. My free hand latched onto her hip to steady her as something that sounded like a groan vibrated in her chest.

Blood rushed to my cock, making it stand to attention. Instead of leaping away, Ivy pressed herself closer and shimmied, a little. Then she purred out another groan, and I knew. She was turned on.

Fuck.

I grabbed the purse Jessa held out to me, nodded in response to her *I will murder you if you hurt her* glare, and led Ivy from the bar. We didn't speak along the way, and I had to fight to keep my pace moderate as Ivy's palm burned against mine.

If anyone was watching, they'd see a couple holding hands as they left The Bullpen. But this wasn't for the lookie-loos or the gossipmongers. This was for me and for Ivy.

I held the door and Ivy climbed into the passenger seat of my Mustang, wondering for the first time why she was being so agreeable. Had that kiss at the shop affected her the way it had affected me? Did she want this as badly as I did?

It had seemed like she did, and though I wanted it to be true when I planned this whole thing, I hadn't truly let myself believe it. There had been this nagging voice in the back of my head telling me I'd read the whole thing wrong, and that Ivy had only been playing a part. But now it seemed like maybe her reaction hadn't been an act at all…just like I'd hoped.

"Thanks for the ride," she said as I climbed in behind the wheel.

Before I could respond, she giggled. I looked over at her with wide eyes. She was still sporting pink cheeks as she laughed at the sexual innuendo in her words—and I had no doubt that was what she was giggling about. Her eyes were slightly unfocused and her head wobbled before she laid it back against the headrest.

"Shit," I muttered under my breath as I started the engine.

She was drunk.

Which meant there'd be no conversation that led to us getting naked and easing the sexual tension between us. Because when I slept with Ivy Anderson, she sure as hell was going to consent to it with a clear mind. And she sure as hell was going to fucking remember it.

During the drive to her apartment, Ivy rambled on about how much she loved girls' night, how she cherished Jessa, Karly, and Felicia, and how much she adored light beer. I chuckled despite my disappointment, because damn, she was a cute as hell drunk.

When she complained about the heat in the car, I turned off the vents, but that didn't stop her from unzipping her jacket and peeling it off her shoulders. I forced myself to keep my eyes on the road after one peek revealed a skin-tight sweater with a low-plunging neckline.

My dick twitched as I imagined running my tongue down that valley between her tits, and I turned up the radio to try to drown out my thoughts. Singing the lyrics in my head helped, but only a little.

After a few beats of silence from Ivy, I could feel her eyes on my face. I wasn't one hundred percent certain I could stop my eyes from dropping to her cleavage if I looked her way, so I kept my eyes on the road and asked, "What?"

"Why do you have to be so fucking beautiful?" she asked, the words slow and slurred.

"I'm sorry, what?" I said, just because I wanted to hear her say it again.

"You heard me," she groused. "It's not fair that an asshole like you should be so beautiful."

I blew out a rough sigh. We were back to this. It occurred to me that in her inebriated state, I could easily get her to tell me why she hated me so much. The words would spill from her lips like a waterfall, but as much as I wanted to know, asking her now felt like a dick move. Like I'd be betraying her trust…what little trust she actually had in me.

"I'm sorry you don't think I'm ugly," I said.

I made the turn into the parking lot of her apartment complex and pulled into the first empty spot. I killed the engine and climbed from the car, jogging around to help Drunk Ivy out before she face-planted on the asphalt.

She didn't pull away when I looped one of her arms over my shoulders and stretched my own around her waist. She actually leaned into me, resting her cheek against my chest in a way that made thoughts of never letting go flash through my mind.

Brushing the errant thoughts aside, I asked, "Do you have your keys?"

"Mm hmm," she mumbled, shoving her free hand into

her bag and digging around for several seconds before yanking it free with a victorious shout.

Taking the keys from her, I unlocked the door and led her inside. As soon as we passed the threshold, she came to life, pulling away from me. Before I could muster a protest, she'd slammed the door, turned the deadbolt, and leaned back against it.

"What are you doing?" I asked, my voice cracking with nerves I hadn't felt since I was fifteen.

She pushed away from the door, stalking me as I backed away, further into her living room. The backs of my legs bumped into the couch, and before I could catch my balance, I fell back into it. Ivy kept coming, crawling onto my lap with her knees straddling my hips.

I sucked in a breath to tell her she shouldn't do this, but all that came out was a low groan when she rolled her hips and rubbed her pussy against my cock. Then her mouth was on me, sucking on the skin of my neck before her tongue trailed a path up to my mouth. It flicked against my lips once before she pulled back a few centimeters.

"Yum," she said, then sealed her mouth to mine.

Her tongue dipped in to brush against mine, and my hands took on a life of their own, latching onto her hips and pushing down to increase the friction between us. She moaned and broke off our kiss, straightening her spine as she rode me while pushing her breasts toward my face like some fucking Thanksgiving feast.

And damn, was I hungry.

I knew I had to stop this. As much as I wanted her— more than any woman I could remember ever wanting—I couldn't do it. Not like this.

Not when she would most certainly regret it in the morning.

My fingers dug into her hips, stopping the bucking

movements while gently lifting her off of me. She growled —fucking *growled*—and gripped my shoulders before biting my earlobe and whispering in my ear.

"Fuck me, Nate. I want to feel your magic dick inside me."

Holy shit. That was the first time she'd said the words "magic dick" without derision. She'd said it with real need as she pressed her tits into my chest, and I almost caved.

Because *I* wanted what *she* wanted. I wanted to strip her clothes off and taste every inch of her skin. I wanted to fuck her with my mouth first, to make her come with my tongue deep inside her. Then I wanted to suck her nipples as she rode me, her hot, greedy pussy milking me as little moans vibrated from her.

"Ivy. We can't."

The words were like stabbing a knife into my own gut, but they had to be said.

She went rigid, panting for a moment before rolling off me and tucking herself into the corner of the couch. Blue eyes filled with betrayal, she pointed toward the door.

"Get out."

"Ivy, please. Let's talk about this."

"Get out!" she screamed, her face flaming with anger.

Or maybe it was shame.

No. No fucking way was I leaving here, letting her think I stopped because I didn't want this. Because I didn't want her.

"Ivy," I said, my voice firm, "look at me." I thought she was going to refuse, but her eyes darted to my face. I shook my head and pointed to my crotch. "Look what you do to me."

Her eyes dipped to the obvious hard-on straining against the denim of my jeans before raising back up to meet mine. Then she shrugged.

"So? It means nothing if you find someone else to take care of it for you."

"Why would I do that?" I asked, tilting my head to study her.

"Because you don't want me," she mumbled, so low I almost didn't hear it. "You never did."

18

_____

Ivy

$\mathcal{J}$ sat up with a groan, rubbing circles on my temples with my fingertips to ease the pain. How much did I drink last night? How did I get home?

Fragments of memories flashed through my mind—drinking at the bar with the girls, talking and laughing, then...

I closed my eyes, gritting my teeth against the pain as I searched my fuzzy memory for what came next.

"Oh, shit," I whispered, my eyes flying wide.

Nate had shown up, offering me a ride home. I vaguely remembered being in his car, then in my living room, where I'd...

"Oh, shit," I repeated, and this time it was a groan of agony.

I'd attacked him like a bitch in heat, straddling him and rubbing my body against his as I begged for his cock. And he'd refused.

My head drooped forward, my eyes stinging with tears

of shame and embarrassment. Why did I do that? Had a succubus demon jumped into my body? What other reason could there be?

"Good morning."

Oh, no. He is not here. No. No. No.

I forced my eyes up to the doorway of my bedroom, and there he was. With sleep-mussed hair and a scruffy-looking five o'clock shadow, he looked sexier than anyone had a right to. I was sure I looked like hell warmed over, and the contrast sparked a fuse of anger within me.

"What are you doing here, Nate?"

"I drove you home last night," he said, tilting his head before leaning one shoulder against the doorjamb. "You're welcome."

"Thanks," I growled. "Now, leave."

"Oh, no," he said, arching one dark brow at me. "I went looking for you last night because I wanted to talk to you about something, but I never got the chance."

"Does it have to do with our deal? Is everything okay with the Bel Air?"

"Yes, and yes," he said. "I'm making breakfast. Come to the kitchen when you're ready."

He disappeared from view before I had a chance to react. His audacity had no equal. He was in *my* house, cooking *my* food after, what? Spending the night on my couch? Uninvited?

In fact, I vaguely remember telling him to get out after...

I flipped the blankets to the side, and a small wave of relief washed through me to see I was still wearing last night's clothes. At least I didn't have to suffer the indignity of knowing Nate helped me out of them when I was too drunk to remember.

The pain flared in my head again, and I groaned. I

swung my legs over the edge of the mattress, my eyes landing on a tall glass of water and a bottle of aspirin. My gaze darted back to the empty doorway, the sounds of banging pans drifting in from the kitchen beyond.

"That was considerate," I mumbled, admitting it to myself as I popped the lid and shook two pills into my palm, tossing them into my mouth and swallowing them before chasing them down with half the glass of water.

I shuffled to the door, closing and locking it before making my way into my bathroom. Throwing my long hair up into a messy bun, I hopped into the shower to wash away last night's makeup and the booze seeping from my pores. Dressing quickly in a pair of loose sweatpants and an oversized hoodie, I brushed my teeth and rolled on some deodorant.

That was all the effort Nate would get from me this morning. I didn't invite him to stay, and as soon as he said what he wanted to say, I was kicking him out and going back to bed.

He greeted me with a cup of steaming coffee and a smile as I made my way into the kitchen, and I grumpily thanked him. I sat down at the bar and he slid a plate of bacon and eggs in front of me.

"Why are you still here, Nate?" I asked, shoveling a bite of scrambled eggs into my mouth.

Damn, these are good, I thought, then frowned. *Of course, he's a good cook. Is there anything he can't do?*

"You don't like them?" he asked, misinterpreting my frown.

"No, they're really good," I said. "Please answer my question."

"I told you, I wanted to talk to you about something. Eat first. Then we'll talk."

"Bossy," I mumbled, taking a sip of coffee.

"You don't know the half of it," he chuckled, sitting down next to me with his own plate.

We ate in silence, and when we were done, he took both our plates to the sink and washed them. My heart fluttered in my chest, and I silently ordered that hussy to stand down. The fact that he cooks *and* cleans is of no consequence to me.

I wandered into the living room and slumped onto the couch. My breath hitched as images of me straddling Nate in this very spot flashed through my mind. He'd felt so good. He'd tasted divine.

And he'd rejected my advances. He'd rejected me.

I startled as he plopped down beside me, leaning back to stare at the ceiling and spreading his legs wide. I leaned away from him, refusing to meet his gaze as I tried—and failed—to scrub those memories from my brain.

"I want you, Ivy," he said without preamble.

"What?" I asked, my mouth falling open with shock.

He took a deep breath and met my gaze. "I came to find you last night because I couldn't stop thinking about you. About that kiss in my shop."

"But...you turned me down last night," I said, my voice no higher than a whisper. "You didn't want me."

"No, Ivy," he said, his expression sincere. "I only said no because you were drunk, and I didn't want to take advantage of you. Turning you down was the hardest thing I've ever done. I wanted you so badly, it was *literally* painful."

To emphasize his point, he reached down and adjusted the bulge in his jeans. My eyes widened even further as I stared at it, his obvious erection straining against the denim.

"This is what you do to me, Ivy."

"But...we hate each other," I said, my words fast and furious. "We're just pretending. For the bargain."

"I assure you, this is not some pretense," he said, rubbing his hand over his package again, and my throat went dry. "I want to add an addendum to our deal."

"What do you mean?" I croaked.

"I want to lick and bite every inch of your body. I want to bury my cock inside you, to pump in and out until you scream your release."

Fuck.

I was panting for breath, my nipples tingling with need. My core clenched, soaking my underwear as his blue eyes held my gaze captive.

"The things you said and did last night... Ivy, I wanted nothing more than to bend you over this couch and sink into you. Never doubt that. But I couldn't. Not when you were wasted."

My heart was pounding, the blood whooshing through my ears as his words washed over me. Confusion and fear warred with lust inside me. Was he being serious?

He looked like he was being serious.

"I thought we could give in to it one time," he continued, his voice soft, yet urgent. "That we could get it out of our systems."

One time? Get it out of our systems?

I tried to muster up some anger. I should have been lashing out at him, declaring that I was not some cheap date he could use and toss away. But I didn't feel angry.

I felt...excited. Maybe Nate was right. Maybe sleeping together would ease some of the tension between us. I couldn't lie to myself. I wanted him. And as long as I went into it knowing nothing would come of it...

"Okay," I breathed before I could stop myself. "One time."

His smile was brilliant as he reached for my hand. Grasping it and jerking me forward, he pulled me onto his lap. I straddled him like I'd done the night before, and his fingers reached up to release my hair from its bun. Twisting his fingers around the strands, he pulled me toward him for a kiss.

His mouth was hot and all-consuming, and every doubt I'd had disintegrated as his tongue brushed against mine. All I knew was heat and pleasure as his fingers squeezed my hips and guided them in a steady, undulating rhythm.

"Just like that," he whispered, encouraging me to keep moving as he released his grip and slid his hands under the hem of my hoodie. I wasn't wearing anything beneath it, and a low growl vibrated from him as his hands explored my naked flesh.

He broke off our kiss to whip the garment over my head and toss it aside. His eyes widened, his hands moving to cup my breasts with near-reverence. My eyes fluttered closed at the feel of his palms brushing over my nipples, and I stopped moving, intent on memorizing his touch.

"Look at me, Ivy," he said, and my eyes popped open. "I want you to see me touch you. I want you to see what it does to me."

Holy fuck.

"Nate," I whispered as a fresh wave of heat rolled inside me.

"God, I love it when you moan my name. Say it again."

"Nate," I groaned louder as his fingertips plucked at my nipples.

"So beautiful," he said, his head dipping forward as his tongue darted out to flick one rosy peak before blowing air against it.

I shivered and started moving against him again, my

need ratcheting up several more notches. He sucked the other nipple into his mouth, his tongue flicking against it, making me squirm.

"Nate, please," I whispered.

With a growl, he wrapped his arms around me and stood up. With his hands kneading my ass, he kissed me with a hunger I'd never experienced before and carried me to my bedroom. Setting me on my feet, he put a little space between us. Before I could protest, he dipped his fingers below the elastic waistband of my sweat pants and pulled them down over my hips, slowly.

He dropped to his knees in front of me, pulling the material down inch by inch, kissing each knew patch of bare skin he revealed, until they were on the floor. I stepped out of them, and he threw them aside before starting the process all over again with my underwear.

Once I was completely bared to him, he paused for a moment, letting his eyes rove over me. His expression filled with something that looked like wonder before he grasped my hips and pulled me forward. He kissed my abdomen as one hand slid down my leg to my ankle. Wrapping his long fingers around it, he lifted my leg and slipped it over his shoulder.

He inhaled deeply, exhaling on a low groan before pressing his mouth against my pussy. His arms gripped my legs, keeping me steady as my fingers clenched in his dark hair, holding on for dear life.

Nate's tongue was pure sorcery, eliciting a series of moans that got progressively louder and louder. The tip would flick against my clit before swirling around it. He licked and sucked, and my legs started to shake as need spiked inside me.

Unhooking my leg from his shoulder, Nate climbed to

his feet and whipped his shirt over his head. My mouth filled with saliva as my hand reached to touch him.

He grabbed my hand before it reached its destination, saying, "Not yet."

He unbuttoned and unzipped his jeans, and my eyes widened, anticipation filling me as I waited to get my first look at his cock. But he only stripped off the pants, leaving his left-very-little-to-the-imagination boxer briefs firmly in place.

"Nate," I begged. For what, I wasn't sure.

"Turn around," he said.

My stubborn streak and previous penchant for arguing with everything he said wanted to ignore the order, but something in his voice, in his eyes, made me quick to obey. I turned my back to him, my excitement ramping up a few notches.

Who knew I'd be into this aggressive, bossy kind of thing?

Nate's bare chest came up against my back, his hands snaking around to knead my breasts as he walked me toward the bed. Once there, one hand slid down to cup my pussy while the other planted in the middle of my back, pushing until I was bent at the waist, my ass in the air.

His body heat left me, and I only had a second to wonder what he was doing before his tongue licked up and down my slit. My yelp of surprise quickly turned into a long moan. Fuck, it felt good.

I felt his fingers on my clit, rubbing gentle circles before his tongue pushed inside me. The world exploded, my orgasm coming unexpectedly fast and hard as I screamed his name. He fucked me with his tongue as wave after wave of ecstasy rolled through me.

I slumped against the mattress, a boneless mess of goo as Nate kissed his way over my ass cheeks and up my spine. My body refused to obey my brain and move, so I just groaned with pleasure as his lips and tongue carved a hot path over my body.

Something hot and hard pressed against my opening, and I stiffened, realizing Nate must've shed his underwear at some point.

"Are you okay?" he asked softly, obviously feeling my suddenly rigid posture beneath him.

"Yeah," I whispered back, glancing over my shoulder to meet his eyes. "I just want to *see* you."

His lips turned up as he straightened, lifting his weight from me so I could push up and stand before him.

"Holy fuck," I murmured, my eyes devouring every inch of him.

He was fucking perfect. In every way. And for today, he was mine.

19

Nate

H oly fuck.

That's what she said when she got her first look at me naked. I'd always been a little cocky about my body, knowing women found it attractive. It wasn't my best quality, that cockiness, but when every female who saw me naked had the same hungry reaction…it had gone to my head, a little.

But those two words hissing from Ivy's lips affected me in a way I hadn't experienced before. Instead of feeling self-assured and cocky, a new sensation rose up inside me. It was primal and possessive, and may as well have been chanting the word *mine* to a constant, heavy beat.

Ivy moved forward slowly, as if approaching a wild animal—which, maybe, I was. She pressed her hands against my shoulders before her palms glided downward, exploring every inch of my chest. I gritted my teeth against the urge to throw her on the bed and fuck her hard and fast. If she wanted to touch me, I wasn't going to stop her. No matter how loudly my cock complained.

Her fingertips danced over my abs, tickling me in the best way before she leaned forward to kiss me. Her tongue delved into my mouth, brushing against mine hungrily as her fingers continued their downward path. I hissed into her mouth as her hand wrapped around my cock, squeezing it lightly.

She moaned like the act of touching it pleasured her as much as it did me. That's when I lost my tenuous grip on my control.

"Ivy," I growled, breaking off our kiss, "I need to fuck you right now."

Her eyes flared with need, and I groaned as I pushed her away from me. Grabbing one of the condoms from the pocket of my discarded jeans, I watched Ivy as I ripped open the wrapper with my teeth and rolled it on slowly.

"How do you want it?" I asked, fighting the urge to shove her face down against the bed and take her from behind. "Tell me what you like so I can give it to you, Ivy."

I'd never felt this kind of need before, and I could barely stand still as I waited for her to answer. I'd always been methodical in my seduction, so detached, but something about having Ivy Anderson in front of me naked, with the taste of her still on my lips, made a beast I never knew was inside me emerge to the surface.

I wanted to mark her. To stake my claim.

Before I could explore those dangerous thoughts further, Ivy moved, turning her back to me before bending over and planting her hands on the mattress. She looked back at me over her shoulder, and her eyes begged me to take her. Now.

I strode forward, slipping my hands between her thighs and urging them apart. Then I slid a fingertip down her slit to her clit, rubbing a few circles before gliding back up and slipping a finger inside. She was so hot, so wet, I groaned with pleasure before pulling out and pushing a second finger back in with it.

Ivy was panting in time with my movements, her pussy filling with even more moisture as I pumped my fingers in and out. I wrapped her blonde hair around my fist, using it to turn her head to the side as I pulled my fingers from her pussy so she could watch me shove them into my mouth.

"Please, Nate," she groaned as I lined up my cock with her entrance.

I slid inside her, my legs trembling slightly as her inner walls clenched around my dick, squeezing me in the most delicious way. I released her hair and dug my fingers into her hips, holding her still as I pulled out slowly. My hips bucked forward, slamming back into her even deeper than before. Ivy yelled something unintelligible, and I rotated my hips before repeating the whole thing.

Out slowly. Ramming back in.

"Nate," she said, and her pleading tone was my undoing.

I lost all sense of rhythm and control, pumping harder and faster until I felt my own orgasm building. Leaning over her back, I slid one hand up to her breast while the other found her clit. She bucked beneath me, her pussy clenching tightly around my cock as she yelled her release.

My whole body stiffened, and I slammed into her one last time. I growled her name as I came, my arms looping around her in a tight embrace. The room was silent save for our harsh breaths, and I felt a sort of peace I'd never experienced before.

Ivy shifted beneath me, and I straightened, pulling her upright with me with her back against my chest. I lightly kissed her shoulder before flipping her hair off her neck and pressing my mouth there.

"That was amazing," I whispered, and a tremor ran through her as my breath tickled her skin.

She muttered something that sounded suspiciously like "magic dick," and I chuckled. Turning her in my arms, I hugged her tightly, reveling in the feel of her naked breasts against my bare chest. My hands slid down to grab fistfuls of her ass, kneading the flesh. Her fingers tangled in my hair, pulling my head down for a kiss.

I broke off the kiss and met Ivy's stare. "Lay down on the bed. On your stomach."

Her eyes widened, but not with fear. No, those blue orbs were filled with nothing but excitement and expectation. As she followed my command, I slipped into her bathroom to toss the condom. I grabbed a bottle of lotion I found on the countertop and took it back to the bed with me.

I climbed onto the mattress and straddled her thighs before squirting some lotion into my hands and rubbing them together to warm it. She didn't move or question what I was doing...she just lay there, her body tense with anticipation.

Applying a decent amount of pressure, I ran my hands up her back from the base of her spine to her shoulders before retracing the same path downward. A quiet moan vibrated from Ivy, and her body melted into the mattress.

It was likely she'd expected something a little kinkier, and my mouth curved up into a grin. Ivy had always acted the ice queen when dealing with me, but she obviously had a dirty side she kept hidden.

And I liked it.

I liked it a fucking lot.

~

*a*fter I'd massaged the tension out of Ivy's back, arms, and legs, I stretched out beside her on the bed. She rolled onto her side, and I slipped my arm under her head and pulled her close. She rested her cheek on my shoulder and pressed a palm over my heart.

We lay there silent for a few minutes before her fingers began stroking my skin. I forced myself to remain unmoving while her fingertips danced over my pecs, swirling around my nipples. Then they tiptoed across my stomach to explore my abs.

My cock hardened as she moved lower and lower. She sat up, and her gaze locked on mine as her hand slipped down to grasp my erection. She sucked her bottom lip in between her teeth, biting it lightly as her hand stroked up and down the length of me.

I wanted to suck that lip into my own mouth, but when I tried to pull her toward me, she wiggled out of my grasp and moved lower on the bed. Before I could object or try to pull her back, her tongue was on my cock, licking upward from the base before swirling around the tip.

My head dropped back to the pillow as I groaned with pleasure. The sound must've encouraged her, because she sucked the length into her warm mouth. My hands fisted the blanket beneath me, my breath whooshing through clenched teeth as my heart raced.

Ivy's fingers squeezed as her head bobbed up and down, her lips and tongue stoking the fire inside me. She hummed with pleasure, and I almost came at the sound of it.

Instead, I sat up and gently pulled her away from me, ignoring the pout on her lips. Grabbing an extra condom I'd dropped to the nightstand, I made short work of rolling it on before yanking her onto my lap. Her legs parted, her knees pressing into the mattress as she straddled me.

I kissed her hungrily, my tongue delving into her mouth as her hand slipped between us to guide my cock toward her entrance. It slipped inside easily, and I growled at how wet she was. From sucking me.

She started to move, rolling her hips as she rode me. My mouth moved down to her neck, lapping hungrily without conscious thought.

Ivy moved faster, her pussy tightening around me as she chanted my name. *Nate. Nate. Nate.* Over and over until she stilled, her inner walls clenching down hard as she came. The sensation of her pussy tightening around my cock, squeezing it deliciously, sent me over the edge. I came with a groan of satisfaction, and every bone and muscle in my body melted.

I fell back, my head landing on a pillow as my arms held Ivy captive against my chest. My fingers traced soft circles on her back as her heartbeat pounded into me. It gradually slowed, and I knew I needed to excuse myself to get rid of the condom still encasing my dick, but I couldn't bring myself to disturb the peaceful serenity of the moment.

Within minutes, Ivy was obviously asleep. Very slowly and gentle enough not to wake her, I lifted my hip and rolled until we were lying on our sides, still chest to chest. I ripped the latex sheathe from my cock with a sigh of relief and tossed it to the floor.

I knew it was gross, but there was no way I was leaving this bed. I wanted to stay tangled up in Ivy's arms as long as possible.

As I lay there staring at her sleep-softened face, I thought about my stupid plan. My idiotic assumption that fucking Ivy once would get her out of my system and ease the sexual tension between us.

There was no future in which I saw that being the case, but as the dark fog of sleep overcame me, I decided not to worry about it today. Maybe I'd want more, maybe I wouldn't. Maybe Ivy would tell me she was done, and that would be the end of it. Or it wouldn't, and I'd fight for more. But right now, I was too tired and sated to run through all the scenarios.

Today was my one day in Ivy's bed, and I wasn't going to ruin it by looking to the future. I just needed a nap, then I'd wake her up with my face between her legs. I drifted off with a smile on my face.

I'd figure out the rest tomorrow.

20

Ivy

*Y*esterday was the most amazing day of my life, and today, I was a wreck. I woke up this morning to find him gone. The only proof that he'd even been here was his scent on my sheets and the slight soreness between my legs.

No goodbye. No sweet note. Not even a text to tell me…anything.

I'd spent an hour soaking in a hot tub this morning, but it had done little to help the fog of confusion I'd been walking around in all day. I was having trouble concentrating, and it was affecting my performance at work.

But somehow, I'd made it through, and I was gathering my things from my locker when Rafe walked in and stopped me from making a hasty exit.

"Do you want to talk about it?"

No. Most definitely not. Especially not with you.

The thought made me cringe. Rafe was my best friend,

and if Nate had been anyone else, I would've unloaded on him over a bottle of wine and a greasy pizza.

"Talk about what?" I asked, hoping my expression was one of innocence.

"Come on, Ivy. You've been a zombie all day, you have dark circles under your eyes, and you look like someone stole your puppy."

"Gee, thanks, friend," I deadpanned.

"Is it Nate?" he asked, tilting his head.

"What? No. What do you mean?"

The words fired from my mouth like gunfire, and Rafe shook his head.

"So, it is Nate. What did he do?"

"It's nothing," I said, trying my best to reassure him. "I just didn't get much sleep last night."

"Are you sure?" he asked, looking unconvinced.

"I'm sure," I said, nodding. "I'm going to head home and go straight to bed."

I swallowed thickly and hoped Rafe didn't notice. I wasn't sure if I'd ever be able to sleep in my bed again. The memories I'd made there yesterday—and into the night—would be hard to forget.

Rafe dropped the subject with a sigh, and I stuttered out a goodbye as I squeezed past him to leave the locker room. I needed to get away from him before I broke down and told him everything. I refused to come between him and his brother.

My apartment felt incredibly empty when I got home, which was ridiculous, because I'd lived here alone for years. Stiffening my spine, I tossed my bag onto the kitchen table and strode into the bedroom. Forcing my mind to concentrate only on the task, I stripped the sheets from my bed and pulled the pillows from their cases.

Keeping the bundle well away from my nose, I carried

them straight to the small washing machine hidden in the hall closet. I dumped them in, added double the usual amount of laundry detergent, and slammed the lid.

I braced my hands against the top of the machine as I took a few deep breaths. The diamond ring on my finger caught my eye, and I stared at it for several seconds before reaching up and turning on the machine. Soon, Nate's scent would be gone.

If only it would've been so easy to clear thoughts of yesterday from my mind.

My phone chimed, alerting me of an incoming text, and I cursed myself for rushing to grab it from my bag. I told myself that it might've been the hospital, needing me to come back because there was a massive accident and an influx of critically injured patients.

Never mind that things like that never happened in Milestone.

When I saw the text was from Felicia in our group chat, I wasn't disappointed. At all. Not one bit.

"And now, I'm lying to myself," I muttered, tapping the screen to pull up her message.

Felicia: *Ok, we gave you forty-eight hours. You can come to us, or we can come to you. Whichever you choose, we're having a girls' night in.*

Before I could type out some excuse, another text came in, this one from Karly.

Karly: *We need details, Ivy! Let my poor, lonely vagina live vicariously through yours.*

Felicia: *Fuck, Karly. No one wants to hear about your cobweb-filled va-jay-jay.*

Karly: *Duh. That's why we need Ivy to give us all the gory details.*

Felicia: *Why would the details be gory?*

Karly: *It's a figure of speech, beeyotch.*

Jessa: *Only if she wants to tell us, ladies. She might be too worn out to talk. ;)*

Their texts came through one after another, giving me no time to respond. And, despite my earlier desire to hide and lick my wounds, having those three over suddenly sounded like the best idea ever. If anyone could pull me out of this funk and help me find some perspective, it was them.

Me: *I'm home now. Give me thirty to take a shower, and bring booze. LOTS of booze.*

Karly: *Yay! See you soon. F, come pick me up, K?*

Felicia: *Why am I always your designated driver? Maybe I want to get sloshed tonight, too.*

Jessa: *I'll pick you both up. See you in a bit, Ivy.*

I sent a smiley-face emoji and tossed my phone onto the table. I'd only taken a step away when I turned back and grabbed it, taking it into the bathroom with me.

You know. In case that multi-car pileup happens and the hospital needs me.

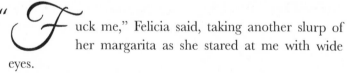

"Fuck me," Felicia said, taking another slurp of her margarita as she stared at me with wide eyes.

I was sitting on the couch next to Jessa, and Karly and Felicia sat in chairs we'd pulled in from the kitchen. Without going into too much detail, I'd told them everything: Nate bringing me home from the bar and refusing the passes I'd made at him, the fact that he'd still been here the next morning, and our deal to have one day together to ease the tension-filled lust between us.

How he'd been insatiable, giving me everything and taking what he'd wanted in return. How he'd brought me to orgasm again and again, making it hands-down the best sexual experience of my life.

How he was gone this morning, and I hadn't heard a word from him since.

"I guess he really is the douchebag I've always thought he was," I muttered, taking a sip of the special cocktail Jessa had made me. It tasted like mangoes and pineapple and made my insides deliciously warm.

"There could be a perfectly logical explanation," Jessa offered.

"Yeah, maybe he is sitting at home right now, wondering why _you're_ not texting _him_," Karly added. "And in a series of bungling missteps and crossed wires, you're both sabotaging this relationship when you really just want to be together."

"No more Hallmark Channel for you," Felicia said, nudging Karly in the arm with her elbow before letting her gaze zero in on me. "You said you both decided that it would be a one-time thing, right? To—and I quote—'get it out of your systems?'"

I nodded, taking another long sip of my drink. I had a feeling I knew where she was going with this, and I didn't know if I could handle this much truth while I was sober.

"And now you're upset because Nate upheld his end of the agreement?"

"I see your point," I said, my shoulders drooping.

"Are you going to continue with the fake engagement?" Jessa probed.

"Of course," I replied, a little shocked she felt the need to ask. "We made a deal, and I plan to see it through to the bitter end."

"Maybe you should just talk to him about it," Karly said. "Tell him you really enjoyed meeting his cock, and you want to get to know it a little better."

She watched me with sparkling eyes as she slurped the last of her drink through the straw. Laughter bubbled out of me as Felicia's hand shot out and shoved Karly, who wasn't expecting it. She fell out of her chair and hit the carpet with a thud, then lay there like one of those old people in the medical-alert device commercials.

As if she read my mind, Karly yelled, "Help! I've fallen, and I can't get up!"

Jessa giggled, turning my light laughter into full-blown hysterical guffaws. I didn't know if it was the depression, the booze, or these delightful people, but tears streamed from my eyes and my side stitched as I bent over laughing.

"Yep, she's lost it," Felicia said, watching me crack up. Then she looked down at the redhead on the floor. "Karly, get up. You're fine."

Jessa laughed louder for some reason, which set off another round of hysterical giggling inside me. Maybe Felicia was right.

Maybe I really had lost it.

21

Nate

It had been a long, busy day—especially after playing hooky the day before—but when the shop closed, I didn't go home. I was out in the garage by myself, cursing as I worked to remove the old bent and rusted rear axle from the Bel Air so I could replace it with the new one that had been delivered today.

The task was made harder by the fact that I couldn't seem to concentrate. I couldn't get lost in the beauty of working with my hands to restore a fine piece of machinery to its previous glory. I was too busy imagining my hands working with much softer parts. Squeezing flesh before running my tongue over it.

"Damn it," I yelled when my wrench slipped off a rusty bolt for the fourth time.

Leaving the car up on the rack, I walked to the bathroom to wash my hands. I wandered into the waiting room and slumped into one of the chairs. Tilting my head back, I closed my eyes and tried to force myself to relax.

I'd been a tense wreck all day, snapping at the techs for the stupidest shit and having zero fucking patience for even my most loyal customers. I needed to get my shit together…I just wasn't sure how to go about doing it.

My day with Ivy had been… Actually, none of the words in my vocabulary were epic enough to describe it.

And now I was left floundering, beating myself up for insisting it be a one-time thing while simultaneously cursing myself for wanting more. I'd snuck out of her apartment while she slept and hadn't texted or called her since. Shame burned my insides as I imagined how that might've made her feel, but I didn't know what to say.

Thanks? That was fun? I hope you enjoyed the orgasms?

I couldn't tell her the truth, so I'd said nothing at all. I knew it was wrong, but I wanted to taste her again. I wanted to feel the walls of her tight, wet pussy clench around my dick over and over again.

My cock hardened as I imagined the feel of her, and I grunted as I reached down to adjust myself. It had been happening all day, and I needed a release. Making the decision, I double checked the doors were locked and went back into the bathroom—the only room in the building without windows.

Dropping my pants and underwear, I braced one hand on the sink while using the other to squeeze my erection. I closed my eyes and pictured Ivy, her naked ass up in the air as she panted with need. My hand pumped as I imagined slipping two fingers inside her to find her drenched with need.

I stroked faster as her phantom voice met my ears, whispering my name and urging me to fuck her. I envisioned myself teasing her entrance with the head of my cock, and my ears rung with her impatient groans as she wiggled her ass and pushed back against me.

The muscles in my arm tensed as I continued to pump my dick, but I didn't slow down because fantasy me was sliding into Ivy's wet pussy.

A growl ripped up my throat as I came, my fingers clenching tightly around my shaft. Harsh breaths echoed off the bathroom walls as my muscles relaxed, leaving me feeling loose-jointed and a bit dizzy. I stared into the mirror for a few seconds, the satisfaction of the orgasm warring with disgust inside me.

I was no horny teenager who needed to whack off every chance he got. I was in a fucking public bathroom, for Christ's sake. Granted, it was in *my* building, but still. I usually had more self-control than this.

Putting my uncharacteristic eagerness out of my mind, I pull my pants up before grabbing some paper towels and disinfectant spray. Once my mess was cleaned up, I washed my hands and splashed some cold water on my face.

"Maybe now I can get some work done," I muttered to my reflection in the mirror before flipping off the light and walking back out into the shop.

I managed to get the rusty bolt off the axle, despite my mind wandering back to Ivy and our time together. This time, though, my body didn't react to the thoughts.

Instead, a dark feeling of foreboding fell over me.

Sleeping with Ivy had been a mistake. She hated me, and if things got weird between us because of what we did, the cost could be too high. If Ivy called this whole façade off, I'd only have two choices—suck it up and date Charity Glasscott, or lose my shop.

Neither of those was an acceptable option.

Ivy and I needed to pretend that whole night never happened. Just put things back the way they were, sell this whole fake engagement until Charity gave up and moved on, then return to our normal lives.

I stayed at the shop until the new rear axle was installed on the Bel Air. By the time I finished, it was late, and I decided to go home and get some sleep. I could talk to Ivy in the morning.

After making sure all the lights were off and the alarm was set, I locked the doors and headed for my car in the lot. A black sedan parked on the street caught my eye, and as soon as I looked in that direction, I saw someone duck out of sight in the driver's seat.

I took a deep breath and let it out on a sigh. Did Charity think I wouldn't recognize her father's car? He's one of my regular customers. While it's less flashy than her bright red convertible, the sedan is still one of the more luxurious models and easily identifiable.

Pretending not to notice her, I added a little pep in my step as I jogged toward my Mustang. I wanted to appear excited. I knew she would follow me, and that meant I couldn't go home. I couldn't pass up the opportunity to reinforce Charity's belief that I was taken. That she couldn't have me, and she should just give it up, already.

So, I started my car and headed out, driving to the only place I could go—Ivy's apartment.

Keeping an eye on my rearview mirror, I saw her following at a distance. I rolled my eyes as I pulled into the parking lot of Ivy's complex, and Charity stopped with a screech of tires, quickly pulling off to the side of the road and killing the headlights.

"You suck at this," I murmured as I climbed from my car.

I slammed the door and locked it, then jogged up to Ivy's door. I could see lights in the window and laughter echoed from inside. She wasn't alone.

I briefly grappled with whether or not to interrupt her and her guests, but one glance over my shoulder showed Charity still parked on the street. I had no choice. I had to knock. I had to go inside.

And I had to stay there until Charity got bored and left.

I raised a fist and rapped my knuckles against the wood. The noise inside cut off instantly, and I heard soft footsteps pad toward the door. After a brief pause, the panel swung open, and I stood face-to-face with my brother's girlfriend.

"Jessa," I said with surprise, "what's up?"

"What's up with you?" she shot back, an edge of venom in her voice.

"Can I come in?" I asked, ignoring her tone. "It's important."

"I don't think so, Nate," she said, and my head flew back with shock.

"Please," I said, leaning closer. "Charity followed me here. I need to come in and see my *fiancée*."

I stressed the title, and Jessa's eyes flicked over my shoulder to surreptitiously search the parking lot behind me. Whether she saw anything or not, her shoulders dropped and she stepped out of the way, motioning me inside.

With a curt nod, I moved past her, then froze. Ivy sat on the couch, a drink in her hand as she stared at me with an unreadable expression. Karly and Felicia were rising from their chairs, mumbling excuses and reaching for their purses.

"You guys don't have to leave," Ivy said, never taking her eyes off me. "Nate won't be here long."

"He obviously needs to talk to you about something," Felicia said, arching a brow at me.

"Yes," I replied simply.

"We'll call you tomorrow," Karly offered as Felicia dragged her toward the door.

"Do you need me to stay?" Jessa asked, her tone filled with some meaning I didn't understand.

"No. I'm good," Ivy said, waving her off. As Jessa grabbed her purse and a pair of shoes by the door, Ivy added, "Thanks, Jessa."

Jessa gave her a firm nod, then narrowed her eyes at me threateningly before walking out the door and pulling it closed behind her.

"What was that all about?" I asked, my gaze searching her face.

"What do you want, Nate?" she asked instead of answering.

She sounded tired. Tired of this whole farce. Tired of me.

And I didn't like it.

"Charity was spying on me when I left the shop tonight. She followed me here and is parked outside. I came in to reinforce our fake engagement. I hope that's okay."

Ivy closed her eyes briefly before refocusing her gaze on me. When she spoke, her voice held a fake cheerfulness I didn't like. Not one bit.

"Sure. Stay as long as you need to."

"What's wrong?" I asked.

"Nothing, Nate," she answered, her voice once again low and weary-sounding.

I didn't like the way she kept saying my name. When women used a man's name like that, it usually meant they were fed up with their shit. Only, I didn't know what I'd done to deserve it.

We'd both agreed to sleep together, and I was pretty

sure she enjoyed it, if the number of orgasms I gave her were any indication. But now, she was back to treating me the way she had before we struck our deal.

And while it shouldn't have been a problem—our bargain didn't mandate that we *like* each other—her attitude struck a nerve in me.

"Obviously, something is wrong," I said, my voice firm. "Only, I didn't do anything, so I don't know why you're acting like this."

"You're right," she said, her nostrils flaring a little. "You didn't *do* anything. Stay as long as you want. I'm going to bed."

With that, she got up and left the room. The click of her bedroom door closing echoed in my head like a death knell, and I stood there staring at it for several seconds without moving.

What the fuck?

Half of me wanted to barge in there and demand she tell me what the hell was going on, but the other half told me to settle down and accept that this distance between us was for the best. It would make things so much easier when we ended the deception. No tangled feelings. No hurt egos.

I knew I should leave her be. Sit down on the couch and wait Charity out. Then leave.

Instead, I stomped to her bedroom door and threw it open without even knocking, only mildly surprised she hadn't locked it. It hit the wall with a bang, startling a yelp out of Ivy. She froze, one knee on the bed as if she'd been in the process of climbing in.

She wore a pair of thin, short shorts and a tight tank top. My eyes zeroed in on her breasts, hard nipples straining against the material. Ivy straightened quickly, standing with a stiff spine as she crossed her arms over her chest to obstruct my view.

"What do you think you're doing?" she demanded.

"Sorry," I muttered, my gaze meeting hers. "I…"

She frowned at me as she waited for me to finish my apology. My mouth opened and closed a few times before I pinched my lips together and shook my head.

"No. You know what? I'm not sorry." I took a couple of steps toward her, but when she flinched back, I stopped. "We had what I thought was an amazing day together, but if you were left dissatisfied, I'd be more than happy to try again."

My tongue darted out to moisten my lips, and her eyes widened at the sight of it. Her chest was heaving, and her harsh breaths echoed in the air between us. I didn't know why I said what I did. Maybe it was my ego, begging for reassurance. Maybe it was a challenge, to make her talk to me. But seeing her reaction, there was no way I was taking it back.

I took another step forward, and other than a slight shudder, she didn't move.

I ignored the tiny voice in my head telling me this was a bad idea. That sex with Ivy was supposed to be a one-time thing.

All that mattered was getting my hands on her. Touching her. Tasting her. Making her scream my name.

And there was no way I was talking myself out of doing all that, and more.

22

Ivy

$\mathscr{I}$ came in here to get away from Nate before I did something I'd regret. Something I knew was wrong. A bad idea that could lead to unwanted ramifications.

Like wrap myself around him and beg him to stick his dick in me again.

Yet, here he was barging into my bedroom, staring at my boobs like they were chocolate cake and he was starving, and telling me he wanted to...what? Prove he could leave me satisfied?

Why did he have to look so good? He stepped closer, and I could smell him. Oil and metal with a hint of rust, and for some strange reason, the scent made my insides clench. I held up a hand, ordering him to stop.

"What are you doing?" I asked, silently cursing the break in my voice.

"I think you know, Ivy."

I must have blacked out for a moment, because the

next thing I knew, my legs were wrapped around his waist, my hands were in his hair, and my tongue was in his mouth. Nate's hands were groping my ass, and his erection rubbed deliciously against my lady bits.

I thought about putting an end to it. Stopping this madness and putting some space between us. I really did consider it. For about two seconds.

But the truth was, I wanted him. Again.

So, instead of breaking off our kiss and saying the words that would end the pleasure building inside me, I rolled my hips to create more friction between us. Nate growled into my mouth and spun around before lowering me to the bed, his weight pressing down on me in all the best ways.

His mouth moved to my neck, sucking and licking until I was writhing beneath him. His hand tugged up the hem of my tank top, and he lifted his weight from me to whip it over my head. He stared for a moment, his expression filled with awe, before mumbling something that sounded like "beautiful."

Then his mouth was on me, sucking a nipple between his lips as he hummed with pleasure. Then he paid the same homage to the other, and my core clenched with need.

"Nate, please," I groaned.

"Tell me what you want, Ivy," he said as his mouth released my nipple and trailed kisses over my stomach.

"I want you to fuck me."

The words popped out of my mouth before I could stop them. My face heated as I squeezed my eyes shut. I'd never been much of a dirty talker, but my embarrassment faded at Nate's heady groan. He pushed himself up to his knees and yanked off my shorts and underwear with impatient hands.

Spreading my knees, he dipped his head and swirled his tongue around my clit. My body jerked at the burst of pleasure, and Nate wrapped his arms around my thighs to hold me still. When his tongue pushed inside me, I chanted his name.

But it wasn't enough. I needed more.

"Please. Nate," I mumbled. "I need you."

He stilled, his grip tightening on my thighs for a moment so brief, I was sure I imagined it. His tongue gave one last stroke up from slit to clit before he released me and climbed from the bed. I opened my mouth to object, but I quickly snapped it shut as I realized he was undressing.

He ripped his shirt off so fast, I was sure he'd popped some buttons. The muscles in his chest and shoulders flexed as he unbuckled his belt, and I propped myself up on my elbows to get a better look as he dropped his pants and stepped out of them.

He started to smile, but it quickly turned into a frown. "Shit," he cursed, then looked at me with pleading eyes. "Please tell me you have condoms."

"What?" I asked, my mind not comprehending the change in his mood as I stared at his cock.

"Condoms, Ivy. I didn't think... I don't have any with me."

"No," I said, my mind finally breaking free from the dick-hypnosis. "I don't have any either."

He sighed, but his expression quickly turned to one of determination. He climbed back onto the bed and stretched out beside me.

"I guess we'll just have to get creative. There are other ways we can make each other come."

He kissed me as his fingers clasped mine and moved them to his hard cock. Guiding them around its girth, he pumped my hand up and down a couple of times before releasing it. His hand landed on my thigh, gliding over my skin until his fingertips hit that sensitive bundle of nerves that ached for his touch.

When he slid a finger inside me and curled it upward, my hips bucked. It felt amazing, and I knew I was close to coming, but my brain rebelled. I wanted more. I needed it.

I turned my head, meeting his eyes. His fingers stilled as he searched my gaze, his forehead wrinkling with worry.

"You okay?" he breathed, then grunted as my fingers tightened on his cock.

"I want this," I whispered, stroking it with meaning. "I'm on the pill, and I'm clean. The hospital tests me every six months, and...I haven't been with anyone besides you in a long time."

"I just got tested last month. I'm clear, too," he said, then stared at me meaningfully. "I've never had sex without a condom before."

"Me, neither," I said, barely any sound coming out.

A tiny little voice chirped inside me, telling me this was a mistake. Not because of the physical ramifications. Those were minimal.

It was the emotional risk that sent a shiver coursing through me. Doing this would bring us as close as two people could get, and the fact that it was the first time for both of us...

"Are you sure, Ivy?" Nate asked, breaking off my train of thought.

I looked into his blue eyes, so filled with wonder and anticipation, and I knew those same emotions were mirrored in my own expression. I wanted to *feel* him. I wanted him to feel *me*.

"Yes, I'm sure. Make love to me, Nate."

My breath hitched as I realized what I'd just said, but it didn't seem to faze Nate in the least. His head dipped, and he gave me a scorching kiss as his finger began to move again, stroking inside me until I was trembling with need.

He pulled his hand free and moved over me, settling between my thighs as his mouth trailed searing kisses across my jaw and down my throat. I wrapped my legs around his hips, pulling him closer until his cock teased my entrance. I bucked my hips to urge him forward, but he held back.

"Look at me, Ivy," he whispered, and my eyes opened to stare into his.

He had most of his weight braced on his arms, and he stared down at me from beneath a halo of dark hair. His hips pushed forward, his dick sliding into me, and my eyelids drifted closed. Nate pulled out, and my eyes snapped back open.

"Keep your eyes on me," he said. "I want to see you. I want you to see me."

My head nodded quickly, and he smiled. I kept my gaze locked with his as he slid inside me, inch by agonizingly glorious inch. Watching the play of emotions on his face, knowing he could see the same on mine—it was the most vulnerable moment of my life.

And the most erotic.

His growl of pleasure as he sank his full length into me was nearly my undoing. My inner walls clenched, making him groan even louder. I tilted my hips, pushing him deeper and holding him there. Nate licked his lips and opened his mouth as if he meant to say something.

Seeming to think better of it, he dipped his head and kissed me. I drove my hands into his hair, clenching my fists in the soft strands as I kissed him back. Our tongues tangled together before he sucked my bottom lip into his mouth and bit down lightly.

Then he began to move. His hips rotated as he pulled

out at a snail's pace, then slid back in just as slowly. He buried his face in my neck, sweat rolling off of him as he moved with controlled precision.

It felt so good. *He* felt so good.

Barely blinking, I kept my gaze locked on his as he picked up speed, doing that little hip-roll thing he knew I liked. Soon, my hips were lifting to meet him thrust-for-thrust as I moaned unintelligible words.

My eyes slammed shut, and a shout flew from my mouth, my orgasm hitting fast and hard before I realized it was even coming. Nate grunted as he slammed into me one final time, then stilled, his harsh breaths fanning against my face.

His arms shook for a moment before he collapsed onto me, his cheek resting against my chest as if he were listening to my heartbeat. My fingers itched to stroke his hair, but I kept my hands firmly at my sides.

As the post-orgasm glow faded, tension spiraled through me, tightening each of my muscles as one thought cycled on repeat through my brain…

What did I just do?

23

Nate

*W*hat did we just do?

I fell back against my couch, a beer in my hand, as memories from Ivy's bed assailed me. She'd clammed up shortly after we finished, the tension between us becoming decidedly *un*sexual. After peeking out to make sure Charity had given up and left, I'd given Ivy a stilted goodbye and practically ran to my car.

Make love to me, Nate.

Her tone, her word choice, the pleading in her voice that told me she truly meant it—that simple phrase had broken something inside me. My control had splintered and cracked, and there had been nothing on the planet that could've stopped me from giving her what she wanted.

What we *both* wanted.

The sex had been amazing, even more so given the skin-to-skin contact, but that wasn't the problem. The problem was my fucking *emotions*. My deal with Ivy was temporary and would be over soon. And while neither of us could deny we had a shitload of sexual chemistry, I was pretty certain this possessive feeling growing inside me was all one-sided.

I needed to shut that shit down before I went right over the edge and did something stupid...like asking Ivy to be mine. For real, this time.

And I couldn't allow myself to go down that road. Not again.

I took a swig of beer, memories of when we first met flashing through my mind. I'd actually begun to fall for her, my stupid early-twenty-something-year-old brain convincing me I had a shot when so many factors stood between us.

She was my brother's best friend.

She was a couple of years older than me, and while the gap was inconsequential to me, to Ivy, it might as well have been a decade or more. I was immature. I knew it, and I'd owned it.

She was fresh out of college, starting her career as a nurse, and I was some kid who'd barely graduated high school with grease stains on my hands.

But despite the obstacles, I'd caught her looking at me more than once, a hunger in her eyes that couldn't be denied. And every single fucking time I'd caught that look, my dick had popped up, begging for attention. I'd had to excuse myself more than once to "use the restroom" when I needed to get myself under control.

I set my beer on the coffee table and leaned my head back, allowing the images of a younger Ivy flood my brain. It was far safer than thinking of more recent times...times like tonight, my bare cock buried deep inside her as she came.

Instead, I thought about the day I'd decided to tell her how I felt. I was going to shoot my shot and ask her out, obstacles be damned. I had the whole thing planned out.

We went to Hero's for a family dinner with Rafe and Lola, and the tension between Ivy and me had been so thick, there was no denying the electricity between us. Her secret smile and pink blush had boosted my confidence, and I'd just known it...great things were going to happen between us. Long-term things.

And while the thought of settling down had scared me —I'd always been a bit of a player—I'd known Ivy was worth it. That she, above all others, was the one girl whose heart was worth it. And also, I couldn't wait to get my hands on her.

Imagining how her skin felt had given me a rise, so I excused myself to "use the restroom." I swung around the corner without paying attention to where I was going, and a pair of hands grabbed me and yanked me into the ladies'. Before I could stop her, our waitress had me up against the wall, her tongue in my mouth as her hand rubbed my cock through my jeans.

And, of course, she thought that hard-on was for *her*.

I gently pushed her away, trying to spare her feelings, and extricated myself from her octopus arms before rushing from the bathroom. I laughed, remembering how I'd smirked at the fact that at least my erection had waned.

But when I got back to the table, Ivy was gone. Rafe said something about her not feeling well, and I couldn't push for details without making him suspicious of my motives. I was disappointed, but not deterred.

My big confession would still happen, it would just have to be another night.

I didn't see Ivy for a while, and she refused to respond to my texts or answer my calls. The next time I did see her, she was...different. Guarded. Belligerent. Hostile.

That's when I knew I'd never get what I wanted. She'd figured out that I was going to make a move and had decided to cut me off at the pass. She didn't want me. All the little signs I'd thought I'd seen weren't real. It wasn't going to happen.

I'd assumed that once I made it clear I'd gotten her point, she'd chill with the aggression, but it had never happened. And eventually, I began to return the hostility, and we got stuck in this never-ending loop of being assholes to each other.

Until now. Until the one time I really needed her help, and she agreed with barely a thought. Sure, I was restoring the Bel Air, but Ivy knew me well enough to know that was no hardship. It was like she was doing me *two* favors—pretending to be my fiancée *and* letting me work on one of my bucket list cars.

I leapt to my feet and shook off the train of thought. I could not let myself get wrapped up in the idea that something real could happen between us. Not again. It had nearly broken me the first time.

And I didn't think my heart could take another hit like that.

❧

*P*retending like something wasn't hell, when it was *very obviously* hell, was problematic, at best. It was the weekend, and this was the first time I'd seen Ivy since the night I showed up at her place unannounced.

I'd asked her out on a date—for appearances' sake—and here we were, strolling hand-in-hand across the parking lot at The Bullpen. I thought about taking her to dinner and a movie, but being at the bar was more likely to get us noticed and have word get back to Charity.

Which was the whole point of this fake relationship.

I held the door for Ivy, and she thanked me politely as she walked inside. We found an empty booth, and I slid in beside her. She didn't outwardly react to the fact that I'd chosen to sit next to her rather than on the other side, but I could sense her discomfort. I stretched out a hand to take hers before bringing it to my lips.

"Thanks for coming," I murmured before pressing a light kiss to her knuckles. "Some of Charity's friends hang out here on the weekends, so word is bound to get back to her. I wouldn't be surprised if she showed up within the hour."

"No problem," she muttered, gently extracting her hand from my grip.

"Welcome to The Bullpen. What can I get you?"

Ivy startled at the server's voice, then cleared her throat before ordering a draft beer. I ordered the same, then turned a questioning gaze to Ivy as the server left with a promise to bring the drinks right out.

"You okay?" I asked, my head tilting as I studied her.

"Yeah," she sighed, shaking her head. "I'm just tired, and it's making me edgy."

"Having trouble sleeping?"

"Sort of," she said. "I've put in a lot of hours at the hospital the last few days, and it's been hard to make my mind settle down once I'm home."

I knew the feeling. Every time I closed my eyes, images of our time in Ivy's bed spun through my mind on a loop, making it nearly impossible to sleep. I wondered if it was work, or those same memories keeping her awake at night.

"Listen, Ivy," I said, leaning closer so she could hear my low voice, "about the other night—"

"Nate," she said in a low voice, cutting off my words.

"I think we should talk about it," I argued.

"I think we should forget about it," she shot back.

Forget about it? Impossible.

"We need to remember this is all an act," she went on before I could respond verbally. "We can act cozy in public, but from now on, we need to keep things strictly platonic in private."

"Platonic?"

She nodded, even as she placed a gentle palm on my cheek. "Now, kiss me. We have an audience."

My eyes widened as she leaned in, then my brain caught up, comprehending her words. Someone was watching us, so it was show time.

I met her halfway, brushing my lips against hers in a whisper-light kiss. She started to pull back, but my fingers slipped behind her neck, holding her still as my thumb skimmed over her jaw to her chin. I applied gentle pressure until her mouth opened, then slipped my tongue inside to brush against hers.

A quiet moan vibrated in her chest, belying her earlier words. There was nothing platonic about her reaction. And there was nothing platonic about the blood rushing to my dick, making it unbearably hard.

I pulled back, just far enough to gaze into her eyes, and asked, "Are they still watching?"

Her gaze darted past me for a moment before she looked back at me and nodded. Her lips turned up into a very wide, very fake smile, and she slid close to my side while pulling my arm around her. Her fingers tangled with mine at her shoulder, and her other palm landed on my thigh.

Before I could react, our server came striding over with our beers. After she set them on our table and confirmed we didn't need anything else, I let my eyes trail after her as she walked away. At least, I pretended to be watching her go. I was really scanning the bar for whoever Ivy saw that made her cuddle up to me.

There she was, sitting rigidly at a corner table with two other women. Charity must have been here all along, and I just didn't see her when we walked in. Good thing Ivy had noticed.

"Stop staring at her," Ivy mumbled as her hand left my thigh to cradle her beer. "Pretend like she doesn't matter. Like she's not even here."

I nuzzled Ivy's neck, placing a light kiss beneath her ear before whispering, "You're right. We should keep this strictly business from now on."

I threw the words out there, knowing she *was* right, but hating every single syllable as it passed my lips.

24

Ivy

*Y*ou're *right. Strictly business.*

Nate's words echoed in my head long after he'd spoken them. After the tingling sensation his lips had left on my skin had faded. Long after Charity got up in a huff and stomped to the exit, shooting daggers at me with her eyes before slamming through the door.

As soon as her friends followed her out, Nate had removed his arm from my shoulders and put a foot of space between us, leaving me cold with the loss of his body heat. I took a long gulp of beer and pretended to listen to Nate's rambling words as he told me about his day.

We were still in public, and even with Charity gone, I still needed to act the part. Any gossip about a coldness between me and Nate would get back to her. Especially in a small town like Milestone.

I knew I should've been happy, or at the very least, satisfied with Nate's response to my suggestion. Despite my inner sex goddess that was quickly becoming addicted to

Nate's touch, I *knew* I was right—we were getting too wrapped up in each other, in the sex that was supposed to be a one-time deal to get it out of our systems. I, at least, was heading down a path that led straight to heartbreak, and I needed to change direction.

But "knowing it" and "doing it" were two different things. The words had cut my throat as I'd choked them out, and Nate's agreeable response had stabbed me right in the gut.

What had I expected? That he would fight me on it? Demand that we give this thing a real go? Tell me he couldn't go another day without touching me again?

And what would I have replied if he did say those things? All my old fears still stood. Nate was a player who fucked random girls in public bathrooms. He would never commit to a monogamous relationship.

A tiny voice in my head whispered that I was being judgmental. That I was assuming the worst just to protect myself, and putting up those walls kept me a prisoner just as much as they kept Nate out.

I ignored that voice. I'd gotten the taste of Nate I'd always secretly wanted, and now it was time to shut it down and get back to normal. Once Charity backed off and moved on, he'd go back to his normal life—the life that didn't include me in his bed *or* in his heart. I needed to prepare myself for that now.

"I'm ready to go home," I said, stroking a finger down Nate's arm.

He shivered, then cleared his throat, giving me a nod. Leaving some cash on the table next to our unfinished beers, Nate held out a hand to help me from the booth. I took it, trying my damnedest to ignore the heat that shot from his touch straight to my core.

To make matters worse, he pulled me into his embrace

and pressed his mouth to mine, giving the crowd one last show before leading me toward the exit. As we walked out, anger flooded up inside me, filling every cell in my body.

I was angry at Nate for not being the man I wanted him to be when we first met. Angry because he was *acting* like that man now, when it wasn't real. Angry that my body refused to recognize the difference.

And angry at Charity Glasscott for brewing up the shit storm that brought us to this point in the first place.

As if I'd conjured her, the bitch appeared. She was leaning against the hood of Nate's car, obviously waiting for him. The fact that she'd seen us together inside, yet still thought it appropriate to loiter around the Mustang like some hooker looking for her next john spiked my anger into some next-level shit.

Nate's hand tightened around mine, letting me know he'd spotted Charity, as well. His steps slowed, but my fight or flight instinct was screaming too loud for me to comprehend what he wanted.

Fight. Fight. Fight.

I wasn't a violent person, and I'd never been in an actual fistfight. But Charity's smug face and low-cut blouse that showed off half her bra made something inside me snap, and my pace picked up, my grip on his hand dragging Nate behind me.

This was *her* fault. Her threats to destroy Nate's business had set this whole plan into motion. And this pretend engagement had shown me how amazing a life with Nate could be. A life I could never have.

The pain of losing Nate all over again—even though I knew I'd never really had him to begin with—made all sense of reason fly out of my head. I shook my hand loose from Nate's grip, and he called my name as I began to run.

Charity straightened, and I could see the fear flash

across her face as I drew near. She quickly hid the emotion behind a smirk. Propping a fist on her hip, she cocked her head at me as I skidded to a halt in front of her.

"I'm here to talk to Nate, not y—"

Her words cut off with a yelp as my palm cracked against her cheek. Her face whipped to the side, her hand coming up to cover the spot I'd struck as she stared at me with incredulous eyes.

"He's mine," I growled before I could even think about my words, "and he will *always* be mine. You need to back the fuck off."

I took a menacing step forward, and satisfaction welled up inside me when she stumbled back a few feet.

"Get away from me, you lunatic!" she yelled, looking past me at Nate with pleading eyes.

"Don't look at him," I snapped, and her eyes shot back to me, widening. "Don't talk to him, don't even think about him. And if you so much as *consider* following through with your threats to go to daddy and mess with Nate's loan, I'll have you both investigated for fraud. If he's so quick to fudge numbers to help you get a man, I wonder what the authorities would find during a real investigation."

My eyes narrowed with warning as I spouted that shit —I was pretty sure I'd heard similar dialogue on a police drama I'd watched last month. The threat, coupled with the not-so-thinly-veiled insult about her needing help to get a man had Charity puffing up her chest.

"I should have you arrested for assault," she huffed.

"I didn't assault you," I said, arching a brow.

"You hit me," she whined, then looked to Nate for support.

"I didn't see anything," he said, backing me up like I expected him to.

"Move on, Charity," I gritted out before she could

accuse him of lying. "We're engaged. You can't have him. Find someone who actually *wants* you, and leave us alone."

She shot one last hopeful glance at Nate, but whatever she saw in his expression made her face fall. She whirled around in a cloud of poufy hair and stalked away, sliding into the backseat of a nearby silver SUV before its driver squealed from the lot.

"That was amazing," Nate muttered, his eyes moving from the receding taillights to my face. "You are amazing."

All the angry energy drained out of me, and I suddenly felt like my head weighed eight hundred pounds. I shuffled around the car and climbed into the passenger seat, shutting the door behind me. After a moment's hesitation, Nate slid in behind the wheel, took a deep breath, and then angled his body toward mine.

"Ivy—"

"Just take me home, Nate," I said, cutting off whatever he'd been about to say.

He stared at me for several seconds, motionless, before heaving a sigh and straightening in his seat. The engine roared as we pulled out of the lot, and I focused on the sound to keep myself from thinking about everything that had happened tonight.

To keep myself from thinking about Nate, and what the end of Charity's scheme would mean for us.

∼

I spent an hour on the couch, the television playing some show I wasn't interested in, as I stewed over everything that had happened over the last several days.

First, I'd had sex with Nate. Multiple times. Then, I did it again, only with no protection. The nurse in me cringed despite the fact that I knew we were disease-free and ninety-seven percent safe from a surprise pregnancy.

And tonight...tonight, I told Nate I wanted to keep things platonic between us. And he'd agreed.

Despite not wanting to admit it to myself, I knew, deep down, that was the crux of my anger. I didn't know what I expected. For him to argue? To fight for me? To at least admit our physical connection was amazing, and he wanted to keep it going?

But he didn't do any of those things. He'd simply agreed, and left it at that.

And now I was feeling a little guilty for taking that anger out on Charity. Not that I didn't think she deserved it, but it just wasn't in my nature to strike out at people like that.

I picked up my phone and pulled up the text thread I had going between me, Jessa, Karly, and Felicia.

Me: *Hey, you guys up?*

Karly: *If this is a booty call, I'll consider it.*

A chuckle burst from me, but before I could reply, another text popped up.

Felicia: *Jesus, K, get a vibrator. What's up, Ivy?*

Me: *I just had a helluva night and needed to talk to someone.*

Jessa: *I heard you were at the bar with Nate. Did something happen?*

Of course, she knew I was at The Bullpen. It was her dad's place, and she was running it for him. She probably called to check in, and one of her employees told her we were there.

Me: *I told Nate I wanted to keep thing platonic from now on, and he agreed.*

Felicia: *He did not.*

Karly: *He didn't even argue? A little?*

Jessa: *Well, if he thinks that's what you really want...*

Felicia: *Don't stick up for him, Jessa! He's an idiot.*

Me: *It is what I really want. It's just…*

Jessa: *You wanted him to argue. To fight.*

Me: *Yeah. Pathetic, right?*

Karly: *Not pathetic.*

Felicia: *You're only human.*

Jessa: *What do you really want, Ivy?*

Me: *I don't know.*

Karly: *I do. You want that Magic Dick.*

Karly: *Sorry. I couldn't resist. I'll behave. I promise.*

Me: *LOL, you're not wrong.*

But I wasn't laughing, not really. Tears stung my eyes as I searched for the words to explain to make them understand.

Me: *I think my feelings got a little more tangled up than they should have.*

Felicia: *Obviously.*

Karly: *Then why don't you just tell him the truth?*

Me: *I can't. He doesn't want more than sex, and opening myself up like that would only lead to more heartbreak.*

Jessa: *I think you're wrong, Ivy.*

Me: *I know I'm not.*

Feeling a strong need to change the subject, my fingers flew over the screen to get in another text before anyone could respond to my last statement.

Me: *J, did your informant tell you Charity was at the bar, too?*

Jessa: *What? No.*

Karly: *Oh, shit. What happened?*

Me: *We put on a good show of being in love. Kissing and stuff. She left in a huff, and I told Nate I was ready to call it a night. When we got outside, she was waiting by his car.*

Felicia: *No, that bitch was NOT.*

Me: *Yep. Said she wanted to talk to Nate.*

Karly: *What did you do?*

Me: *I hit her.*

Felicia: *Holy shit.*

Karly: *Yaaasssssssss.*

A series of emojis popped up on the screen from Karly and Felicia, ranging from laughing faces to shocked faces, from explosions to hammers. Finally, Jessa cut in with a text of her own.

Jessa: *Are you okay?*

Me: *I'm fine. I told her Nate was mine, and she needed to back off or I'd file charges against her and her father that would launch an investigation into his questionable business practices.*

Felicia: *Brilliant.*

Karly: *You go girl!*

Jessa: *Are you really okay, Ivy? Do you need us to come over?*

Me: *I'm good, really. I'm gonna head to bed. Thanks for listening.*

Felicia: *Any time.*

Karly: *Sure thing. We'll always have your back. Just call me next time you're gonna jump her. I want in on that action.*

Felicia: *OMG, Karly.*

Jessa: *Call me if you want to talk.*

I really did have the best friends. Between those three and Rafe, what more could a girl ask for? Nate's face popped into my mind, and I groaned, pushing it away with thoughts of a hot shower and my cozy bed.

Thoughts of my bed conjured memories of what I'd done there with Nate, and I groaned again.

Tonight, I'm sleeping on the couch.

25

Nate

Platonic.

He's mine.

Platonic.

He's mine.

Ivy's voice rang in my ears all night, making sleep nearly impossible. The way she shut things down between us and my grudging agreement to it filled me with anger and regret. Her possessive claiming of me in front of Charity made me feel...good.

Too good.

The constant back and forth of my emotions was exhausting, so when Rafe knocked on my door the next morning, he was met with a snarl as a greeting before I spun and stalked back to the couch.

"Is that any way to greet your brother?" he asked, closing the front door behind him.

"Sorry," I sighed. "Didn't get much sleep last night."

"Did it have anything to do with why Ivy was texting Jessa at an ungodly hour?"

"She did? What did she say?"

Rafe shook his head. "I don't know, man. It's none of my business. Yours, either. If Ivy wants to tell me, she'll tell me."

"Except she won't, because your my brother," I added, slumping further into the couch. "I'm sorry, Rafe. This has to be weird for you."

"Ivy is my best friend," he said, his words slow and tactful, "but you're my brother, Nate. If you need someone to talk to, I'm here for you. Whatever you say stays between us."

"Thanks, brother," I said. "I appreciate that."

He gave me one firm nod, then raised a hand to rub the back of his neck. It was one of his tells. He wanted to talk to me about something, and it was making him nervous.

"Spit it out," I said, arching a brow at him.

"What?" he asked.

I just stared at him, knowing if I waited him out, he'd tell me what was on his mind. I didn't have to wait long.

"I'm going to propose to Jessa," he said in a rush.

He reached into his pocket, then held the hand out to me. In his palm rested a diamond ring. My eyes widened with shock. Not because Rafe was going to propose—I'd been expecting that for a while, despite the fact that they'd only been together for a few months—but because the ring was familiar.

It was our mother's.

"Where did you get that?" I asked, pushing myself off the couch and plucking it from his hand to study it closer.

I hadn't seen it in almost a decade...not since before

Mamá died. But I knew I wasn't mistaken. I could clearly remember seeing it on her finger.

"Mamá gave it to me…that day, in the car. She told me to give it to my girl, and I've had it ever since. I considered giving it to Papa, but you know how he was. He would've destroyed it. Or sold it for booze money."

Our mother had been killed in a car accident when I was sixteen. Rafe, who was eighteen at the time, had been in the car with her. They'd been headed to the mall to buy a Christmas gift for his girlfriend when the accident happened, and I knew he'd carried a massive amount of guilt about it for a long time.

It was what kept him focused on me and Lola for far too long. It was what drove him to become an emergency room doctor, so he could save people who'd been injured in accidents like the one that took Mamá from us.

He'd spent his entire adult life neglecting himself in order to take care of others—until Jessa.

"I had no idea you had this. I thought she'd been buried with it," I murmured, my eyes still glued to the sparkling ring.

"I want to give it to Jessa," he said, his voice soft and low, "but I wanted to clear it with you and Lola first. Just because Mamá gave me the ring doesn't mean…"

His voice trailed off, and I lifted my gaze to meet his. He looked nervous. And sad.

I took one last look at the ring, ignoring the vision of Ivy that popped into my head for a millisecond, then handed it back to him.

"Of course, you should give it to her. Mamá would've loved her. Papa, too."

Our father had become a nonfunctioning alcoholic after our mother had died. He couldn't handle her absence, and had lost himself at the bottom of a bottle of whiskey…hundreds of bottles. He eventually spiraled so far that he lost the will to live and committed suicide after striking our sister.

But before that, when things were good, he was a good father. He loved Mamá, and he loved us, and were they both alive today, they would've adored Jessa Maddox. Would've welcomed her into the family with zero qualms.

And Mamá would've given Rafe this ring to give to her. No doubt about it.

"You don't think it's selfish of me? You and Lola have just as much right to this as me."

"Rafael," I said, using his full name to emphasize my sincerity, "she gave it to you in her final moments. She wanted you to have it." I gave him a small smirk, adding, "Besides, you and I both know I'm probably never getting married, and Lola's future husband will want to buy her a ring. It's all good."

"I don't believe the part about you never getting married, but you're probably right about Lola. Of course, if and when she ever starts dating, the poor guy is going to have a hell of a time passing muster with the two of us."

I laughed, having a hard time imagining our sister dating, much less in a serious relationship. She'd always been so focused on her future, there just wasn't any time for boys. She was set to graduate college a year early, after which she'd come work at the shop for me—I'd promised her an internship to get some work experience to go with her business degree.

I'd feel sorry for whatever guy she'd pick when she finally decided to date. Rafe was right. With Rafe's papa bear mentality and my personal experience as a bit of a womanizer in my younger years, poor guy didn't stand a chance. We'd eat him for breakfast.

"Congratulations," I said, refocusing on the present. "I mean, you're pretty sure she'll say yes, right?"

His fist flew forward and popped me in the arm, and I fell back a step, laughing. He shook his head at me with a smile, but I could see a spark of worry in his eyes. It was no secret that before Rafe, Jessa had been a commitment-phobe, scared to trust anyone with her heart.

But Rafe had broken down those walls as surely as he'd overcome his own obstacles, and they were deliriously happy living together in our childhood home. As far as I could tell, Rafe had nothing to worry about, and I told him as much.

"I know you're right," he said, "but it's still scary. Just wait until it's your turn."

Ivy's beautiful face flashed through my mind again, but I shook it off. The thought was ridiculous. She barely tolerated me, and I couldn't see that changing any time soon... despite our undeniable physical connection.

"So, asking you about the ring isn't the only reason I came over," he said, rubbing his palm across the back of his neck again. "I wanted to ask you—if Jessa says yes, of course—if you'd be my best man."

I smiled and stepped forward to clap him on the shoulder before pulling him into a hug.

"Of course, I will, man. I'd be honored," I said.

"Thanks," he said, a smile stretching his own lips before it fell. "Now that we have that settled, do you want to talk about Ivy?"

I motioned for him to take a seat on the couch as I headed toward the kitchen. "You want anything to drink?"

"I'll take some water," he called out.

I brought two water bottles back and slumped onto the couch next to him before handing him one of them. I screwed the top off mine and took a long swig from it before dropping my head to the back of the couch.

"We had sex," I admitted, knowing what he'd said before was absolute truth—whatever I told him would remain between us. Well, between us and *Jessa*, maybe.

I saw Rafe's head rear back in my peripheral vision, which surprised me, a little. I knew for a fact that Ivy had told the girls—including Jessa—about our first night together. That much was obvious when I'd shown up at her apartment the other night while they were all there. I was a little shocked Jessa hadn't told Rafe. Must've been some girl-code thing.

"I know this puts you in a weird spot," I continued, "with Ivy being your best friend and me being your brother, so I'll spare you the finer details. Just know that it happened more than once."

"Was Ivy...sober?" Rafe asked, his word slow and measured.

"Rafe!" I snapped, my heated gaze frying him on the spot. "What the fuck?"

"Sorry," he said, holding up his palms in surrender. "It's just...Ivy kind of hates you, so I just can't imagine..."

His words trailed off as a shiver wracked his body. I shook my head at him with a sigh.

"She was sober, and she wanted it just as much as I did. *Both* times."

"Okay," he said slowly.

"But now, she wants to keep things strictly platonic between us. We'll keep up the act in public, but in private, we're back to barely tolerating each other."

"And that's what has you in such a foul mood?" he asked. "I thought those were the terms of your deal to begin with."

He wasn't wrong. But one taste of Ivy had shot that

deal to hell as far as I was concerned. Her putting on the brakes was confusing and frustrating.

"What do you want, Nate?" he asked, pulling me from my thoughts.

"I don't know," I said, leaning back against the couch and closing my eyes. "I wish I did."

"Well, here's my advice—figure it out, and when you do, tell Ivy. Life's too short to waste time on fears and doubts."

He stood, looking down at me. His brown eyes bore into mine for a long moment, then he nodded.

"I'll call you when I decide how I'm going to ask Jessa. See you later."

"Bye," I called out as he walked out the door and swung it closed behind him.

I sat there for a long while, sipping water and thinking about what Rafe said. He was right about one thing. I needed to decide what I wanted.

I knew I wanted more sex with Ivy. That was a given.

I liked hanging out with her, even when we weren't naked. She was fun when she wasn't trying to strike me dead with that wicked tongue of hers. And now that I thought of it, I even liked her taunts and insults.

But I wasn't so sure telling Ivy how I felt was the right thing to do. She might've been attracted to me physically, but there was no doubt she'd spent the last few years hating my guts.

And I didn't know if getting past that hate was even a possibility.

26

Ivy

"*Y*ou've got this, girl."

I felt silly, giving myself a pep talk in the bathroom mirror, but I desperately needed one. And there was no one else here to give it to me. I rolled on a coat of lip balm and flicked off the light before heading out to the living room to wait.

Nate was picking me up for a public appearance—a movie date—and I was irrationally nervous. It was the first time I'd see him since the night I hit Charity in The Bullpen's parking lot...the same night I told Nate we should keep our private time platonic.

And he'd agreed...with zero argument.

He'd texted me yesterday, asking if I was available tonight, and while I'd been tempted to lie, I'd ultimately decided to go out with him. The more we were seen, the more people would talk, and the quicker Charity fucking Glasscott would get the picture and leave Nate alone. This farce would be over, and my life could go back to normal.

The thought of going back to life without Nate made my stomach pitch uncomfortably, but I ignored the sensation. I did *not* want to think about what it meant. I refused to be upset by the loss of fake kisses, forced embraces, and the constant temptation of touching Nate's skin—

The sound of knuckles rapping against wood cut off my errant thoughts. *Thank God.* I shook off the negativity as I strode toward the door, swinging it open with a counterfeit smile.

"Hey," Nate said after a second's pause, his eyes roaming down my body before snapping back up to meet my gaze. "You ready?"

"Yeah," I breathed, grabbing my small purse from the table and stepping out of the apartment.

I turned my back to Nate, taking an inordinate amount of time to close and lock my door so I could get my emotions under control. Seeing him, looking like a tasty snack in loose jeans, and a black t-shirt under an unbuttoned flannel shirt, made me want to do things I'd sworn to never do again.

Things he'd quickly agreed we shouldn't do again.

"Need any help?" he asked when I didn't move for several moments.

"No, I'm good," I said, spinning around to give him that fake smile again.

He stepped forward, right up into my personal space, and I shuffled backward until my shoulders hit the door. Nate kept coming, leaning into me as his hands landed on my hips. My heart tried to pound its way out of my chest as his lips brushed softly against mine.

"In case someone is watching," he whispered, then kissed me again.

His tongue brushed against the seam of my lips, which fell open without my permission. Nate's weight pressed harder against me as he kissed me, the heat between us building up to a near-unbearable degree.

The tiny moan that purred in my throat gave Nate some kind of signal, because he groaned and moved his mouth to my neck, sucking greedily. My insides clenched, moisture soaking my panties as one of his hands slid upward and his thumb brushed over the side of my boob. When it circled over my hard nipple, I gasped and pushed against his chest.

He stumbled back a step, and the loss of his body heat left me feeling cold. We were both breathing hard, and I leaned against the door heavily. There was no way my weak knees would hold me upright without assistance.

Nate lifted a hand to the back of his neck, scrubbing it the way his brother Rafe did when he was nervous or embarrassed. He shook his head before meeting my gaze.

"Sorry. I guess I got a little carried away."

Words escaped me, so I just nodded. His chest heaved with a deep sigh, and he held out a hand toward me. I slipped my fingers between his, lacing them together loosely as I mentally berated myself for losing control of my desire. Again.

Platonic. Business agreement. Less than friends. No benefits.

The words scrolled through my mind over and over as we made our way across the parking lot to his Mustang. He opened the door for me, gently assisting me inside before swinging it closed. Then he jogged around the hood and hopped in behind the wheel.

"Are you hungry?" he asked. "We have some time before the movie starts. You can pick the place."

As he inserted the key and cranked the engine, I grappled with the idea of eating. My stomach was a mass of nerves, the constant fight to hold onto my dislike of Nate making me nauseous. I sucked in a small breath as a thought occurred, then steeled my spine.

"Let's go to Hero's," I suggested, ignoring the aversion that welled up inside me at the thought of going there with Nate again.

He nodded in agreement and pulled out of the lot. I fiddled with the radio, looking for some decent music to keep myself busy. The sour taste in my mouth was exactly what I needed. Going to the place where all my hopes for something to happen between Nate and me had been shattered was...perfect.

The reminder of why I'd started hating him in the first place was just what I needed.

Nate was a player. A whore. And thinking about his *magic dick* pleasuring that waitress in the restaurant's bathroom was the cure for my ever-softening heart and traitorous lady bits. And it would stop me from thinking about what that magic dick did for me.

"I love this place," Nate said as he pulled into a spot near the front door. "I'm glad you like it, too."

I nearly choked on my own spit as he exited the car with those words. He wasn't totally wrong—the food was excellent—but until our first date, I hadn't been here in years. I hated this place and the memories of a dream life I'd wanted and could never have, thanks to Nate and his exhibitionistic ways.

And why would he care if I liked it or not? This thing between us was almost over. If Charity hadn't given up already, she would soon. Then we'd just have to play it out a little longer to make sure she moved on to her next conquest.

This whole thing would be for nothing if we "broke up" too soon and she sunk her claws right back into him. We needed to make sure Nate was no longer on her radar, at all. There was no guarantee that my threats of having her father investigated would do any good. Or that, if I followed through with them, the police would find anything of interest.

My door swung open, and Nate's honey-brown hand reached inside to offer assistance. I took it, ignoring the sparks his strong grip sent through my entire body. Once I was on my feet, Nate tucked my hand into the crook of his elbow and closed the car door behind me. His lips whispered across my cheek in a soft kiss before he pulled me toward the pizza parlor's front door.

We found an empty booth, and just like before, Nate slid in next to me. He pushed the menu toward me, and I picked it up and glanced it over before setting it back down.

"What are you getting?" I asked.

I didn't look at him. I knew I should, but after that kiss at my apartment and his gentle handling of me since, I didn't know if I would be able to keep my feelings out of my expression. My resolve to keep Nate at an arm's length was evaporating. Even being at Hero's didn't lessen the tense need building inside me.

"I'm thinking a calzone tonight," he said. "They're really good here. I get mine with pepperoni, bacon, mushrooms, and jalapenos."

"That does sound good," I said.

"We can share it, if you want," he offered. Then he quickly added, "Or you can order your own. They're pretty big."

Sharing an entrée seemed…intimate, but I found myself agreeing to it. Images of Nate feeding me from his fork flashed through my mind, and my heart flip-flopped in my chest. I silently chastised myself, gritting my teeth as I demanded that my body get it together.

"Oh, hey there, Nate."

I looked up to find the owner of that husky voice, and my vision swam for several seconds. I knew my breathing had turned harsh, but there was nothing I could do about it. I felt like I was on the verge of hyperventilating.

It was *her*. The waitress from the bathroom. The one who'd helped Nate destroy any fantasies I'd had about a future with him.

How is she even still working here? It's been years.

"Anna. Nice to see you," Nate said, his hand slipping over the table to cover mine.

I would've pulled away from his touch, but I was frozen. My eyes searched her face, looking for some hint of the carnal knowledge I knew she held of Nate and his body, but I only saw longing. And disappointment as her eyes travelled from his face to the hand that was holding mine.

"Anna, this is my fiancée, Ivy. Ivy, this is Anna. Her father owns this place."

She was the owner's daughter? No wonder Nate came here all the time. She was probably here a lot, and he could have dirty bathroom sex whenever he wanted.

I tried to pull my hand away, but Nate's fingers tightened. He lifted it toward him and pressed his lips against my palm, his tongue darting out to tease the sensitive flesh before pulling it down into his lap. Under the table. Where *Anna* couldn't see.

It was a message, and she obviously got it, if her frown was any indication.

"We'll have the calzone with pepperoni, mushrooms, bacon, and jalapenos, please," he said before adding, "to share." Then he looked at me. "Do you want anything else?"

"Just iced water," I croaked past the lump in my throat.

He looked back up at Anna. "Make that two. Thanks."

He turned his attention back to me, his fingers brushing over my knuckles under the table as his eyes stared into mine with loving intensity. I met his hot gaze, my heart thumping in my chest as he flipped my hand over and rubbed circles on my palm with his thumb.

I didn't know why he was doing that. It certainly wasn't for Anna's benefit. Or anyone else's. No one could see our hands, making it feel entirely too intimate.

The waitress stood frozen, watching us like she'd forgotten where she was and what she was supposed to be doing. Irritation spiked inside me at her incredulous expression. She looked like she couldn't believe Nate was ignoring her, despite his introducing me as his future wife.

So I did what any civilized woman would do.

I darted my tongue out to moisten my lips before biting down on the bottom one and gave Nate my best "come hither" look. He didn't hesitate. He lunged forward, sucking that lip in between his own teeth before soothing it with his tongue.

On some subconscious level, I was aware of Anna's huff and hasty departure, but Nate's hot mouth felt too good. His breath mingled with mine, and a quiet growl vibrated in his chest.

His hands slid into my hair, gripping it tightly and using it to tilt my head to a better angle. As his tongue slipped in to caress mine, my hand that still lay limply in his lap flipped over to grip his thigh with tight fingers.

Nate groaned, and his left hand slipped from my hair to reach down and curl around my wrist. Applying the slightest of pressure, he guided my hand where he wanted it, right over the bulge straining against his jeans. Then his fingers curled over mine until I was cupping him. He broke off our kiss, trailing his lips along my jaw until they brushed against my ear.

"I want you, Ivy," he whispered between harsh breaths. "Do you want to get out of here?"

Reality came rushing back in, and I snatched my hand away from his erection. I glanced around the restaurant and, after confirming none of the other customers were watching the show we'd been putting on, I put some space between us. My face was hot. My chest burned with fire. And my lady bits were screaming with disappointment.

"I'm sorry," Nate said, taking a deep breath and letting it out slowly.

"You are?" I asked, tensing at the streak of disappointment flaring through me.

"No," he said, one corner of his gorgeous mouth tugging upward. "It just felt like the thing to say." He leaned toward me, bringing his lips so close, they brushed against mine when he spoke again. "I never regret kissing you."

Then our lips met, a short, chaste kiss that left me wanting more. This was stupid. I was a grown-ass woman, and there was no reason to deny myself the pleasure I knew Nate could give me.

My heart squeaked in fear, knowing that it could end up shattered into a million pieces, but I brushed that fear aside. I'd worry about that later.

Right now, other parts of my body demanded attention. And I was tired of fighting off the need.

"Take me home, Nate," I said, my voice raspy.

His face fell, disappointment written across each of his features as he backed off, putting at least a foot between us. He obviously thought I'd meant to end this date with my words, but that was the furthest thing from my mind. I followed him, sliding closer as my hand moved back to the bulge in his jeans.

"Take me to *your* home," I clarified, tightening my grip on him.

He grunted and gave me a hard kiss before sliding out of the booth completely. He pulled out his wallet and dropped enough cash on the table to cover the food we'd ordered, then held out a hand to me.

I stared at it for moment as some mix of fear and excitement set my blood on fire. Nate wanted me. Not Anna or any other woman he may have previously hooked up with. He wanted me, and I wanted him.

I couldn't deny either of us the pleasure I knew would come. I slipped my hand into his and gave him a heated look. He pulled me to my feet and out the door before I had a chance to change my mind.

Not that I would.

Tonight, I was living for the present. I'd worry about the future later.

27

Nate

I needed to touch Ivy. To keep her so hot and bothered that she wouldn't even consider changing her mind about letting me take her home. But my fucking car had a manual transmission, and I needed both hands to drive.

I couldn't believe this was happening. As much as I longed to bury myself inside Ivy again, I'd been sure she didn't feel the same need. She was the one who put an end to our physical relationship.

And I hadn't meant for things to get carried away the way they had at Hero's. Anna was looking at me with too much lust, just the way she always did, and I thought my "engagement" to Ivy was the perfect way to put an end to her advances. I'd turned that woman down more times than I could count, yet she came onto me every time she laid eyes on me. Fighting her off was becoming exhausting.

When Ivy had played along, looking at me with those blue eyes shining with desire, I'd lost my senses. There was nothing fake about that kiss or my body's reaction to it. I could tell she'd been caught in the web, too, and I'd uttered those words before I could think better of it.

I was so sure she'd been denying me when she told me to take her home, and I'd silently cursed myself for being so stupid and pushy.

But here we were, speeding along the quiet roads of Milestone, my dick throbbing with need as it pressed against the zipper of my jeans. A tiny bead of panic shivered through me, wondering if Ivy would come to her senses before we got to my apartment. Would she let her brain take over and convince her that this was a bad idea?

I needed to touch her. To keep that fire stoked and burning. Fucking stick shift.

My breath caught in my chest when Ivy's hand landed on my thigh, her palm brushing down toward my knee before travelling upward. Her fingertips grazed my cock, and even through my jeans and boxers, I could feel the heat of her touch.

"That feels so good, Ivy," I groaned, pressing my head back against the headrest as my foot pushed harder against the accelerator.

"Does it?" she asked, her voice breathless as her hand cupped me the same way I'd guided it to in the restaurant.

"Yes," I croaked, then cleared my throat. "You should touch yourself with those fingers. See how it feels."

She froze, and my heart pounded double-time as I waited for her reaction. Was it too much? Had I taken it too far? I knew some women were shy about bringing pleasure to themselves in front of their lovers in the privacy of their own bedroom, much less in a muscle car careening through town at speeds well above the posted limit.

I opened my mouth to take it back as Ivy pulled away from me and faced forward, but my words choked off when she pulled the lever to recline her seat back. When her fingers slid down her thighs, then dragged the hem of her skirt upward as they returned, my mouth went dry.

"You should keep your eyes on the road," she said, her voice low and husky as her hands pulled the skirt up higher before latching onto the top of her black tights.

We were less than five minutes from my apartment, and I was torn between ordering her to keep going and begging her to stop until we got to the parking lot so I wouldn't miss a second of it. Thank God I was watching the road, because the last traffic light between me and my bedroom turned yellow, then red, forcing me to stop.

My eyes darted over as Ivy lifted her hips and shoved the top of her tights down to her knees. I swallowed thickly, unable to take my eyes off her fingers as they trailed a path up her inner thighs with agonizing slowness.

I glanced up at her face to determine if she was actually enjoying this, and my heart pounded against my ribs. Her cheeks were stained a ruddy pink, her plump lips were parted as she panted in tiny breaths, and her eyes were closed.

My dick hardened to a near-unbearable degree as my gaze moved downward. One hand cupped her pussy, her middle finger rubbing in slow circles as the other hand squeezed the bare flesh of her thigh.

Holy shit.

The honk of a horn startled me from the trance I'd fallen into, and I tore my eyes away from Ivy to look into the rearview mirror. A small sedan idled behind me, and I couldn't for the life of me figure out why the driver was honking.

"The light's green," Ivy whispered, the words abbreviated with a small moan of pleasure.

I slammed my foot on the gas pedal, making the

Mustang's tires squeal when I didn't let off the clutch quick enough. Taking a deep breath, I eased off the gas and shifted into second gear, determined to drive like a normal, law-abiding citizen.

The last thing I needed was to get pulled over with Ivy half-naked in the passenger seat.

By the time I pulled into my parking spot outside my apartment, I thought I was going to explode. Ivy moved her hands, her fists clenching the fabric of her tights as if she meant to pull them up.

"Don't stop," I ordered, my voice deep and husky with desire. "I want you to make yourself come."

"But...someone could see," she stuttered, her gaze darting from side to side.

"No one will see."

I leaned over and slipped my hand between her legs and groaned. Her folds were slick and swollen with need, making me want to slide my aching cock inside and feel her come apart around it. But not yet.

"You're so wet, Ivy." She groaned and writhed in her seat, and I slid one finger inside her. "So tight and hot."

I pulled my hand away, and she grunted in disappointment. "Nate, please."

"Show me how you make yourself come," I ordered, barely hanging onto the threads of my own control.

Her right hand released the fabric of her tights and started to glide upward. I held my breath, sparing a glance through both the windshield and the back window to make sure we were still alone before looking back at her.

In the dim light of a nearby streetlight, I watched as Ivy rubbed two fingers against her clit. Her knees fell open even further as her other hand moved up to slide a finger inside. My mouth went dry as my heartbeat pounded in my ears, and I couldn't take it anymore.

"Ivy, stop."

She froze, looking over at me with wide blue eyes. "What? I thought…"

"I know," I said. "I thought I could handle it, but I can't. I need to be inside you. Now. Pull those off."

I motioned toward her tights, and she shoved them down to her ankles without hesitation. Kicking off the flat shoes she wore, she pulled her feet free of the tight material while stomping it into the floorboard.

Fuck. It was times like these that I wished I had a bigger car. If there was more room, I'd pull her into my lap and have her ride me right here in this lot—possible spectators be damned.

I leaned over and kissed her, and her hands wove into my hair. Before we could get too carried away, I pulled back and looked into her eyes.

"Let's go inside."

She nodded, unbuckled her seatbelt, and climbed from the car on shaky legs. I grabbed her purse from the floor, leaving the discarded tights and underwear. She wouldn't need those. Not tonight.

I rounded the car and came up behind her, wrapping one arm around her waist as my stiff cock rubbed against her ass. She moaned and pressed back against it, making me groan in return.

She snatched her purse and the keys out of my fingers and ran. I chased after her, but she made it to the door of my apartment before I could catch her. As she tried to unlock the door, I slammed into her back, pushing her up against the wood as my hands explored her bare thighs.

She must've managed to turn the key in the lock, because the door swung open and we stumbled inside. I kicked it closed behind me, then bent over and scooped Ivy up, tossing her over my shoulder. I trotted toward my bedroom, not giving her time to protest my barbaric hold on her before I was dropping her onto the mattress.

She hadn't even gained her bearings when I buried my face between her legs. She moaned with pleasure as my tongue stroked up her slit. I spent some time flicking her clit with the tip of my tongue before moving back down to push it inside her.

She was so hot. So wet. So delicious.

"Nate," she said, and I could feel her thighs tightening with tension.

Giving her pussy one last kiss, I pushed myself up and stripped out of my clothes faster than should've been possible. As I kicked off my boxers, Ivy rolled off the mattress to stand beside me. She motioned for me to sit on the edge of the bed before pulling off her shirt, skirt, and bra.

My hands itched to grab her, but the look of determination on her face made it clear she wanted to be in charge of this rodeo. She moved between my legs and fisted her hands in my hair. Then she pulled my head down, angling my mouth toward one pert nipple.

I sucked it between my lips, swirling my tongue around it as Ivy threw her head back in pleasure. I moved to pay the same attention to the other nipple, and Ivy whispered my name as she straddled my lap.

My cock slid into her easily, and my mouth popped off her breast to kiss her. As my tongue brushed against hers, Ivy lifted her hips before slamming back down. Then she did it again. And again.

Growling noises echoed around us, and I wasn't sure who was making them. All I knew for sure was that Ivy's greedy pussy was throbbing around me, and if I wasn't careful, I was going to come. God, I wanted it, but I needed to make sure Ivy finished first.

I stood up and turned, laying Ivy on her back. As I

pumped into her, I spread the folds of her sex and rubbed my thumb against the sensitive bundle of nerves nestled within. Her back arched as her moans grew louder, and I pumped faster, racing for climax.

Ivy came with a scream, the inner walls of her pussy clenching down hard. I shouted my own release, my fingers digging into her hip as my movements slowed and I collapsed on top of her.

"Fuck," I breathed into her ear.

"Yeah," she agreed, her hands gliding over my shoulders and down my arms.

Sex with Ivy was…good. *Too* good.

And when this was all over, I had no idea if I'd be able to settle for less.

28

Ivy

"Holy fuck."

Karly's eyes were glazed over with a mix of reverence and jealousy when I finished speaking. We were seated at Felicia's Kitchen table, with Karly next to me and Felicia and Jessa on the other side. Those two looked at me with the same wide-eyed expression.

I'd been tightlipped and vague at first, but Karly and Felicia had managed to drag every single detail about my "date" with Nate out of me. It should've been particularly weird with Jessa—her boyfriend was my best friend and Nate's brother—but Jessa had a way of making people comfortable enough to spill their guts…including me.

Probably because she was a bartender.

"So. Hot," Felicia muttered, fanning herself.

"So what does this mean for the two of you?" Jessa asked.

"Nothing," I said, trying to ignore the pit forming in my stomach as I said the word. "This thing between us isn't real. When Charity lets go of her threats against Nate, and I get my mom's car, it's over."

"Sounds pretty fucking real to me," Karly said.

"It's just sex," I argued.

But the words left a sour taste in my mouth. I knew it wasn't true. Not for me. But Nate was another matter. I was pretty sure it was just sex for him, and I'd been trying to convince myself I could enjoy it without letting my heart get tangled up. Well, any more than it already was.

"Bullshit," Felicia said, giving me a wicked side-eye. "We haven't known you long, but it's pretty obvious you're not the type to jump into bed with someone when there aren't any real feelings present."

"What do you mean? I'm an enlightened, modern woman. I can have casual sex."

"Of course, you can, Ivy." Karly's words said she had my back, but her tone implied there was some thick smoke being blown up my ass.

"I can," I insisted, elbowing her in the side.

"Maybe you could…if it were anyone other than Nate," Jessa said.

They all fell silent, giving me a moment to process her words. I knew she was right, but I'd convinced myself I could sleep with him and keep my feelings out of it. That I could get through this whole charade and go back to my normal life with no repercussions.

I'd been so sure I could pretend to be in love with Nate Walton and not *actually* fall in love with him.

"Oh, God," I moaned, crossing my arms on the tabletop and burying my face in the crook. "I'm so screwed."

"That's what she said," Karly threw out, giggling at her own joke. Then someone must've hit her, because she added, "Ow! Shit, it was a joke. Just trying to lighten the mood here. Sheesh."

"Your timing is terrible," Felicia drawled. "Ivy." I lifted my head and met her eyes, and she gave me a sincere smile. "The solution is simple. Tell Nate how you feel."

"I can't do that," I said, shaking my head vigorously.

The last time I'd decided to tell Nate how I felt, I'd ended up in bathroom-sex hell. He didn't care about me then, and I was pretty sure he didn't care about me now. Not in the way I was starting to feel about him. Again.

This was nothing but a business arrangement...with benefits.

Maybe he'd want to be friends when this was all over. Maybe—at some point—I could be his friend. Yeah. We'd be able to hang out with Rafe, Jessa, and Lola at family dinners and actually get along. No more fighting. No more hateful words.

Yeah, right. Who the fuck was I kidding? I'd never be able to look at Nate again without thinking about his mouth on me, his hands...his goddamned *magic dick*.

"Maybe he feels the same way," Jessa said, yanking me from my spiraling thoughts.

"What?" I blurted, thinking she'd somehow read my mind.

"If you tell him how you feel, maybe he'll say he feels the same way," she said, her expression filled with hope.

"I don't think so," I said, my heartbeat accelerating.

The thought that Nate might actually share my feelings was exciting, but I quickly tamped down the feeling. I couldn't risk it. If he rejected me again, actively or passively, like before, I didn't know if my heart could take it.

"Fuck it, let's drink," Felicia said, raising her shot glass into the air.

Jessa had raided the bar's stash of top-shelf tequila, and after clinking my glass against the other three, I poured it down my throat. Smooth, minimal burn, and a pleasant warmth in my belly told me is was some good stuff.

"Ooh, I know," Karly shouted, slamming her empty shot glass down onto the table. "Let's play truth or dare."

"Ugh, not again," Felicia mumbled.

"What are we, twelve?" Jessa asked, laughing.

"Come on, it'll be fun," Karly whined.

Jessa looked at me, and I shrugged, not caring what we did as long as the tequila kept flowing. Felicia groaned and took another shot as Karly clapped her hands and bounced in her chair.

"You guys can crash here tonight so no one needs to drive," I offered.

"Slumber party!" Karly sing-songed. "Now, we *have* to play truth or dare. It's like, federal law, or something."

"Federal law?" Felicia asked, arching one black brow at Karly.

"Shut up," Karly said as she brought her glass to her lips and tossed the tequila back. "I'll go first. Jessa. Truth or dare?"

"Truth," Jessa answered, an unsure expression on her face.

"Boo. No fun," Karly shot back. "Okay, truth. How old were you when you lost your virginity?"

Jessa's cheeks turned a light shade of pink. She knocked back a shot, then cleared her throat as she stared at Karly. "Twenty."

"No shit?" Karly gasped.

I half expected Felicia to push her out of her chair, but the dark-haired beauty only stared at Jessa with wide eyes. I had to fight to keep the shock out of my own expression.

Though twenty wasn't old, by any means, most of the girls I knew in high school became sexually active at fifteen or sixteen.

"No shit," Jessa confirmed. "You guys know I never had any friends in high school, much less boyfriends."

That was right. I'd forgotten these three went to high school together.

"Yeah, but…" Karly sputtered.

Jessa shrugged. "I slept with a couple of guys in college, just to try it. I found it…underwhelming, to say the least. I never really got what the big deal was until Rafe."

Her pupils dilated as her blush grew brighter. She was obviously thinking naughty thoughts about my best friend, and I couldn't help but get a little misty-eyed at how happy they made each other.

Sheesh, this tequila is making me sappy.

"Okay, my turn," Jessa announced, snapping me out of my thoughts. "Felicia, truth or dare?"

"Dare," Felicia said firmly.

"Ooh, let me pick. Let me pick," Karly begged.

"No, it's Jessa's turn," Felicia said firmly, making Karly sag in her chair.

"You always say truth when it's my turn," she pouted.

"Exactly. You know everything about me, and your dares are ridiculous and mostly illegal."

My head reared back at those words, and I wondered just what kind of dares Karly liked to issue. I needed to remember to never accept a dare from her.

"I dare you to call the hottest guy you know and tell him you want him," Jessa said, narrowing her gaze at Felicia like she knew she'd never do it.

"Okay," Felicia said, pulling out her phone. "What's your dad's number?"

"Ew. Come on," Jessa groaned, balling up a napkin and throwing it at Felicia's face.

Laughter burst out of me as Karly nodded in vigorous agreement. Mr. Maddox truly was a silver fox, but I knew Felicia was just fucking with Jessa.

These girls were too much, and I loved it. I loved being part of their group, and I knew that no matter what happened with Nate, I'd always have them to lean on.

And that meant the world to me.

29

_____

Nate

𝒯he repairs on the Bel Air were finished. The windshield had come in today, and it was the last part I needed to install before taking the car to the body shop to be completely repainted. After that, I'd take it to have the seats and carpet reupholstered, and she'd look good as new.

I was cleaning the last of the fingerprints off the glass when Dane walked in and gave a low whistle.

"Hey," I said, stuffing the rag in my pocket as I stepped back to admire the car with him.

"It looks good," he said.

"You think Ivy will be happy?" I asked.

He nodded, then gave me a knowing look. "I think Mrs. Anderson will be happy, too."

"That's what I meant," I said, pulling the rag from my pocket and scrubbing it over an imaginary smudge on the driver's window.

"Mm hmm," Dane replied.

"Shut up," I shot back, making him laugh.

He was right—I should've been thinking about Ivy's mom and whether or not the car would please *her*. It was her car, after all. Not Ivy's.

"Ivy will be pumped that it's going to be done before Christmas," Dane mused. "She wanted to give it to her mom as a Christmas gift, right?"

"Yeah," I said, and uneasy feeling slithering into my gut.

Thanksgiving was next week, which meant Christmas was just over a month away. If everything went to plan, and Charity lost interest in me in the near future, my deal with Ivy would be over in a few weeks.

No more smiles. No more kisses. No more intimate encounters that led to the best sex I'd ever had.

Maybe I should break something that will take weeks to get replacement parts for, I thought, my gaze scanning the car.

"Stop it," I muttered, shaking my head.

"What?" Dane asked, peering at me.

I looked back at him, my shoulders drooping. "I need some advice."

Dane pointed a finger at his chest as his mouth fell open. "Advice? From moi?"

"Yes, asshole. From you," I said, motioning for him to follow as I made my way to my office.

The shop was closed and all the other techs had gone home for the night. There was no one to overhear, so I left the office door open. I slipped into my chair, and Dane took the one across the desk from me.

"Okay, shoot," he said, rubbing his hands together.

"This thing with Ivy has me tied in knots," I said without preamble.

"Do you like her?" he asked.

"Yes, of course I like her, but that's beside the point."

"Why is that?" he asked. "Seems to me that *is* the point."

I was shaking my head before he finished. "She doesn't like me."

Dane's head tilted as he looked at me with incredulous eyes. "Haven't you guys been sleeping together?"

"Yes."

"Well, that would indicate that she likes you, at least a little. Right?"

"She's so hot and cold, it's hard to tell," I said with a sigh. "I know she likes the sex. But you and I both know you can enjoy a physical relationship without any feelings between you."

"Speak for yourself," Dane shot back with an indignant expression.

"Please," I deadpanned, "you're an even bigger player than I am. *Was*. Fuck."

"We're not talking about me," he said, shaking his head. "We're talking about you and Ivy. Maybe you should just tell her how you feel."

A faraway look crossed his features for a split second before he wiped it away. I started to ask him about it, but shook off the urge.

"I don't know, man," I said in response to his statement.

"You don't know how you feel? Or if you should tell her?"

"Both," I answered, but it came out as more of a question.

"It sounds like you have some things to figure out."

"Well, that's helpful," I grunted.

"Hey, don't take your cluelessness out on me," he said, holding his palms up. "I can't tell you how to feel. The only advice I can give you is to decide what you want, then be honest with Ivy about it."

"But…what if I decide I want to be with her, and she shoots me down?" I asked, the words quiet and unsure.

"Then you'll have to accept her decision."

I sighed and scrubbed a hand down my face. "I don't know if I can handle the rejection."

"Then you've already lost her," Dane said, then stood. "I'll see you tomorrow, man."

I watched him go, my thoughts running over everything he said. Could he be right? Could it be that simple? If I told Ivy I wanted to give this thing between us a real shot, and she agreed, we could be a true couple by Christmas.

But what if she laughed in my face?

I groaned and leaned back in my chair, closing my eyes. No. What was happening between Ivy and me—it wasn't real. We were *acting* like a couple, and it had gone to our heads. The sex was amazing…we couldn't fake that if we tried.

But the rest was just pretend.

Maybe Ivy had been right all along. Maybe we needed to erect some boundaries. Put everything back into perspective and stick to the rules of our original bargain. Keep everything clear cut. Safe.

Yeah. That would be for the best.

～

"Thanks for letting me come over."

Ivy nodded as she stepped aside to let me into her apartment. My stomach was queasy, and my skin itched, but I knew what needed to be done. I'd called Ivy from the shop, and when she said I could come over, I drove straight here.

I knew I must stink of motor oil and sweat, but that wasn't a bad thing. I could use my dirtiness as a shield. A suit of armor to keep Ivy at an arm's length.

"Do you want something to drink?" she asked, walking toward the kitchen.

"No, thanks. I won't be here long. I just...wanted to talk to you about something."

She stopped and turned around, backtracking to the living room. Taking a seat on the couch, she looked up at me with expectant eyes. I shifted my weight from foot to foot as the nausea grew even more pronounced.

Taking a deep breath, I said, "So, I've been thinking."

"Did it hurt?" she asked, smirking. At my serious expression, her face fell, and she nodded. "Sorry. Go on."

"Things between us seemed to have gotten out of hand," I said in a slow, measured cadence. "When we entered into this deal, we set clear rules—most of which, we've broken. The sex..." I paused to clear my throat, "... has been amazing, but it's clouded our judgment."

"What are you saying, Nate?" she asked, her tone unnaturally neutral.

"I'm saying I think you were right. I think we should keep things platonic between us in private."

"Platonic," she said, as if she'd never heard the word.

As if she hadn't said it first.

"Yeah," I replied. "I can't see Charity going much longer without giving up on me and moving on. Once she does, everything between us will go back to normal. No more pretend dates. No more fake engagement."

Ivy was silent, her head nodding slowly as if she agreed. I wasn't sure how I felt about the response. My emotions were all over the place. I wanted to be relieved that she wasn't fighting me on this, but I couldn't deny the disappointment welling up inside me.

"Okay," she said simply.

"Okay? That's it?" I asked, flinching at the frustration in my voice.

"What do you want me to say, Nate?"

I want you to argue. I want you to fight.

"Nothing, I guess," is what came out of my mouth instead.

"So, I'll see you on Thanksgiving?" she asked, her voice still quiet and slightly monotone.

"Thanksgiving?"

She nodded. "Rafe invited me and my mom to family dinner…unless you don't want us to come?"

"No," I said quickly. "I mean, yes. Yes, of course, I want you to come."

"Okay," she said. "See you then."

"Okay," I replied.

When she stared at her lap and didn't say anything else, I turned and headed for the door. Pulling it open, I looked back at Ivy. She glanced up and gave me a small smile. I smiled back, gave a little wave and walked out.

That had been easier than I thought it would be. Too easy.

And, fuck, why did it hurt so badly?

30

Ivy

*N*ate was right. Things *had* gotten out of hand, and we needed to reestablish our boundaries and focus on our priorities. He needed me to help him get out of the dumpster fire he'd fallen into with Charity Glasscott. I needed him to finish restoring my mother's beloved Bel Air.

That was all.

But no matter how many times I repeated those facts, the hollow feeling in my chest refused to go away. I knew, without a doubt, that my feelings had gotten tangled up with Nate. I'd let my guard down, invited him inside, and offered him fucking refreshments—metaphorically speaking.

What I'd *actually* done was let go of the hate I'd been harboring for years while letting myself remember why I'd liked him in the first place. He was charming, funny, considerate, and hotter than hell. And the sex—I wasn't going to think about that right now.

Steeling my spine, I got out of my car and headed into the hospital. I was due to work a double, and there was nothing like a busy emergency room filled with patients who needed serious help to get my mind off my emotional baggage...and to put that baggage into perspective.

When I arrived at the nurse's station, I was almost disappointed to see how empty the place was. There were a few patients—one broken ankle, two unusually high fevers, and a guy who looked like he might puke at any second. I grabbed a blue disposable emesis bag from the counter and carried it over to him. He thanked me with a weak voice before closing his eyes with a groan.

I had just returned to the nurse's station and pulled up the lineup of patients on a tablet when Rafe found me.

"Hey, Ivy. You okay?"

"I'm fine," I said, looking at him with a curious expression. "Are *you* okay?"

He looked keyed up, filled with nervous energy as he ran his fingers through his hair. I could tell it wasn't the first time he'd done that today. He shook his head and motioned for me to follow him into the employee locker room.

"What's going on Rafe?" I asked when he stared at me for several seconds without speaking.

"I need your help," he said.

"Of course. Anything."

"Can you take Jessa to the movies tomorrow afternoon, and maybe get Karly and Felicia to go, too? I know you're working a double, but you'll be able to get enough sleep before then, right? It's not too much to ask, is it? If it is, just tell me."

"Rafe," I said, wrapping my fingers around his wrist to ground him and stop his spiral of...whatever this was.

"Sorry," he said, taking a deep breath. "I'm kind of a mess."

"I can take Jessa," I said. "It's no problem, but I have to ask, why?"

There was obviously some reason he wanted her out of the house. Otherwise, a simple afternoon out with the girls wouldn't be such a big deal.

"I'm going to ask her," he said in a low, almost reverent voice.

My mind blanked, not really understanding what he was saying. "Ask her what?"

He shoved a hand in his pocket and pulled it back out, holding his fist toward me. When he uncurled his fingers, a dainty, vintage-looking diamond ring rested in his palm.

"Oh," I said, then more excitedly, "Oh!"

I threw my arms around his neck and squeezed him tightly. When I let go, some of his anxious energy seemed to have dispelled.

"You don't think it's too soon?" he asked.

"No, I don't," I said, shaking my head. "You two were made for each other. She loves you *almost* as much as you love her."

I laughed at his arched brow and plucked the ring from his still-outstretched hand. As I stared at it, my eyes started to burn. This was the real deal. Rafe and Jessa were building a life together, and his proposal was the next step.

As I handed the ring back to him with a smile, the ring on my own hand felt like it weighed about eight hundred pounds. It was bigger and fancier than the one Rafe had— the one I knew was his mother's—but it meant nothing.

It was a fake. Maybe not literally—I was pretty sure the diamonds were real—but my ring was a prop meant to perpetrate a lie.

"Thanks, Ivy," Rafe said, pulling me back to the

present. "There's a five o'clock showing of that romantic comedy she wants to see. That'll give me a couple of hours to prepare everything and surprise her when she gets home."

"Of course," I said, pulling him into another hug. "I'm so happy for you, Rafe. You both deserve all the happiness a life together will bring you."

My eyes burned with emotion, and as I pulled away, I laughed as though my tears were only ones of happiness. And I *was* happy for him and Jessa. But I was also sad that I might never know the same joy and excitement he was feeling right now.

Because Nathaniel Walton was the only person who'd ever made my heart stutter and my insides melt. And he simply wasn't an option.

~

I was bone-tired after my double-shift. Physically. Mentally. Emotionally. I just didn't have an ounce of energy in me, and I couldn't wait to collapse on my bed. To welcome the sweet relief of unconsciousness.

So, when I walked through the automatic doors to see someone leaning against the hood of my car, I grunted with impatience. I didn't care who it was. I was too tired and too grumpy to deal with anyone right...now...

"Charity?" I asked as I drew closer, unable to believe it was her. "What are you doing here?"

She smirked, and my hackles rose, a burst of angry energy coursing through me. I stopped in front of her, bristling as I waited for to speak. The fact that she thought she could, what? Harass me at my place of employment? It was unreal, the gall this woman had. How did she even know what time my shift ended to be here?

"I just came to warn you," she said, her smug little smile still firmly in place.

"Warn me about what?" I gritted out.

This was all her fault. The pain and confusion, the anger and sadness. All of it lay on her bony shoulders, and some part of me wanted to lash out. Violently.

"Nate," she said, holding a hand up to study her long, glossy-red fingernails before focusing back on me. "I know you think you have him wrapped around your pretty little finger, but he's got you fooled, honey. He's a man-whore, and he'll *never* keep his dick in his pants. Even for you."

My body flashed cold and then hot, her words voicing my own thoughts, however crassly. If I was actually in a real relationship with Nate, I knew that no matter how hard I tried to dismiss them, those fears would forever reside deep inside my heart.

I'd seen his loose and easy ways first-hand years ago when I'd found him fucking the owner's daughter, hadn't I? That's why I'd hated him for so long—because he wasn't the man I'd thought him to be. He was just what Charity had called him…a man-whore.

"You'll never be enough for him," she went on, unaware of my internal monologue. "And when he tires of you, he'll come to me."

I knew what she was doing. Her claims of one day having him didn't have two legs to stand on—Nate despised her—but even if it wasn't her, it would be someone else. Despite the convoluted truth in her statements, her motives were as black as her soul.

She was trying to tear apart an engagement that *she* thought was real. She was trying to destroy my confidence in my relationship, my belief that my fiancé really loved me and that I was everything to him.

She was spilling bile, hoping to find a notch in my

armor that she could exploit and tear me down with. She was a vile human being, and I was suddenly filled with so much rage, there was nowhere for it to go but out... directly toward her.

Before I knew what I was doing, I stepped closer, up into her personal space, making her flinch back against my car. There was real fear in her eyes, like she'd somehow forgotten that I'd already lost my temper once and hit her.

I'd never had violent tendencies before, but Charity Glasscott's manipulations had brought forth a viciousness I'd never known existed inside me.

"If you hit me again, I'm calling the cops," she said, injecting confidence into her words that was belied by her body language.

"Go ahead, bitch," I snarled. "My father was a cop and had connections all over the county. They might take me down to the station, but I'd walk in the front door and right out the back." *Lie, but she didn't need to know that.* "But while I'm there, maybe I'll tell them a little story about a certain banker's daughter, extortion, and harassment."

I'd already made this threat, but obviously, she needed reminding. And the fear that crept into her eyes told me if I did follow through on that threat, the investigators would definitely find something. Something that would hurt Charity's family.

"You know what," she said, slipping out from between me and the car, "Nate isn't worth this bullshit. I'm done. Tell him to lose my number and never look at me again. I hope the two of you are very happy together."

The venom dripping from her voice belied the well-wishes, but I wasn't thinking about that as she spun on her six-inch stilettos and stalked away.

It was over. Nate's plan had worked, and he didn't need me anymore.

I looked down at the diamond engagement ring on my left hand. He was going to take it back, and things would go back to normal. To the way they used to be.

I should've been happy. Mission accomplished. The only thing I felt was numb.

Like there was an endless black void where my heart used to beat.

31

Nate

*I*vy: *Charity confronted me today. It's over. She said she's done, and you can move on with your life. Congratulations.*

I stared at the text for the hundredth time, then at the one below it where I'd responded, "Good news." That was our last communication, and it was three days ago. I'd typed out a dozen other text messages, only to delete them. I pulled up her number to call her half that many times, only to change my mind.

It was Thanksgiving, and I knew I would see her at Rafe and Jessa's place. I'd talk to her in person, thank her for everything, and tell her that her mother's car would be done next week and she could pick it up whenever she was ready.

I shoved my phone into the pocket of my jeans and grabbed my wallet and keys before heading out to my car. It was almost time for dinner, and I didn't want to be late.

When I pulled up to the curb in front of my childhood

home, Lola was parked in front of me, getting out of her car.

"Hey baby sister," I called out, slamming my car door and jogging to catch up to her.

"Don't call me that, Nate," she said, but her words carried none of the teasing lilt that they usually did.

"Hey," I said, placing a hand on her arm to stop her. "What's wrong?"

"Nothing," she said, giving me a weak smile. "I'm just tired. I have finals coming up, and I've been up late every night studying."

"You need to take care of yourself, Lola," I said, slipping into overprotective-big-brother mode.

"You take care of *yourself*," she shot back. "What's going on with you and Ivy?"

"What do you mean?" I asked failing to keep a slight edge of panic out of my voice.

"The whole *fake engagement*," she said, using finger quotes. "How's that going?"

"How'd you know about that?" I asked, deflecting.

"Rafe told me," she said, crossing her arms over her chest. "He didn't want me to be blindsided if I heard the rumors. You should've told me, Nate."

"I know. I'm sorry. It's over, anyway. The woman blackmailing me believed it and backed off, so…"

Lola stared at me, her dark brown eyes intense, like they were trying to penetrate my mind and my heart. I fought to keep my expression neutral, and finally, she looked away with a shake of her head.

"Whatever. I'm glad it all worked out."

Then she turned and headed toward the front door. I caught up to her just as she was knocking—something we did now that Rafe had Jessa. Walking in on our brother buck-assed naked one time was more than enough. Jessa opened the door with a wide, welcoming smile, and Lola hugged her while demanding to see the ring.

That was right. Rafe proposed to Jessa, and I'd been so wrapped up in my own shit, I'd forgotten all about it. Guilt washed over me. I was a terrible brother and an even worse best man. I'd congratulated Rafe when he texted to tell me she'd said yes, then promptly put it out of my head.

I hugged Jessa after Lola moved on to find Rafe. She squeezed me back, then pushed me away to look into my face.

"You okay?"

"Don't I look okay?" I shot back, turning from side to side so she could see both profiles.

She smacked me on the arm. "I'm serious, Nate. You seemed…uptight while Lola was gushing over my engagement to Rafe. Are you not happy about it?"

"What?" I asked, honestly shocked by her question. "Of course, I'm happy. I love you, and I think you're perfect for my big brother. If I seem off, it has nothing to do with you. I'm happy for you both. I swear."

"I know. I'm sorry," she said with a wave of her hand. "The holiday is making me emotional, I think. Come on in."

I tried to be cool, I really did, as I scanned the room for Ivy, but apparently, I wasn't as smooth as I thought I was.

"She's not here, yet," Jessa said, a knowing smile on her face. "She had to go pick up her mom, but she should be here any time."

"That's cool," I said, keeping my voice light and disinterested.

Jessa shook her head and walked away. I spotted her friends, Karly and Felicia, chatting in one corner. Jessa's dad, Greg, and his long-time business partner and new girlfriend Janice sat on the couch. Rafe came out of the kitchen with a big smile on his face and hugged Lola, and I couldn't miss how happy he looked.

Why wouldn't he be happy? He was engaged—*for real*—to an amazing woman who adored him. He had a great job, wonderful friends, and a new extended family that included everyone here.

There was a knock at the door, and I turned back, swinging it open. My breath caught in my throat as my eyes landed on Ivy, her cheeks pink from the brisk late-November air and a smile on her face that didn't quite reach her eyes.

I must've lost track of time as I stared, because a throat cleared. Trance broken, my eyes snapped toward the sound to see an older woman standing next to Ivy. Same blonde hair, same ocean-blue eyes.

"I'm sorry," I mumbled, stepping aside quickly to let them in.

"Mom, this is Nate. Rafe's brother. Nate, this is my mom."

"Mrs. Anderson, it's a pleasure to meet you," I said, stretching out a hand for her to shake.

She made huffing noise and pushed my hand away, going in for a hug instead. My arms looped around her waist with uncertainty, but I was soon squeezing her tightly as the full effect of her embrace hit me. Full of warmth and acceptance, it reminded me of the way Mamá hugged me when I was little.

"None of this *Mrs. Anderson* stuff. Call me Barb," she said as she pulled away.

"Barb," I said, smiling as I rolled the name around on my tongue.

She gave me a light pat on the cheek and moved away, calling out to Rafe. He was the only person she'd met before, and I heard her ask for a hug and to be introduced around.

"She's amazing," I whispered to Ivy, forcing my eyes to remain on her mother.

"Yes, she is," Ivy agreed before moving away from me.

I wanted to stop her. To tell her…something. But I managed to restrain myself. The lines were clearly drawn between us, and blurring them again would only make things messier. It didn't escape my notice that she wasn't wearing the ring and she introduced me to her mother as "Rafe's brother."

She obviously hadn't told Barb about our fake engagement…I just hoped everyone else here knew that and didn't mention it. I would hate for Ivy and I to have to explain something like that over turkey and dressing.

Other than a few menacing stares shot my way from Karly and Felicia, the dinner was fun and relaxing. Everyone seemed to feel comfortable, we ate until our stomachs tried to pop, and the wine and beer was freely flowing.

I caught myself staring at Ivy multiple times, but I never once saw her look at me. She was determined to ignore me, and I wasn't sure how I felt about it. My brain knew it was for the best, but the rest of me…the rest of me wanted her to *look at me*.

"Attention, everyone," Jessa called out, tapping a fork against the rim of her glass of water. "Rafe and I would like the thank you all for coming. You've made our first Thanksgiving together one to remember, and we love you all."

A chorus of thanks and declarations of how great dinner was rang out, and Jessa looked at Rafe, who gave her a small nod. She took a deep breath as she waited for everyone to quiet down, and I wondered what was happening. I tilted my head, watching her.

"As you all know, Rafe asked me to marry him, and I said yes," she said, her adoring eyes moving back to my brother. "We've been talking about a New Year's wedding."

My head reared back with surprise. They were obviously in love and wanted to get married as soon as possible, but New Year's was only five or six weeks away. Why the rush?

"We know it's quick, but…I don't want to be as big as the side of a house on my wedding day."

She rubbed her belly and several gasps rang out, but I was just confused. Was Jessa *planning* on packing on some weight?

"That's right," she said. "We're pregnant!"

Cheers erupted around the table, and Jessa moved from her place to squeeze in between Greg and Janice and hug them both. They both had tears in their eyes, which made Jessa cry even as she laughed with joy.

Congratulations were passed around as Rafe told the story of his proposal and how it almost went south because of pregnancy hormones. Everyone laughed as Jessa gave him a stern look, then moved around to hug everyone at the table.

When she hugged me, she whispered in my ear, "Are you ready, Uncle Nate?"

An image of her snuggling a tiny baby flashed through my mind. She was sitting in a rocking chair, with Rafe gazing down lovingly over her shoulder. The image morphed, and it was Ivy holding a baby.

My baby.

Fuck. What the hell is wrong with me?

"I was born ready," I said quickly, giving Jessa what I hoped was a sincere-looking smile.

It must've been convincing, because her grin widened, and she gave me another quick hug before moving on. Rafe caught my eye, and the look of sheer happiness on his face was damned-near blinding. I smiled back at him, giving him a nod and mouthing, "Congratulations."

"Thanks, man," he mouthed back.

He'd done it. My brother, the one who'd spent his entire adult life concentrating on me, Lola, his patients, and everyone else around him had finally found someone who would look after *him*. Someone who would love him unconditionally and bring him the happiness that had been missing since our parents died.

He'd been acting as a father-figure since Lola and I were young, and now he was a father, in truth. I knew he'd make an amazing dad. And I was going to make an awesome uncle.

"When are you due?" Barb asked after Jessa hugged Ivy and moved on to her.

"July," Jessa replied, smiling widely.

"Oh, a summer baby. How wonderful," Barb said.

My gaze moved from her to Ivy, and I met her stare for a half a second before she glanced away. An ache formed in my chest, and I rubbed the heel of my hand against it to ease the burn.

Ugh. Must've eaten too much food. Heartburn is the worst. Yeah. It's heartburn.

32

———

Ivy

$\mathcal{T}$hanksgiving weekend came and went, and other than a quick greeting from Nate at Rafe and Jessa's, I hadn't spoken to him since the day I texted him about Charity. I kept telling myself the separation was a good thing. Better to break ties and move on before someone really got hurt.

I'd taken off his ring before Thanksgiving, and it winked at me from its resting place on the kitchen counter. I knew he'd be wanting it back, so I left it there to be easily accessible once he asked for it. I certainly didn't leave it out so I could stare at it with longing and disappointment.

Definitely not.

I stretched out on the couch and tried to concentrate on the movie I was watching, but memories of my time with Nate kept distracting me. Our dates, his considerate actions, the longing in his eyes when he looked at me.

The sex.

I couldn't stop thinking about it. And it wasn't just the

physical pleasure that I missed. It was that connection, the feeling of being right where I belonged, wrapped around Nate's body while he pleasured mine.

There was something so intimate about it, some key ingredient that I'd never experienced before with another man. Maybe it was because I'd wanted him when we met, and that desire had been pushed down into a locked box after the incident at Hero's. Maybe it was his total devotion to making sure he made me feel good, both physically and emotionally.

Maybe it was because I...loved him.

Oh, no. No. No. No.

I didn't love Nate Walton. I couldn't.

Shit.

The seed had planted somewhere inside me, and now I couldn't shake it loose. I muted the television and closed my eyes, going over every interaction Nate and I had since the day he proposed this fake engagement.

The nervous energy, and the way he calmed it. The fun, the laughter. His smart mouth and his chivalry. His inherent love of family and, despite our past differences, considering me a part of it. The way he set me on fire with just a glance from those baby blue eyes.

The way he worshipped my body like ensuring my gratification was more important than his own.

All of those things flashed through my mind on repeat, spinning faster and faster until I sat up with a groan.

"Fuck," I mumbled, rubbing my temples with my fingertips.

Something was wrong with me. Maybe I needed a CT scan. Or a lobotomy.

Because there was no way I'd let myself fall in love with my fake fiancé. I couldn't possibly be that stupid.

~

*T*he text from Nate came in a few hours later, as I was trying for the fifth time to get into the movie I'd been watching. I snatched up my phone, ignoring the little thrill that shot through me when I saw his name on the screen.

Nate: *I think we should be seen in public again. You know, just in case Charity is still paying attention.*

I tamped down the disappointment that tried to rear its ugly head inside me. Of course, Nate didn't want to see me. He just wanted to be seen *with* me so Charity wouldn't come sniffing back around.

Me: *Of course. When were you thinking?*

Nate: *Are you free for dinner tonight? Or we could get drinks at the bar.*

Me: *Drinks sound good.*

I was definitely going to need alcohol to get through this "date" with Nate. Particularly after all the soul-searching I did today and the revelations it uncovered. Revelations I still refused to fully accept.

Denial wasn't just a river in Africa.

Nate: *Great. Pick you up at seven?*

Me: *Sure thing.*

I tossed my phone down beside me and hung my head. I could do this. I could maintain an emotional distance from Nate while pretending to be in love with him.

Pretending. Not actually in love. Don't forget that, Ivy.

I hopped into a scalding hot shower, attempting to wash away my troubled thoughts. Once I was finished, I blow-dried my hair into fat waves and applied some mini-malistic makeup. I pulled on some jeans, a conservatively flowy shirt, and a black leather jacket.

Perusing my boot collection, I chose a black pair with

high heels and stitched accents that matched the pink of my top. I stared at my reflection in my full-length mirror and realized I was as ready as I was ever going to be.

This night was going to be hell.

Because no matter how successful I was at pushing away thoughts of strong feelings for Nate now, I knew being with him was going to destroy all my defenses.

Unless…

I perked up as a plan started to formulate in my mind. If I could somehow trigger Nate's asshole side, it would remind me of why I hated him for so long. And maybe those feelings of dislike and disgust would overrule the more tender feelings I'd been plagued by for the last few weeks.

Maybe it would poison that seed of love I was having such a hard time destroying.

I sat down on the couch to wait for Nate, ideas flowing through my head. It could work. If I could breed animosity between us again, things would go back to normal.

There'd be no more longing. No more regrets.

I'd be able to move on. Maybe I'd start dating more and find someone I could truly love, who loved me in return. I ignored the way my stomach turned at the thought.

I got up and went to the kitchen. Plucking the ring from the counter, I slipped it back onto my finger.

It was what I needed to do if I didn't want to spend the rest of my life alone, pining over what might've been. I needed to get over Nate Walton. And that process would begin tonight.

33

Nate

Ivy looked amazing. She always looked beautiful to me, but the leather jacket and boots somehow gave her an air of badass confidence I hadn't seen before. It was sexy as hell.

We kept ourselves at a distance and made polite conversation until we got to the bar. Then it was show time.

I helped Ivy from the Mustang and wrapped an arm around her waist. She stiffened at my touch while the smile on her lips contradicted her discomfort. We walked into The Bullpen like that, outwardly affectionate while inwardly cringing.

This was fucking harder than I thought it was going to be.

Ivy slid into a booth, and this time, I took the bench across the table from her. The questioning look in her eyes vanished the moment I noticed it, and she looked down to peruse the drink menu. As our waitress neared, I stretched a hand across the table, and Ivy took it without even glancing up at me.

"What can I get you?" the waitress asked, popping out a hip as her eyes devoured me.

I was used to that reaction, but tonight I found it particularly distasteful. Didn't she see me holding hands with Ivy? The girl across from me who outshined every other woman in the place, including her?

"I'll have a light beer. Whatever you have on tap is fine," I said, then turned my gaze to Ivy.

She was staring at the waitress with a critical eye. Nothing negative, but like she was sizing her up for some reason.

"I'll have the same," she said, dropping the drink menu to the table. "And some chips and salsa."

"You got it," the server said, writing on her notepad before looking back at me and shooting me a wink.

"She's pretty," Ivy said as the girl sashayed away.

"I guess," I said, feeling distinctly uncomfortable.

"Maybe you should hit that," she said, her face completely blank.

"Excuse me?" I replied, incredulous. *Hit that?*

"Why not?" she asked, turning her gaze back to the waitress as she put in our order at the bar. "She's hot and obviously interested. Isn't that the kind of girl you usually go for?"

What in the actual fuck?

"What are you doing, Ivy?" I asked, and she slipped her hand out of mine and dropped it to her lap.

"I'm trying to be your friend. You know, like a wing-man, or something."

"I don't need a wing-man, or a wing-woman for that matter," I said, sighing.

What had gotten into her? Real or no, I would never

hit on another woman while I was on a date. Especially not while on a date with Ivy.

"I was just trying to let you know I wouldn't be upset if you decided to make a move. That's all."

"Thanks, but I'm good," I said, but she just shrugged and looked away.

We sat in silence until the waitress returned with our beers, chips, and salsa. As she approached, Ivy perked up. Thanking her for the beer with a big smile, Ivy stopped the waitress from leaving with a hand on her arm.

"Excuse me, what's your name?"

"Amber," the server said, raising a questioning brow.

"So, Amber," Ivy said, chancing a quick glance at me before refocusing on the woman, "are you single?"

"Are you hitting on me?" Amber asked, popping out a hip and resting her hand there. "Because if you are, you should know I'm straight as a fencepost."

"You know, moisture can warp the wood, making it not so straight," I chimed in, shooting Ivy a wink. If she was going to play games, so could I.

She narrowed her eyes at me before looking back at Amber. "I'm not hitting on you. I was just wondering, because I might have a *friend* who'd be interested."

"Really? Is he good looking?"

"Eh," Ivy said, tilting her hand back and forth, "he's all right."

I crossed my eyes and bucked my top teeth out, but Ivy didn't laugh. She just gave me another irritated look before turning her attention back to her conversation.

"But I hear he's excellent in bed. Some might even say his dick is…magic."

"I think those reports are grossly exaggerated," I cut in.

"I don't know," Ivy said, tapping a finger against her

chin. "You can only hear something so many times before you start to believe it."

"That's the danger of rumors. Wouldn't you agree, Amber?" I replied, looking up at the waitress.

"I…uh…" she started, but Ivy saved her.

"I assure you, these rumors are true."

"Are you telling me you know from first-hand experience, my love? Who is this *friend*? And how long has it been since you fucked him?"

"Ex-c-cuse me. I have to get back to work," Amber stuttered before rushing away.

"What the hell, Nate?"

"I should be asking you that," I retorted, leaning over the table so I could keep my voice down. "What the hell do you think you're doing?"

"I told you," she said, most of the fire draining from her. "I was just trying to help you."

"And I told you I don't need your help."

"Of course you don't," she said.

She looked away from me, taking a sip of her beer as if those words settled something in her mind. I just wasn't sure what.

"Ivy—"

"Just drop it, Nate. This is our last date together. Might as well enjoy the food and drinks."

We sat in silence after that, drinking our beers and eating the snacks. Outwardly, we appeared civil. Ivy made sure to smile if she felt someone looking at us. She flashed her ring around, and my mood grew sourer by the minute.

I didn't like how fake she was acting. I didn't like her refusal to make any further eye contact with me. I didn't like how she said it was our "last date," like it was no big deal to her.

Or that she was in a hurry for this to be over with.

And I especially didn't like how my chest hurt at the idea, or how my stomach dropped at the end of the date when she slid the ring off her finger and handed it to me.

It really was over.

~

"Hey."

"What are you doing here, Rafe?"

I spun around and stalked back to the couch, leaving the front door open. That was the only invitation Rafe was going to get. I was in a foul mood, and didn't feel like having company.

"Jesus, what crawled up your ass and died?" he asked as he stepped inside and closed the door behind him. "This is the second time you've answered the door like that."

"If you're just going to be an asshole, you can leave," I growled.

"I think you cornered the market on dickish behavior today, little bro," he replied, moving to stand in front of me. "What's going on?"

I closed my eyes and sighed. "I don't know, man. I'm sorry. I'm just in a mood today."

He went into the kitchen, grabbed two bottles of water, then came back and plopped down on the couch next to me. Handing me one of the bottles, he twisted the top off his and took a long swig.

"Tell me what happened. Maybe I can help."

"I doubt you can fix this, Rafe."

"Try me," he said.

Taking a deep breath, I set my water on the coffee table and told him about my date with Ivy the night before. He sat quietly, listening to the whole thing without interrupting.

"So she was actively trying to set you up with your waitress?" he asked when I finished.

"Yep," I said, popping the "p" for emphasis.

"And how did that make you feel?"

I arched a brow at him. "What are you, my shrink?"

"You're deflecting, Nate. Answer the question."

How *did* it make me feel?

"Angry, at first. Then amused. I tried to play along like it was a big joke, but Ivy was dead-serious. Then I just felt...wounded. Like she stabbed me in the chest and jiggled the knife around to cause a little extra damage."

He nodded thoughtfully, then asked, "Why do you think she was trying so hard to hook you up with someone else?"

"Hell, if I know," I said, throwing my hands into the air. "I told her to stop. I told her I didn't need her help."

"And what did she say to that?"

"She said, 'Of course you don't. Let's enjoy our last date,' and refused to speak to me the rest of the night."

Rafe tilted his head to observe my expression. "So... are you more upset that she was trying to set you up with another woman, or that she said it was your last date?"

"I don't know. Both?" I said, shaking my head. "It doesn't matter. It's over, anyway. Charity is done toying with me, and Barb's car is being delivered from the upholstery shop tomorrow. The terms of our deal have been met."

My stomach dropped as I said the words, and I unconsciously rubbed the area with my hand. Something was wrong with me. Maybe I needed to see a doctor. With that thought, I looked back at Rafe.

"Can you give me a physical, or something?" I asked.

"What? Why?" he blurted, looking confused.

"I don't know. Something is wrong with me."

"What are your symptoms?" he asked, narrowing his eyes.

"Intermittent chest pains—could be heartburn. Nausea. Lack of energy."

"And when did these symptoms begin?" he asked.

"I don't know…a couple of weeks ago?"

"I don't think you're sick, Nate," he said, crossing his arms over his chest.

"What's wrong with me, then?"

"It sounds like you're in love."

My first instinct was to scoff, but the laughter died in my chest. My breathing became erratic as my heart pounded out a staccato rhythm.

"No," I whispered.

"Yes," Rafe said. "These so-called symptoms started after you and Ivy decided to put a halt to things between you and keep things platonic, right?" He held up his palms at my questioning look. "Jessa told me. And they keep getting worse as the distance between you spreads?"

My wide eyes stared at him, and something inside me clicked into place. Could he have been right? Was I in love with Ivy Anderson?

I knew the answer before I finished thinking the question.

The new question was, what was I going to do about it?

34

Ivy

$\mathcal{I}$ put on some clean clothes, brushed my teeth, and tried to pinch some color into my cheeks. Rafe had called and asked if we could hang out, and he was on his way over. It had been far too long since we'd spent any quality time together, and I was trying to perk myself up so I wouldn't be a total downer.

I put on a pot of coffee, and as I watched the thin stream dribble into the pot, I tried not to think about Nate.

My attempt to lure out the asshole in him had been a complete failure. He'd been rightfully offended that I'd be so brazen as to try to hook him up with another woman instead of taking the bait like I was sure he would.

So I'd latched onto one thing he said—that he didn't need any help getting women—and ran with it as a last-ditch effort to harden my heart against him. The problem was, I *knew* he didn't mean it the way I was trying to interpret it. I thought I could convince myself he meant he could get any woman he wanted with his *magic dick.*

That my time with him didn't matter. That he'd be onto his next conquest without my help. And soon.

But hard as I tried, I just didn't see him that way anymore. I saw the sweet, funny guy he'd introduced me to over the last few weeks. I saw his secret smiles that were only for me. I saw the man that gave me the greatest pleasure of my life.

I was in love with him. And that depressed the hell out of me, because I couldn't have him.

A knock sounded at the door, and I shook off my dark thoughts. Infusing a little pep in my step, I hurried over and swung it open for Rafe.

"Hey, you," I said. "Come on in. Want some coffee?"

"Sure," he said, looking at me strangely as he stepped inside.

I ignored the look and breezed into the kitchen. Pulling two oversized mugs from the cabinet, I poured two cups of coffee, adding cream and sugar to mine.

When I met him in the living room, Rafe asked, "How many of these have you had?"

"This is my first one," I said, handing his cup to him. "Why?"

"You're acting a little manic. You're not taking diet pills or anything, right?"

"No, Rafe," I groaned.

We were both in the medical field, and we both knew how ineffective and possibly dangerous so-called weight loss drugs were.

"Is it meth, then?"

"Shut up," I said, nudging him with my toe. "Tell me, how is Jessa? Did she have her first prenatal yet?"

"Yesterday," he said, grinning. "We heard the baby's heartbeat."

He was positively glowing, which made me smile. It was the first real one I'd formed in a while.

"I'm so happy for you, Rafe."

"Thanks," he said, then cleared his throat. "So, enough about me. What's going on with you? We've been on opposite shifts for so long, I feel like it's been forever since I saw you."

"It's been a week," I deadpanned. "And nothing new here. Same old, same old. How are plans coming along for the wedding?"

"Nuh-uh," he said, shaking his head. "I've known you for a long time, Ivy, and I know when you're trying to hide something. Out with it."

"Rafe. I can't," I said, my breaths puffing out erratically.

"Ivy, listen to me," he said, setting down his coffee mug to lay a hand on my knee. "I'm your best friend. You can talk to me. I won't judge, and nothing you say will leave this apartment."

"Not even when Jessa asks?" I countered, one side of my mouth lifting.

"Not even then," he stated. "Though, if I were a betting man, I'd put my money on the fact that she already knows whatever it is."

It was true. At our last girls' night, the truth had been torn from me no matter how tightly I tried to hang onto it. Jessa and the others were the ones that made me face the fact that my feelings for Nate had evolved.

"It's your brother," I mumbled.

"I figured as much. What did he do now?"

"He didn't *do* anything," I said, perhaps a little bit too vehemently.

"So, what did he *not* do?" Rafe countered.

He didn't love me.

I didn't realize I'd said the words out loud until Rafe's head jerked back. I could feel my face heating with a blush, and one look at me had Rafe's expression smoothing out.

"How do you know?" he asked.

"How do I know what?"

"That he doesn't love you," he clarified.

A sardonic laugh burst from me, but Rafe didn't smile.

"You can't be serious," I said.

"Do you think he's incapable of love?"

"I…uh…no. I've seen his love for you and Lola. His love for his work. I just think he's incapable of loving *me*."

"Why would you think that, Ivy? You're an amazing woman. Beautiful. Caring. Fun as hell."

"He ended things, Rafe."

"Didn't you try to end them first?"

"Yeah, but—"

"But, nothing," he cut in. "People make mistakes. Stupid judgment calls when they think they're doing the right thing. Have you told him how you feel?"

"No. Of course, not."

"Why not?"

"Because I don't want to get hurt."

"And yet, here you are," he said, gesturing a hand to encompass all of me.

"An outright rejection would hurt worse," I argued.

"If you say so."

"Damn it, Rafe. Don't patronize me," I gritted out between clenched teeth.

"Ah, there she is," he said, a hint of a smile playing on his lips. "Don't lose that fire, Ivy. It's what makes you…*you*. Now, what would the girl who told my asshole brother off on a regular basis do?"

"Hide under the covers while eating all the ice cream?"

I offered. When he just stared at me, I slouched down. "I don't know if I can."

"Tell him how you feel, Ivy. Let the chips fall where they may. Otherwise, you'll spend your whole life wondering what might've been."

~

My conversation with Rafe lingered in my thoughts the rest of the day, plaguing me with indecision. I decided to run out and find Nate no less than seven times, but my doubts and insecurities kept me firmly planted in my apartment.

Not knowing what else to do, I sent out a nine-one-one via my group chat with the girls, and they were on their way over now. I wanted to lay everything out on the table for them and get their opinions. They'd already dragged most of the details out of me the last time they were here, and had advised me to tell Nate how I felt.

But that was when I only thought it was a strong sexual attraction with a fair amount of affection. It was before I realized I *loved* him.

"We have arrived," Karly called out dramatically when I opened the door for them. She whooshed past me bearing two bottles that she held up like prized trophies—margarita mix and a fifth of tequila. "And we come bearing gifts."

"Don't mind her, Ivy," Felicia said as she followed Karly inside. "She's been streaming that new historical romance series everyone is talking about and *fancies herself a duchess.*"

I laughed at the terrible British accent she affected with those last words, then turned to say hi to Jessa.

"Hey. Thanks for coming," I said, closing the door behind her.

"Of course," she replied, shrugging out of her coat. "I've got your back. Besides, I have a feeling these two are going to take full advantage of this pregnancy and make me their designated driver on a regular basis."

She motioned toward the others. Karly was raiding my freezer for ice while Felicia set up the blender.

"Make Jessa a virgin," I called out to them as she and I settled on the couch.

"Too late for that!" Karly quipped, laughing at her own joke.

Jessa rolled her eyes before settling her gaze on me. "How are you holding up?"

Her concerned expression and low tone immediately put me on the defensive. I knew I was being irrational, but these were special circumstances.

"Did Rafe tell you he came to see me?"

Jessa cocked her head at my tone. "He did say he came by, but he didn't tell me what you guys talked about…and I didn't ask."

I groaned and closed my eyes. "I'm sorry, Jessa. I don't know what's wrong with me."

"Something is obviously bothering her, and I'd bet my last dollar it has to do with N-A-T-E," Felicia said, whispering the letters as she handed Jessa her virgin margarita.

"You know I can hear you, right?"

"That's why it's called a stage whisper," she shot back with a wink before rejoining Karly in the kitchen.

Once everyone was settled with a drink in their hand, the three of them turned their attention to me. I took a drink of my margarita, cringing a little as the tequila burned my throat. Then taking a deep breath, I spewed out the words in one long run-on sentence.

"I'm in love with Nate but I'm scared because he doesn't love me and I don't know what to do and it's driving me crazy."

The silence was deafening as they absorbed my words. I nervously took another long pull off my drink, bracing myself for their response.

"How do you know he doesn't love you?" Jessa asked, her words slow and careful.

"Because I just know," I said.

Real eloquent, Ivy.

"But *how* do you know?" Felicia asked. "We need all the details if we're going to make an informed decision on how to advise you."

"Have you asked him?" Karly added.

"What? No," I blurted.

"Have you told him how you feel?" Felicia asked.

"No."

"Then how do you know?" Jessa repeated.

"It's obvious, isn't it?" I asked, my tone getting defensive again. "He had his fun with me, and now he's done. He said it himself, that the sex clouded our judgment. That I was right, and we should end our arrangement the way it started—a business deal with zero benefits."

Those weren't his exact words, but close enough.

"Maybe he was only saying what he thought you wanted to hear," Karly offered. "You did try to end the physical aspect of your relationship first."

"That's because I was getting swept up by my feelings. It was confusing. And dangerous."

The three of them gave me matching pointed looks that I didn't understand.

When it was apparent I wasn't getting it, Felicia huffed. "Who's to say he wasn't experiencing the same dangerous confusion? Ivy, it's obvious you have a connection. We've all seen it. There is no way Nate is not feeling it."

"And that's the real problem," I murmured, looking at each of their faces. "If he does have feelings for me, and he surrenders to them, then he'll lose his freedom."

"Love is not a prison," Jessa muttered.

"It is when you have to contain the basic characteristics that make you who you are. Nate is the type to have random sex with random girls in public places. If he were to commit himself to me, that would end. Or it wouldn't, and I'd be devastated."

Again.

35

Nate

The Bel Air was ready, and I'd texted Ivy to let her know she could come give it a final inspection and set up the delivery to her mother. I hoped she would agree to let me drive it out myself, rather than setting up a flatbed to transport it out there. I'd spent so much time making sure everything was perfect, and I wanted to experience driving this beauty before it slipped out of my life.

Like Ivy.

I'd been in a foul mood for days. Torn between storming over to her house to demand she give us a real shot and letting her go to live her life the way she wanted, I'd been on a never-ending carousel. I felt like I was constantly moving up and down while spinning around and around with no clear destination. No resolution.

I was in love with her. The concept was so simple, yet it was the most complicated situation I'd ever been in. Despite the fun we had together and our obvious physical chemistry, Ivy had gone back to hating me.

I wished I could say I didn't know why. But honestly, I knew this was all my own fault.

I got scared and ruined everything by telling her we should backtrack. Make things simple and *non*sexual. Why did I even do that? Why did I hit the brakes on something I never wanted to end?

Because I was an idiot. Because my feelings were intense and alien, and rather than tell Ivy the truth, I decided to cut and run to save myself from any possible pain if and when she ultimately rejected me.

And by not fighting for me, for what we had, she'd proven—at least in my mind—that I'd been right to do it.

"Fucking idiot," I mumbled, running a soft cloth over the hood of the car.

Ivy deserved better than that. She deserved the truth. She deserved to be loved.

"Hey, Nate. Is she ready?"

I looked up to see Dane walking toward me, his eyes glued to the Bel Air. A smile spread across his face as he circled the vehicle, examining every inch of her for flaws or imperfections.

I had put down the top and hung some red fuzzy dice that matched the paint job on the rearview mirror. The seats were white leather trimmed with red and the steering wheel had been covered with leather of the same shade. Clean and shiny whitewall tires threaded with chrome and red rims completed the look.

"Yeah, she's ready," I said before mumbling, "I'm not so sure I am, though."

"Are you going to tell her?" Dane asked, no longer referring to the car.

"I think I have to," I admitted. "I'm miserable without her. I know chances are slim to none that she'll give me a chance to prove I can be a good partner. But I have to try."

"I think you might be surprised," Dane said, but before I could ask him what he meant, Ivy's voice called out from the waiting room. "That's my cue. Good luck."

He slapped me on the back and headed inside. I heard him tell Ivy she could find me out in the garage before the tap-tap-tap of her booted heels echoed around me. The sound mimicked my pounding heart as I waited for Ivy to get her first look at the Bel Air.

A frown crinkled her forehead as she moved closer, her eyes on the floor in front of her. When she finally looked up, she froze in her tracks. Her mouth fell open and her chest heaved, followed a second later by a stream of tears splashing on her cheeks.

"Ivy," I said, rushing toward her. "Are you okay?"

Pulling her eyes away from the car to look at me for the first time, she shook her head. Turning her gaze back to the car, she moved toward it, her steps slow and measured like she was afraid it would disappear if she moved too fast.

"When I was young, my dad showed me pictures of these cars from the fifties. He would tell me that one day, *this car* would look like that again." Her eyes met mine as she reached inside to stroke the buttery leather of the driver's seat. "It's perfect, Nate. Better than I ever dreamed."

"I'm glad you like it," I said, moving to stand beside her.

"I feel like you did too much," she said. "All of this couldn't have been cheap. Let me give you some money to help cover the costs."

"No, Ivy," I said, wrapping my fingers around her elbow to stop her from digging in the purse hanging from her shoulder. "I don't want your money. You earned this."

Her body seemed to petrify, and all the color drained from her face. She jerked her arm out of my grip and stumbled backwards. I tried to follow, but she held up a hand an ordered me to stop.

"What's wrong? What did I say?" I asked as the blood rushed back to her face, turning it an angry red.

"I earned it?" she asked, her voice laced with venom.

"Yeah," I said, sure this was some kind of trap but unable to pull myself free of it. "You held up your end of the deal and helped me get rid of Charity. I held up *my* end of the deal and restored this car."

"You obviously put a lot more into this than either of us expected when we made that deal, Nate. Is this some kind of payoff for the sex?"

My head jerked back as if she'd struck me. "Woah. What the fuck, Ivy? Why would you say something like that?"

She seemed to wilt in response, and I took the opportunity to step closer to her. Something was very off with her, and I was not going to let her leave here until I found out what it was and we hashed everything out.

It was time for the truth. From both of us.

"Why would you ever think I'd treat you like some kind of prostitute?" I asked, keeping my voice low and gentle.

Her anger was gone, but I wasn't sure this new emotion was better. She reeked of dejection. Like she was tired of fighting and ready to give up. Unacceptable.

"I'm sorry, Nate. I don't know what got into me. I'm just tired and not thinking straight."

I shook my head. "No. You're not doing that this time."

"What do you mean?" she asked, giving me a quizzical look.

"You've always been so quick to think the worst of me. Whatever I say or do, your mind immediately takes the leap to *Nate's an asshole, doing asshole things.* But it wasn't like that in the very beginning, Ivy. I felt a connection between us—the same connection that ties us together now—but something changed. It's time you told me what."

"It doesn't matter—" she began, but I cut her off.

"It does matter. Tell me, Ivy."

She seemed to struggle with some internal battle, then heaved a sigh. She let her eyes trail over the Bel Air for a moment, then her blue gaze collided with mine.

"We were at Hero's for dinner. You, me, Rafe, and Lola. I was so sure there'd been sparks flying between us for weeks, but you wouldn't make a move. I thought maybe it was because I was Rafe's best friend, and you considered me somehow off-limits. So *I* decided to make a move on *you.*"

"Was this the night you disappeared while I was in the bathroom?" I asked, remembering that as the turning point in my relationship with Ivy.

"You remember?" she asked, tilting her head. At my nod, she said, "I followed you, Nate. I was going to…I don't know. Tell you the truth. Kiss you. Something."

My heart picked up its pace until it was trying to pound its way out of my chest. Ivy wanted me from the beginning. I hadn't imagined it. The connection between us was really there.

"Wait," I said, grinding my excitement to a halt. "Why didn't you? When I got back to the table, Rafe said you weren't feeling well and had gone home. Nothing was the same after that. You went from flirty to ferocious overnight. What happened?"

"I walked into the bathroom and saw you fucking that waitress!" she shouted. "Anna. The owner's daughter. Right against the wall for anyone to see."

The bottom dropped out of my stomach, and I staggered back a step. "I never fucked anyone in a bathroom. Not at Hero's. Not anywhere."

"I know what I saw," she said, her voice edged with despair. "That's why I've always hated you Nate. I was catching real feelings for you, and you made me think…it doesn't matter what I thought. I was wrong. You went from making me hot and wet with flirty words and heated gazes to fucking some random in a public bathroom."

Holy shit. All these years, and this was the reason? She hated me because of a mistake? A misunderstanding? So much time had been wasted while Ivy lived under the misconception that I'd somehow trifled with and betrayed her.

Well, no more. I refused to waste another minute. The rest of my life started now.

36

Ivy

hile I stood there bleeding, the old wound I'd ripped open painful and oozing with pus, Nate's expression flickered from confused to shocked to determined.

"I never fucked her, Ivy."

The honesty in his voice was unmistakable. My entire body shuddered as I struggled to maintain the belief that my anger had always been justified. That I hadn't been a fool, hating him for nothing.

"But I saw—"

"What you saw," he said, cutting me off, "was a woman attempting—and *failing*—to get into my pants for the hundredth time. I got up to go to the bathroom because you had my dick so hard, it was painful, and I needed a minute to get myself under control. Do you really think I'd sleep with someone else when it was *you* that had been driving me crazy for weeks?"

"I…"

I didn't have an answer. I had thought that. I was sure it had been true for years. But now... Could I really have been so stupid?

"She was coming out of the ladies' room as I walked by. Before I knew it, she had me inside and backed against a wall with her tongue down my throat."

"That's what I saw," I mumbled, feeling a bit shell-shocked.

"Well, if you'd stayed another two seconds, you would've seen me push her off. I told her to leave me alone. That it was never going to happen. She assumed that because she's the owner's daughter, she's untouchable and could do whatever she wanted...including me. I disabused her of that notion, and I left. I went into the men's room, washed my hands, and rinsed out my mouth. When I got back to the table, you were gone. I was so disappointed, because I'd planned on finally asking you out after dinner."

"You didn't..."

I couldn't finish my sentence. My mind was spinning out of control as it tried to make sense of his explanation. If he didn't do what I'd thought, then my hurt and hatred all those years had been for nothing. I'd shut him out, treating him like scum all that time, over a mistake?

"I wish you would've just asked me about it," he said quietly, "but I understand why you didn't. I'm so sorry, Ivy."

Why was he apologizing? This was all my fault.

"Stop it," he said, moving close enough to prop his hands on my shoulders. "I can see the wheels turning in your head, and this is just as much my fault as it is yours. If I hadn't let my ego get in the way, I would have made you tell me what happened to change your attitude so drastically back then. Instead, I let my own hurt and disappointment over your sudden disgust get the better of me and started treating you just as badly as you treated me. After a while, I guess it became habit. But I never really hated you, Ivy."

"You didn't?" I squeaked, then cleared my throat. He shook his head, and I said, "I never hated you, either. Not really. I hated what you did—what I *thought* you did—and how it made me feel, but I could never hate you. I love you, Nate."

The words slipped out before I could stop them. I sucked in a sharp breath as fear spiked through me. What had I just done?

I was getting ready to work myself into a real panic, but Nate's smile stopped me from uttering the litany of backpedaling words building in my throat. I blinked, and his arms were wrapped around me, pulling my body against his. His mouth sealed over mine, his tongue darting between my lips to taste me gently, yet somehow fiercely at the same time.

My fingers clenched in his shirt, pulling him closer as our kiss grew more heated. It was always like this with Nate. One kiss, one touch, and I was a goner. Nothing else existed but the two of us. Nothing else mattered.

Nate broke off the kiss abruptly, putting a few feet of space between us. We were both panting, and the fire banked in his blue eyes held promises of things to come. As if he'd read my mind, he began to speak.

"I'm going to take you to my bed and show you exactly how much I've missed you and how much you mean to me, Ivy Anderson. But first, I need to tell you something. When I came over that day and told you I wanted to keep everything between us platonic, I was lying."

"Lying?" I asked, my brain still not firing on all cylinders after that searing kiss.

"I only said what I did because I was scared."

"Scared of what?" I asked, finally catching up.

"Scared of what I was feeling. I realized I never wanted this thing between us to end. That I was falling for you, but you didn't feel the same way. I thought if I put up that wall between us, my heart could start to heal, and it wouldn't be so awful when this deal between us was over and we went our separate ways."

My heart fluttered as he spoke, beating faster and harder with each word. He thought I didn't feel the same way as him? Did that mean…

"What, exactly, are you saying, Nate?" I asked, not wanting there to be any more confusion or misunderstandings between us.

"I'm saying," he said, pulling me back into his arms, "that I am truly, madly, deeply in love with you, Ivy. I want to be your partner, your lover…your boyfriend. For real this time. No bargains. No end date. Just you and me, seeing where this might go."

"You love me?" I asked, feeling a little shell shocked as tears burned in my eyes.

"I love you," he whispered. "And you love me."

Then he kissed me, and everything else faded away. All that mattered was Nate, how I felt about him, and how he felt about me. Somehow, I ended up sitting on the hood of the Bel Air with Nate's tongue in my mouth as his hand slid under my shirt.

"Stop," I said, breaking off our kiss and slipping out of his grip.

Nate's questioning gaze was laced with a slight edge of fear, like he was half-convinced I'd changed my mind about him. About us.

"Sorry," I said, pulling down my shirt. "I am *not* having sex with you on top of my mother's car."

He laughed with relief, reaching out to tangle his

fingers with mine. "I hope you don't have any plans for the next day or two, because I'm taking you home, and I'm not letting you leave until I'm done showing you exactly how much I love you."

A smile so big, it made my cheeks hurt spread across my face as he pulled me toward the office. He made short work of closing everything down and locking the doors, despite stopping to kiss me every few seconds.

Before I knew it, we were in his car, speeding down the streets of Milestone toward his apartment. It was already dark outside, but that didn't stop it from feeling like a brand new day.

The first day of the rest of our lives.

~

"*M*erry Christmas, Mom!"

It was the morning of Christmas Eve, and Nate and I made plans to spend today with my mom and tomorrow with his family and our friends. I'd driven here alone, and after giving me a hug, Mom craned her head to search the driveway.

"Where's Nate?" she asked.

"Oh, he's on his way. He had an errand to run, so we decided he'd meet me here."

"Oh, maybe he's stopping to buy an engagement ring," she teased, nudging me in the side with her elbow.

"Mom," I scolded, making her laugh.

After meeting Nate on Thanksgiving, Mom had hit me with a hundred questions on the car ride home. Since I'd told her previously that Nate and I were dating, she demanded to know why we'd acted so weird around each other. Had we broken up? Did he hurt me? Should she get Dad's gun from the safe?

The tension between me and Nate, Jessa and Rafe's baby news, and my mom's obvious concern had eventually worn me down, and I'd spilled all the details about our fake relationship and the phony engagement. When she asked why I'd agreed to it, I'd rattled off some bullshit about helping him simply because he was Rafe's brother. I couldn't mention the car, and I hadn't been in a place to admit my real feelings at that point.

Now that Nate and I were a couple, for real this time, Mom never missed an opportunity to tease me about getting engaged. She said we'd had plenty of practice, so the real thing should be a cakewalk.

"Are you going to let me inside?" I asked, hoping my nerves weren't obvious in my voice.

Nate would be here any minute with the Bel Air, and I didn't want Mom to see it and ruin the surprise. She stepped back to let me pass, and I took one last peek up the road before closing the door firmly behind me.

"Is that coffee I smell?" I asked, hustling Mom toward the kitchen, away from the front windows.

Once we each had a warm, steaming mug, we sat down at the table to chat. I told her about work and updated her on Rafe and Jessa's baby journey. We talked about Lola, and how she was only one semester away from graduating college—a year early.

"She's going to intern at Nate's shop when she graduates. She'll manage all the books, payroll, and human resources, giving her some experience while she searches for the perfect job."

"Speaking of Nate," Mom said, ignoring my groan, "how are things going with you two?"

"Things are good. Really good," I said, unable to contain my smile.

"Has he asked you to move in yet?"

"Mom," I said, my tone filled with warning.

"What? Can't a mother worry about whether her daughter is settled and happy?"

"Worry all you want," I said. "Just don't bring it up in front of Nate."

"I wouldn't," she started, but a knock at the door cut her off.

"Hello?" Nate's deep voice called out from the front of the house.

"We're back here," I yelled before Mom could stand up to go greet him.

"Hi, Nate," she said as he strode into the kitchen.

"Merry Christmas," he replied.

He bent over to kiss her cheek, giving her shoulders a squeeze before sliding into the chair next to mine. Taking my hand, he lifted it to his lips and kissed my knuckles. I could feel the energy crackling off him, and his excitement fueled my own. We'd planned to wait until after lunch to show Mom the car, but I didn't think I could wait.

I met Nate's eyes, trying to convey my thoughts, and he shrugged. I narrowed my gaze, and he chuckled. Leaning in to kiss my cheek, he whispered, "It's your gift. It's up to you."

It may have started out that way, but Nate had put so much work into that car, so much love, it seemed like the surprise was more from him than from me. I may have come up with the idea, but he'd done all the work.

"You know, it's rude to share secrets in front of people," Mom said, taking a sip of her coffee, her eyes shining over the rim of her mug.

"Nate brought your Christmas gift," I said, keeping my eyes on his. When he gave me a small nod of encouragement, I looked back at Mom. "I was going to give it to you after lunch, but I can't wait."

"Well, I'm always up for gifts," she said, setting down her mug and smiling. "Let's go into the living room. Yours are under the tree."

Nate and I sat next to each other on the couch as Mom dug around under the tree for our gifts. I pulled a small box from my purse while she was distracted, and Nate discreetly passed me the Bel Air's key. I'd stuck another gift for her under the tree, just to throw her off, and she came out with it and three more wrapped boxes.

Mom opened hers first, a silk scarf I'd picked out with the car in mind. She could tie up her hair with it when she wanted to cruise around with the top down in the summer. She gushed over its beauty, wrapped it around her shoulders, and handed Nate and I our gifts from her.

She gave me a pair of white cowboy boots with little blue flowers embroidered all over them. They were so beautiful, I kicked off my shoes and pulled them on so she and Nate could admire them.

"I know you probably don't have room in your closet, but I saw those and knew you had to have them," she said, smiling.

"Thanks, Mom. I love them."

"Merry Christmas, baby," she said.

Nate opened his gift to reveal two sets of wrenches—one standard and one metric.

"I wasn't sure which kind you use, so I got both!" Mom laughed.

"They're perfect. Thank you, Barb," Nate said, smiling at her. "I use both, so these will come in handy."

My fingers wrapped around the box I'd stashed between Nate and me, but Mom picked up the last present she'd pulled from under the tree. She held it out toward me, and I took it from her with a shake of my head.

"Mom, the boots are perfect. You didn't have to get me anything else."

"I didn't," she said, then shot Nate a pointed look. "This one must've slipped it under the tree before he met us in the kitchen."

"Nate?" I asked, my gaze shooting over to meet his.

"Open it," he said, but his smile seemed tense.

Like he was nervous.

I unwrapped the rectangular box, taking a deep breath and holding it as I opened the hinged lid. Nestled inside was a platinum keyring with two charms—a stethoscope and a monkey wrench—and one new-looking key.

My eyes darted back to Nate. "What is this?"

"It's a key," he said, shooting me a wink.

"A key to what?" I asked.

"My apartment," he said, his face growing serious. "But I want it to be *our* apartment. You don't have to give me an answer now. I know it's a lot. I just…don't want to be apart from you any more than we have to be. I want you to move in with me, Ivy."

I looked over at Mom, whose grin stretched from ear to ear. I thought about our earlier conversation and how she asked me if Nate had brought up moving in together.

"Did you know about this?" I asked.

She held up her palms in surrender. "Purely coincidence. I swear."

I turned back to Nate, his hopeful expression warming my heart. "How much closet space are you willing to sacrifice? I have a lot of boots."

Nate jumped to his feet with a whoop of joy. Pulling me up into his arms, he pressed a quick, hard kiss to my mouth before spinning me around. He set me back on my feet, saying, "We'll make the closet space work. I promise."

"I'm so happy for you," Mom said, tears in her eyes.

"Oh! Mom, Nate and I have one more gift for you."

"Oh, honey, this wasn't necessary," she said as she took the small box from me.

She pulled off the lid and stared into the box for a moment, obviously confused. Tears stung my eyes as she lifted hers to me and gave me a small smirk.

"Isn't this the key to the Chevy?" she asked, shaking her head like she thought I might've lost my marbles.

"It is," I said, my voice cracking with emotion. "It's out front."

"What do you mean? It's in the barn—"

"Just go look, Mom," I said, hustling her up and pushing her toward the front door.

Nate beat us there, swinging open the door so I could lead Mom out onto the porch. There, glistening in the sun, sat the cherry-red Bel Air. Even though it was too cold to drive that way, Nate had put the top down before he came inside so Mom would see the fully-restored interior, too.

"Is that?"

"Nate fixed it," I said quietly. "He finished what Dad started, making it perfect—just like you. Merry Christmas, Mom."

She started to cry, which made me start to cry. Nate laughed at us, so I gave him an elbow to the gut. He wrapped an arm around my shoulder, and we watched Mom climb inside the car and sit behind the wheel.

She looked so happy, running her fingers over the steering wheel and dash, and I could tell she was thinking about Dad. That car was his dream realized. A gift that was always meant for his wife.

Nate had made that dream a reality…just like he was slowly making all of *my* dreams come true.

"I love you," I whispered, leaning my head against his chest.

His arm tightened around my shoulders, and I felt the fingers of his free hand under my chin. Tilting my head back, he pressed his lips to mine before pulling back to meet my gaze.

"I love you, Ivy. And I promise I'm going to do my best to keep you as happy as you are right now. Always."

I smiled. "I know you will. I can't help but be happy when I'm anywhere near you."

"Now, that is," he said, and I shook my head.

"Even when I thought I hated you, and I groaned and griped and acted like I couldn't stand to be in the same room with you, you still had the ability to take my breath away and make my heart beat fast."

"Same," he said.

"Let's make a deal," I proposed.

"Uh-oh," he replied, faking a shudder.

I chuckled, pushing my fingers into his hair. His hands fell to my hips, his fingers digging in as he pulled me in closer.

"Let's resolve to never keep our feelings bottled up again. Don't assume we know what the other is thinking, and really talk things through if we ever feel upset or feel like we're not getting all of our needs met."

"Deal," he said, pressing his lips to mine. "Speaking of needs—"

"Thank you so much, you two!"

Mom ran up the steps, tackling us in a group hug before Nate could finish his sentence. We embraced her, and I could feel the joy vibrating in her bones. I recognized it, because I'd felt that kind of joy myself.

Every time Nate Walton looked at me the way he was looking at me right now. Like he couldn't live without me, and he wouldn't want to anyway.

I returned his smile as warmth spread through my

whole body. I'd finally gotten everything I'd ever wanted. I was happy, in love, and I finally felt like I had a life outside work with real friends and a sweet, sexy boyfriend.

Mom went back inside, and Nate pulled me to a stop out on the porch.

"When we get home, we're going to christen every room in our apartment."

"Haven't we already done that?" I asked, grinning.

"That was when it was my apartment. Now that it's *ours*, we need a do-over."

"Okay," I said, "but only if you do that one thing with your tongue—"

He growled, and I squealed as his fingers tickled my ribcage. "Don't tempt me, woman, or we'll have to make excuses to your mother and cut out early."

"How about we eat lunch, and then I'll show you the hayloft in the barn?" I teased, making him growl again.

"It's a deal," he said, pressing his lips against mine.

"Deal," I repeated.

And that was one bargain I'd happily see through to the end.

EPILOGUE

Ivy

The ceremony was perfect. There wasn't a dry eye in the church as promises were made—promises filled with love, laughter, and several impatiently stolen kisses. When the minister finally declared Rafe and Jessa husband and wife, the whole crowd went wild with applause and cheers.

Jessa had asked me to be her maid of honor, so I spent a lot of the ceremony watching Nate. Though he looked calm and composed on the outside, I could see tension in the set of his shoulders, how tightly he kept his hands clasped together in front of him, and the way the muscle in his jaw kept ticking…like he was grinding his teeth.

I tried to talk to him on the ride to The Bullpen—where the reception was being held—but he just held my hand and told me he was fine. That he'd just been nervous, being in front of the whole town like that.

"Guess what? I got a new job!"

Karly plopped down in the chair next to me with those words, sipping a glass of champagne. Felicia was right behind her, a "Happy New Year" paper crown on her head and some gold plastic beads around her neck.

"A new *temp* job, you mean," Felicia said, sliding into her own chair.

"Don't mind her bitchiness," Karly said, nodding her red head in Felicia's direction. "She's just jealous."

I took a drink of my own champagne and wisely held my tongue. I'd seen these little spats turn physical with these two more than once, and I, for one, did *not* want to get tit-punched.

"Jealous? Why on earth would I be jealous? I have a stable, well-paying job."

"Yeah, with old Bobby Sumner. He's as old as a dinosaur and has the arms to match."

Karly set down her glass. Tucking her elbows tightly against her sides, she waved her hands up and down—the universal sign for t-rex arms. I managed to swallow the drink of bubbly in my mouth without choking, but just barely.

Felicia gave Karly a narrow-eyed look, but the redhead ignored it. She picked up her flute, took a sip like nothing had happened, and turned her attention back to me.

"Where is the job?" I asked.

"That's the best part," Karly squealed. "I'm going to be a receptionist for Milestone's newest law firm—Parker and Parker. They're twin brothers from Texas, according to Jessa. I haven't seen them yet, but I hear they're hot."

Felicia rolled her eyes. "Jess never said they were hot, Karly. She only met the one, and all she said was he wasn't ugly."

"They're *twins,* Felicia. And Jessa only played it down

because Rafe was giving her the side-eye while we were talking about it. I could see it in her face—he's hot, which means his brother is hot, too."

I hadn't met the Parker twins, but Rafe had. I heard all about how he saw Jessa with the handsome Max Parker at an early-morning meeting at the local coffee shop. His mind had immediately gone to a dark place, assuming Jessa and Max were on a "morning after" date. Then he met Marshall at Jessa's house and, not knowing he was a twin, assumed it was the same guy, claiming to have never met Jessa. He told me he'd nearly punched the guy's lights out before the whole thing was cleared up.

There was no "night before the morning after." Jessa had been meeting with Max because he and his brother wanted to rent out The Bullpen for a grand opening party for their new law firm. And Marshall really had never met her.

"So when do you start?" I asked before Felicia could start arguing again.

"Next week! I know it's just a temp job," she said, rolling her eyes at her dark-haired friend, "but I'm hoping it will turn into so much more."

That gleam in her eyes scared me, a little. It was obvious she was talking about more than just a permanent position. As a mischievous smile tugged at her lips, I knew I was right.

"Be careful, girl," I warned.

"Yeah, sexually harassing two big shot lawyers is a great fucking idea," Felicia grumped.

She seemed off, especially considering we were at the wedding reception of one of her best friends. I opened my mouth to ask her what was wrong, but warm lips landing on my neck made me lose my train of thought completely.

"Dance with me," Nate whispered, his breath tickling my ear.

I was on my feet in a second, wrapped in Nate's arms as he twirled me to the center of the room. Tables had been cleared away, leaving a makeshift dance floor. Twinkling white lights were strung above it and soft music played from the jukebox.

"You're so beautiful," Nate said, his fingertips brushing the skin bared by the low-cut back of my dress.

"You clean up good, yourself," I said, smiling at him.

Nate in regular, everyday clothes was too handsome for his own good. Nate in a tux? Holy hell. I'd caught myself drooling more than once.

"You like this look, eh?" he said, his face tightening the tiniest bit.

"I like every look on you," I said, pressing my mouth to his.

I smiled as some of the tension drained out of him. Did he think I wanted him to start dressing in suits and ties? No fucking way. I loved his casual look, his calloused hands, and the smell of motor oil and sweat that permeated around him when he got home from work.

Home. We'd been living together for a month, and I'd never been happier.

"What's that smile about?" he asked, pulling me closer.

"I'm just happy and in love," I said.

"I love you, too," he whispered.

He kissed me lightly, then withdrew. His face was tight with tension again, but before I could ask him what was wrong, he was pulling me across the dance floor toward the bar.

"Where are we going?" I asked as he walked around the bar and through the door that led to the back rooms.

"I need to talk to you. In private," he said.

His voice was strained, his grip on my hand was tight, and his pace was almost too fast for me to keep up in these heels.

Panic gripped me as I let him drag me along. This couldn't be good.

Nate

I knew I was sending all the wrong signals, but the nervous energy inside me was pulling me in ten different directions at once. I knew what I wanted, but going for it was the scariest fucking thing I'd ever done.

I pulled Ivy into the office that Jessa, as bar manager, now shared with her dad. I turned to face her, and the look of trepidation on her face nearly undid me. I jerked her forward, and her body slammed into mine. My fingers threaded into her hair as I devoured her mouth, kissing away any fear she might have had about my intentions in bringing her here, away from the others.

"I thought you wanted to *talk*," she murmured between kisses, her fingers plucking at my belt buckle.

Oh, shit.

I stepped back quickly, refastening my belt as my eyes darted to the still-open door behind her. When I looked back at Ivy, her expression was filled with disappointment. I ran a hand through my hair and huffed a breath. I needed to keep my desire—and Ivy's—under control.

For the moment, at least.

"I did. I mean, I do." *Fuck.* "I *do* want to talk to you."

"Okay," she said slowly, her expression changing from disappointed to confused. "What is it, Nate?"

I swallowed thickly before clearing my throat. Keeping my eyes on Ivy's face, I focused on my love for her to get me through this. Her strength, love, and compassion were unparalleled, and remembering that brought a sense of calm over me.

"Ivy," I said, reaching out to take her hand, "making a home with you this last month has caused me to do some real soul-searching."

Her breath hitched, and her entire body tensed up. "It has?"

"Yes," I said. "Having you there, going to bed with you at night, and waking up next to you in the morning...it's like a dream I never remembered having."

Her hand tightened on mine, but her shoulders were still stiff, like she wasn't sure if what I was saying was a good thing, or not. God, I hoped I wasn't fucking this up.

"I love our life together," I said quickly, and I could see some of the tension draining out of her. "I love you *now*, but what I've realized is that it didn't just begin during our fake relationship."

"What are you saying, Nate?" she asked when I paused to gather my thoughts.

"I'm saying that I fell in love with you when we first met. All those heated glances and flirty encounters hooked me and reeled me in like no one had ever done before. And when you...misunderstood what you saw, it broke my heart, but it did not diminish the love there. I loved you when you were distant and quiet. I loved you when you were spitting venomous words and hate. I may have spent my time with others, hoping to extinguish the flame I carried for you, but it never worked. You were always there, stopping me from taking anyone else seriously.

"*You* are why I've never had a girlfriend or settled down. Not because I'm some kind of player or afraid of commitment. I'm not afraid. I was just waiting for you."

Tears streamed down her face, making my own vision blur with emotion. I ran a hand across my eyes to clear them, then reached into the pocket of my pants.

"I'm tired of waiting," I said, pulling my hand free.

Holding my fist out, I slowly uncurled my fingers, revealing the ring I'd given Ivy at the beginning of our fake engagement. Her breath caught in her throat, and her fingernails dug harder into the hand she was now holding in a death grip.

"When I bought this for you," I said quietly, "it didn't feel like a sham. My palms were sweating and my heart was pounding, and I made the jeweler show me every diamond ring he had so I could pick the perfect one—not for my fake fiancée, but for *you*, Ivy."

Her lungs fluttered back to life as she inhaled a deep, shaky breath. "You did?"

"I did," I said. "And when I saw this one, I knew it was perfect. Just like you."

I paused to let that sink in, then licked my lips. I waited until Ivy lifted her eyes from the ring to meet mine. Then I spoke from the heart.

"I love you, Ivy, and I want to spend the rest of our lives proving it to you. I want to be your rock, your companion, your lover, and everything in between. I want you to have my babies, and I want us to raise them with all the love and joy we can possibly give them."

She started fully sobbing at those words, and panic lanced through me, making me curse myself and backtrack.

"If you don't want kids, that's okay, too."

"I d-do," she stuttered between breaths. "I do want kids."

"Good," I said, relief washing over me.

Inhaling deeply, I dropped to one knee. Ivy's breaths were coming fast and furiously, and I could only pray it was a good thing.

"This time, it's real," I said, swallowing hard. "Ivy Marie Anderson, will you marry me?"

"Yes," she breathed, laughing as I leapt to my feet and hugged her. "Yes, I will marry you, Nate."

"I love you so much," I said, slipping the ring back onto her finger...for the last time.

"I love you," she replied, then pressed her lips to mine.

"Oh, God," she said, pulling back in a panic. "We can't say anything, Nate. This is Rafe and Jessa's day. I don't want to ruin it by making it about us. We'll tell them later, okay? Maybe next week?"

"Too late," I said, grinning.

I spun her around and pulled her back against my chest with arms wrapped around her middle. She gasped at the sight before her just before a loud cheer rang out with shouts of happiness and congratulations.

Crowded in the doorway were Rafe, Jessa, Karly, Felicia, and Lola—the people we cared most about. Lola had a tablet in her hand, with Ivy's mom's face openly weeping on the screen.

"What are you—? Mom?" Ivy said, sounding flabbergasted when she spotted the tablet.

"I wanted everyone we love to see me pledge my life to you, Ivy. Jessa insisted I should do it today because weddings make people feel romantic, you'd be less likely to laugh in my face."

Jessa shot me a wink and smirked, making me chuckle. Then she shooed everyone away. They called out more best wishes as they turned to go, leaving only Jessa behind. As she grabbed the doorknob and started to pull the panel closed, she froze and cocked her head.

"This door has a lock. Use it."

With one last wink, she was gone, the door firmly closed behind her. Ivy turned in my arms and wrapped her hands around my neck.

"You planned that whole thing?" she asked. At my nod, she added, "They were there the whole time?"

"Yes," I laughed. "Thank God, I came to my senses when you were trying to take my clothes off."

I pulled away from her and strode toward the door. I turned the lock, then leaned back against the wood with a grin on my face.

"We're alone now, Future Mrs. Walton."

"We are," she agreed, swaying her hips as she moved toward me. "Whatever shall we do?"

"I think," I said, as she pressed her body against me, "we should practice making those babies we talked about."

"Oh, yeah," she groaned as my hands found her ass and kneaded it. "Lots of practice."

Then she kissed me, her mouth igniting a fire in my blood. Just like she always did. Just like she always *would*.

Forever.

Thanks for reading Faking With the Enemy! I hope you loved it, and if you have a moment, can you please leave a review?

∾

Want more Nate and Ivy? Sign up for my newsletter to receive a bonus scene: The Wedding

∾

Follow Piper James on Facebook and join her reading group: Milestone Mischief Makers

∾

Read ahead for a sneak peek of Karly and Max's story: Teasing Mr. Moneybags

teasing
MR.
M💰NEYBAGS

milestone
MISCHIEF

PIPER JAMES

TEASING MR. MONEYBAGS

CHAPTER ONE

Karly

Have you ever had one of those dreams where you were so immersed, the sound of your alarm clock became a natural part of the landscape? Like the honking of a horn as you walked down a busy city street wearing Jimmy Choo heels while sipping a latte and getting catcalled by hot, bare-chested construction workers? Or the beeping of the timer on that bomb you were so valiantly trying to disarm to save an entire fishing village in Japan, including a hot, bare-chested martial arts master? Yeah? Me, too.

And today was the worst possible day for it to happen.

The temp agency I worked for set me up as a receptionist for Parker & Parker—Milestone, Georgia's newest resident attorneys. It was my first day, and I overslept.

I knew being late wasn't going to give Max and Marshall Parker the best first impression of me, but I wasn't too worried. I'd just have to win them over with my sparkling personality. Easy-peasy.

But just in case, I grabbed my phone and texted my friend Jessa. She'd met the twin brothers a couple of months ago when they came to town to scope out office space. She'd gone to coffee with Max Parker to discuss the possibility of them renting out The Bullpen, her father's bar, for a grand opening party for the law firm.

Me: *Emergency!! How does Max Parker take his coffee?*

I tossed my phone onto the counter and grabbed my toothbrush. I stared at my reflection as I brushed my teeth, groaning at the sight of my hair. I'd showered and gone to bed with a wet head last night, so my red hair stuck up all over, making me look like I'd walked through the eye of a tornado and lived to tell the tale…but only barely.

Spitting out the toothpaste, I grabbed a spray bottle of water and spritzed it all over my head. Scrunching the damp strands in my fingers, I tried to shape it into some semblance of order before giving up with a sigh.

I grabbed my phone and texted Jessa again.

Me: *911!!! Please answer me. It's a matter of life and death.*

Running back out into my bedroom, I dropped the phone onto the bed and pulled the outfit I'd picked out the night before from my closet. Leaning against the mattress for support, I pulled on the electric blue pencil skirt and smoothed the material over my hips. It was my favorite, hugging my curves in just the right way while making my ass look like a million bucks.

I paired it with a white, flowy, long sleeved shirt that was cut low enough to tease the slightest amount of cleavage. Sexy, but professional.

I toyed with the idea of skipping the panty hose, but it was January—too cold for bare legs. Besides, whatever tiny amount of color I managed to burn into my pale skin over the summer was long gone. So I took a few extra minutes to pull on some nude hose before sliding my feet into a pair of black heels.

My phone chimed, and I snatched it up to read the incoming message.

Jessa: *Max took his black, but I'm not sure about Marshall. Please tell me you're already at the office.*

I glanced at the time on my phone and groaned. I was officially late, and I hadn't even left my apartment yet.

Me: *Thanks. Call you later.*

I ran back into the bathroom and squirted some foundation into my palm. Rubbing my hands together, I smeared it all over my face. Archaic, I knew, but desperate times called for desperate measures. I swiped on some mascara and dusted a little blush on the apples of my cheeks before calling it good.

I was washing my hands when my phone chimed again.

Felicia: *Jessa told me you're running late on your first day. I hope they don't fire you.*

Me: *Gee, thanks for the support, bestie.*

Felicia and I had been friends since kindergarten, and I loved her, but her pep talks were shit. Usually, her responsible, dependable demeanor complimented my free-spirited, fly-by-the-seat-of-my-pants shenanigans. But this morning, I didn't have the time nor the patience to deal with her superior work ethic.

Felicia: *Hey, that was me being supportive. Hurry up, and make sure you have a viable excuse when you get there…like a fifteen car pile-up, or something.*

I snorted. Like that would ever happen in Milestone. Two-lane blacktops spotted with law-abiding, slow-ass driving citizens weren't really prone to massive accidents or traffic jams. Plus, with the efficiency of the gossip mill in this town, the brothers would probably know I overslept before I even stepped foot out of my apartment.

Gotta love small town life.

I locked up and ran to my car while silently praying to the god of stilettos that I wouldn't trip in my haste. I made it safely to my piece of shit sedan—I couldn't afford anything better with my measly temp-job pay—and slid in behind the wheel.

Chucking my bag into the passenger seat, I stuck the key in the ignition and twisted it. Nothing happened. I tried again. Still nothing.

"What the—" I murmured, trying a third time. "Mother fucker."

Of all the days this hunk of junk could've died, it *had* to be today. Grabbing my bag, I climbed from the car and slammed the door closed with excessive force. Taking a few deep breaths, I ordered myself to calm down and think.

I pulled out my phone and scrolled through my contacts. Ivy Anderson. She could help me. Her boyfriend was the best mechanic in Milestone.

"Hey, Karly. How's your first day going?"

"I wouldn't know. It started without me," I mumbled, then cleared my throat. "Ivy, my car is dead, and I'm late. I don't know what to do."

"Hang on," she said.

There was a shuffling noise before a much deeper voice came through the speaker.

"Karly, what's happening when you try to start the car?"

"Nothing," I said, my voice on the verge of being whiney. "It's totally dead."

"No clicking noise?"

"Nope."

"Sounds like a dead battery. I can come test it later this morning. Just leave your key in the car. I'll bring a new battery, just in case a jump start won't work."

"Thanks, Nate, but I don't know if I'll be able to pay

for it," I said. "I've probably lost my new job because I'm so late."

"Rafe is a block away." Ivy was back on the phone, giving me the lifeline I needed. "He's coming to get you."

"He drives like an old lady, so good luck," I heard Nate laugh in the background.

"Thanks, Ivy," I said. "And tell Nate thank you. I'll leave the key in the cup holder."

It's not like anyone could steal this non-starting piece of shit anyway.

I'd just slammed the door closed for the second time when Rafe's SUV pulled into the lot. I let out a sigh of relief and rushed forward, hopping in the car the second it stopped moving. Rafe greeted me as he backed into an empty spot and executed a perfect three-point turn.

"Thanks for coming," I said. "You're not going to be late, are you?"

I noticed he was wearing hospital scrubs, and I'd feel really shitty if some poor injured person in the emergency room didn't get the help they needed because I overslept.

"No, I just got off. Had to work a double, so I was there all night."

He looked fresh as a daisy and fine as hell. I'd look like a deranged hyena if I stayed up working all night. Jessa was one lucky woman. She and Rafe had gotten married a couple of weeks ago and were expecting their first child in the summer.

"Can we stop by the coffee shop?" I asked as we pulled into town.

"Aren't you already late?" he asked, arching one black brow in my direction.

"I'm hoping fresh coffee will butter them up enough that I won't get fired on the spot."

Rafe didn't respond but pulled into a parking space in

front of Milestone's only coffee shop. With a promise to be right back, I ran inside, plowing right into someone who was trying to exit. I managed to twirl away unscathed by spilled coffee—a great feat considering the height of my heels—and called out an apology before hurrying to the counter.

I ordered three black coffees, asking the barista to include a bag of sweeteners, creamers, and stir sticks. I tapped my toe as I waited, looking back toward the door. Whoever I'd run into was gone.

Good thing, too. Because I didn't have time to listen to someone bitch at me about what was *obviously* an accident. Sure, it was all my fault, and on any other day, I would've offered a more solemn apology and a replacement coffee.

But not today. I was late, and every second counted.

Get your copy of Teasing Mr. Moneybags today!

ACKNOWLEDGMENTS

Thanks to everyone who loved Playing With the Doctor and couldn't wait to get their hands on this book. You made it so easy to write, knowing you love these characters as much I do.

Thanks to Molly Phipps at We Got You Covered Book Design for yet another amazing cover.

Thank you to my amazing husband for encouraging me to go for this dream. I love you.

ALSO BY PIPER JAMES

Playing With the Doctor

Teasing Mr. Moneybags